HYBRIDS

VOLUME FOUR | HOPE

JENNIE DORNY

HYBRIDS

VOLUME FOUR | HOPE

Set in a future where human values are more important than technology, *Hybrids* weaves a science-fiction world with a story of love, friendship and tolerance.

Hybrids is published in four volumes, which cannot be read separately or in a different order: *Trouble, Vengeance, Fear* and *Hope.*

SUMMARY OF VOLUME 3 | FEAR

In Gambling Nova, the federal planet-prison, Theo makes her peace with her father and discovers the importance of the orgacomps' legacy, while an increasingly sick Jack is reunited with his beloved Farren.

Compromised, Donatella has fled to Eridan to obtain the promised light for herself and the Families, but Keith is not as easy to manipulate as her friend Mogud. In Eridan, Terri organizes the people's resistance against Keith.

When Nand, the Face Changers and Farren are rescued by Theo, Jack, Smanul and Ashta, the mental battle that takes place in Pit 3, inside the Dome, generates a destructive wave in Eridan.

While the Eridanis, Farren and Jack escape the Dome through a paradox door into the desert, Theo confronts Mogud before fleeing with her mother.

HOPE
VOLUME FOUR OF HYBRIDS

Is there any hope for Eridan's living ocean to be saved and for the special link between Eridanis and their ocean to be restored?

After the Guild's ship crashes in Redland's desert, Theo faces her hardest trial, while Jack fights the poison burning through his veins.

In Eridan, Mocean is freezing – a consequence of the mental battle in Gambling Nova's Pit 3 and Keith's decision to launch Mindrule.

But when Nand, Ashta and the Face Changers reach their home planet after leaving Gambling Nova, they are forbidden to land: Eridan has been put in quarantine.

Powerless, unable to reach Kaipekak, Nand watches her beloved ocean slowly choking as ice covers its surface.

Never one to give up, Ashta calls Farren to the rescue …

Set in Redland's deserts and Eridan's icefields, entwining the creation myths of both planets, the final volume of *Hybrids* concludes Theo's search for belonging.

The glossary and list of characters are available at the end of the book.

Keep in touch and join the Distinguished Readers' Club to learn more about the worlds of *Hybrids* and to receive the latest updates about my books.

For information, visit my website:
www.jenniedorny.com

For Hélène de Coustin, of course.

Crash

1 May 3077, Standard Time (ST), Sixth Federal Era
Redland—Esk Strath

Farren straightened in his chair as he snapped out of his sleep, full of a nameless, stark terror. His heart pounded in his ears. He glanced at Jack. His brawan lay in his bed, twitching and tossing in his sleep: alive, delirious.

The drapes surrounding Jack's bed fluttered and Cowan slipped inside.

"Theo and her mother made it out of the Dome safely. Theo is in the Guild ship, and Fern in Kirby's. Lonetom is in touch with Clobb. Everybody's safe," he said.

"No!" Farren stood up as he remembered. "The Guild ship crashed in the desert!"

"How do you know?"

He ruffled his hair. "I've no idea! But it happened." He frowned at the man whose cheery voice had pulled him from despair when he was under the Dome. "I wasn't dreaming. I was awake in my sleep. Conscious. Connected to Theo."

"And you … felt the ship crash?" Cowan leaned against the wall.

Farren couldn't blame his friend's skepticism. "No. She blanked out. I experienced her fear."

"Could it be a projection? Your concern for her turned into a nightmare?"

"Yeah … Still … Lots of strange things happened in Pit 3 …" In the Dome's depths, his intimacy had fissured when he battled Xë.

"What are you talking about?"

He rubbed his eyes and searched for words to skirt around what he didn't want to reveal. "Xë, Mogud's second-in-command, was felled by the force of the Eridanis' minds. I was part of it. So was Theo."

"Really?"

"She lived in Eridan for nearly a year. She obviously learned a thing or two over there."

Cowan nodded. "Well, whether this happened or not, Malcolm should be informed. Let's go to headquarters."

Farren found Alk, at a desk near the ward entrance, busy writing.

"I must talk to Malcolm," he said. "Can you stay with Jack?"

"Of course." She smiled up at him. "I'll sit by his side. If anything changes, I'll send someone to warn you."

Tension fizzed inside headquarters. Its wide, rectangular opening embraced the embedded valley's clouded outskirts.

Erlend stood confidently in the middle of the room. Malcolm

and Lonetom watched him. Several Redlanders Farren had never met stepped aside when they entered.

"Erlend, what are you doing here? I thought you were with the Eridanis," Cowan asked.

"He was, for all the good it did him. We now have the proof that your brother can't be trusted." Livia directed her anger at Cowan and scowled at Farren. She addressed herself to the young man who bore an uncanny resemblance to his older brother. "Didn't you get what I told you the other day? Druskas aren't welcome here."

"Livia!" Farren exclaimed, shocked to hear his sister hurl the ugly insult.

"Your cousin is aboard that ship," Erlend told Malcolm. "Don't you think it's crucial to check if it happened or not?"

Cowan and Farren exchanged glances.

"Check what?" Cowan asked.

"The Eridani woman had a vision. She claims that the Guild ship was shot down by Mogud's fleet," Malcolm explained.

"It's true." Farren realized with a pang that not only Theo but also Rory was in danger. "Theo is in an emergency capsule that got ejected on impact. She lost consciousness."

"How would you know?" Livia's scorn scarred her voice. "You talked to your warrior friend?"

"Ashta? No. I was with Jack." He hesitated. "I was asleep, but I perceived Theo's fear."

"How could you?" His sister considered him from head to foot, a smirk on her face.

"It's hard to believe, I grant you that. I can't explain it rationally," he said. "It's the first time something like this has ever happened to me. I experienced Theo's fear as if I were with her, in her mind."

Lonetom stepped closer. "What about Rory?"

He shook his head. "Nothing." He eyed the Redlander chiefs. "Listen, I know this is mind-boggling, but it wasn't a dream. And if Ashta, an Eridani who's used to mental contacts, experienced the same, there must be some basis of truth. Something happened to the Guild ship." He glanced at Lonetom. "What does Clobb say?"

His friend pulled a face. "I lost contact with him shortly before the two ships left the Dome. And Captain Kirby isn't answering either. I'll take my Xen4 and see for myself."

"The hell you will!" Malcolm snapped. "Mogud's fleet is in the sky!"

"I'll run the risk," Lonetom said curtly. "I don't take my orders from you."

"Malcolm's right." Farren walked to the opening and took a pair of binoculars. "Mogud's showing off." He glanced back at his friend. "If you go now, your ship will be shot down. Anyway, where would you go? Do you know the direction Rory took?"

"Both ships flew towards Sky Cradle," Little Whale, one of the watchers, said. "The *Purple Thistle* swerved and went into orbit to shake away its pursuers. The Guild ship used lots of engine power to force its way out of the Dome. It was flying closer to the ground and went straight into the storm to escape Mogud's Fudrons. We lost it on the monitors as soon as it entered the zone." The woman frowned. "This is a habook, a massive sandstorm, and it's moving fast."

"If Theo's in an emergency capsule, she'll be safe," Lonetom said. "It's Rory I'm worried about. He flew that ship. He could be seriously injured."

Malcom stepped forward. "Lonetom, I prefer that you receive confirmation from the Guild that you're authorized to fly. We don't want Mogud's Fudrons creating havoc in the valley. Livia, can you check that everything is in order? Dag, a word."

Farren joined his brother-in-law in a recess.

"How's Jack?"

Malcolm's grumpy solicitude went straight to Farren's heart.

"He's unconscious. But in good hands now."

According to Smanul, Jack had survived on Fern's mhuol tablets. Despite its potential danger and Jack's possible allergy, the Suni Sisters intended to treat him with the Reddish plant.

"Did you feel … pain when you were … in communion with Althea?"

"Dread, mostly."

"Let's decide that she's alive and unhurt. We'll get to her as soon as we can. And the pilot too. But the Guild's interference in our business …" He scowled. "Not good. Livia's right. If Redlanders are traveling, losses could be huge if Mogud retaliates."

"Casualties would be higher if you had attacked the Dome."

"We'll never know … I hate to be hostage of a situation I can't control."

"If it were possible, the Guild would've done things differently. Thank you for this morning. Without you …"

Malcolm patted Farren's shoulder. "Your friend Lonetom won't talk. What can you tell me about the stakes?"

"It's the story of three ambitious and powerful leaders who have created an alliance to overthrow the federal government in Nuong. The brain behind all this is Donatella Simpson, the SpaceSS leader."

"Your boss?"

"Yes. When she found out Jack and I had discovered her plans, she sent me here for a so-called undercover mission and got rid of Jack by condemning him for my murder."

"Bitch."

"Yeah. Simpson and Mogud have known each other for years. Jack found out they both participated in the Neriyya-yana battle. Mogud served under Simpson. He saved her life. That creates bonds. Mogud became Gambling Nova's gover-nor thanks to her."

"Who's the third guy?"

"He's the youngest. His name is Keith of Rain Forest. He's an Eridani. Yep …" He nodded. "Like Ashta and the others. A man of power—ambitious. A recent leader. I don't know how he can be stopped."

"What do you mean?"

"His ambition is to enslave entire populations with mind power."

"Can he?"

"Maybe. He's the one who frightens me the most."

"Farren? Malcolm? We need to talk." Lonetom joined them, Cowan in tow.

"Something new?"

"I talked to Clobb. The Guild ship was indeed shot down by Mogud's fleet. All communication with Rory stopped be-fore the ship crashed. I know you're against it, but I'm taking the Xen4 out now."

"No!" Malcolm exclaimed.

"Does Clobb realize what the situation is down here?" Farren asked. "Can't he send one of his own ships for reconnaissance?"

"They can't show themselves before the spaceport explodes."

"He's the one who ordered you to fly here?"

"I did it for Jack. Rory has worked for Clobb since he left SpaceSS."

"That's not what I'm asking," Farren said.

"Rory's my friend too," Lonetom said. "Is this what you want to hear? If I was sent here it was precisely so I could intervene when the Guild couldn't."

"It's a bad idea," Farren said. "You'll be intercepted, and then what?"

"The Xen4 is easy to fly, and fast."

"But you haven't flown in a long time."

"I never stopped simulations."

Farren glanced at Malcolm. "Do you own long-range weapons?"

"If your friend takes his ship out, it's at his own risk. I refuse to put our people's lives in danger."

"I have everything I need on board," Lonetom said.

"Perfect. Then let's do it." Farren headed for the door.

Malcolm stopped him. "Where are you going?"

"With Lonetom."

"Don't!" Lonetom said. "I can handle this on my own."

"You can't fly the ship and shoot."

"Dag." Malcolm held him back. "Don't go!"

"I must. I can't let Lonetom go alone. And the pilot is a very good friend. If he's in danger and I haven't helped him … I … and there's Theo."

"I know." Malcolm sighed. "You're right. Go. But, by the Winds, be careful! And fly faster than the storm. It can be as deadly as a Fudron."

CHAPTER 185

Apologies

1 May 3077, Standard Time (ST), Sixth Federal Era
Redland—Esk Strath

"Stay here," Lonetom said as they strode through the wind-filled valley to where the Xen4 was parked. "Jack needs you."

"I can't let you go alone."

"Have you looked at yourself?"

Farren shrugged. "I'm fine. I slept."

They walked in silence through the empty grounds where goats grazed. From time to time one of them raised its head, ears pricked.

A Fudron left its squadron high above Esk Strath and dove towards the valley center.

"Careful!" Lonetom shouted.

Noiselessly the aircraft hedge-hopped as shots rattled through Esk Strath. Greenhouses shattered one after the other. The goats scrambled away, bleating.

"Bastards!" Farren straightened and craned his neck. "Mogud

won't get away with this."

"I disagree with your brother-in-law on many things, but as far as Esk Strath's security goes, he's good."

"Strategy and architecture. That's what the MacDougals are good at." He stared down, as his vision, weakened by weeks in the prison cell's obscurity, blurred easily.

He stumbled, and Lonetom held him up.

"Are you sure you're all right?"

"Positive."

"Is your body as much of a mess as your face?"

"I'm fine."

"Tell it to the others …"

Farren stopped. "What do you want me to say? The Dome is a prison. I was an inmate like everybody else."

"I thought Jack murdered you."

"It was a set-up."

He marched on. Lonetom followed him.

"But I believed it. I was convinced he was guilty. I helped Simpson arrest him."

"Jack told me you cleared things up."

"I want to talk to you too. You must wonder why I thought Jack could harm you."

Farren faced his friend. "I don't want to discuss this. You're right, I'm exhausted. I have a killer headache. I hurt everywhere. I made a bad decision last night, and now Theo could be dead. And Rory too. As for Jack, his chances of survival are frightfully small. The mhuol-based treatment might finish him off. So, what happened in E-Met months ago, what you did, what you didn't do, your remorse …" He shook his head and met Lonetom's troubled eyes squarely. "I don't give a damn."

Lonetom nodded and stalked towards the Xen4, whose wings sparkled under the suns.

"Dag!"

Farren whirled, shading his eyes with his hand. Smanul jogged towards him.

"Let me go in your stead!"

"I can't …"

He waited for his friend to join him.

Smanul raised his fist. "Do I need to do the same thing you did to me in the Gold Mines?"

"You wouldn't dare."

"Try me. You've done enough for today, and for the rest of the week. Go back to Jack. He needs you."

"But—"

"I know nothing about flying, but fighting, that's my area." Smanul's fist still loomed menacingly. "So, do I need to knock you down or will you be reasonable?"

Farren stepped backwards. "I've taken enough blows for now."

Smanul lowered his arm. "Good move." He chuckled. "Your friend must wonder what we're up to. I'll go with him."

Lonetom waited at the foot of the Xen4. He retrieved two helmets from a large bag.

"Hi." Smanul held out his hand to Lonetom. "Smanul. I'm a friend of Dag's, and I'll replace him."

"Fine. Clobb says that the Styx5 and Fudrons are back inside the spaceport. We have a free range."

"It's a ruse," Farren said. "He knows we want to get to the Guild ship."

"We still need to get out now."

"At what time will the Dome blow up?"

"14:00. Shortly." Lonetom handed a helmet to Smanul and pushed the bag towards Farren. "Your brother-in-law will have a fit when he finds out what's inside." His curt laughter matched his grim features. "The day after I landed, he explored the Xen4 and confiscated some weapons. Yet Guild ships contain multiple stashes."

Farren unzipped the bag and whistled his appreciation as he took out the heavy weapon.

"A portable R-Laun, version 8.3. Charged. With ammunition." He weighed it and put the R-Laun in shooting position, his eye in the lunette. "Being on the Guild payroll has its perks."

"I'll feel better if you cover us," Lonetom said. "The Xen4 flies well but is slow to lift from the ground. Do you see that opening?" He pointed towards a bunch of dried-up mhuol husks. "There's a path behind that stack. It gets you to the summit. There are at least a hundred steps. In the hideout, you can access the spurs outside as well as inside the valley. It's the watchers' spot. You won't be alone."

"Give me a fifteen-minute head start. Good luck to both of you."

CHAPTER 186

Meeting Erlend

1 May 3077, 17:00 Standard Time (ST), Sixth Federal Era
Redland—Esk Strath

Nand woke up. Dim light; fresh air. She lay on a bed in a large empty room. Her memories stopped at a galloping horse's pointed chestnut ears, the stringy mane she clutched, a yelling rider.

She sat up, her eyes watering at her stiffness. Checkered green-and-straw-colored hangings covered the walls. On a stool beside the bed she found a pitcher, a glass and a plate filled with pastries. She slowly drank two whole glasses, savoring each sip. She nibbled at the round, pink cake and the sticky pyramid covered with pepper-tasting seeds, and ate two small tarts—a lemony one and another with a crackling nutty spread. She finished with a square filled with a red crispy paste.

She examined the room. She stroked the tufted hangings, pressed her fingers on the cool, uneven stone walls, and peeked inside a wardrobe at stacks of neatly folded blue and black clothes. She opened a red door by the wardrobe. A sail-flapping noise erupted. She went up an abrupt flight of stairs. The higher she climbed, the louder the rumble.

At the top, she stepped onto a narrow terrace nestled against the mountain and surrounded by three thick rails. The sky and wind-swept air were colored orange.

Coughing, she leaned over the rail to her right: the ground, far below, proved strangely seductive. Too seductive. Heart beating, she pressed her back against the mountainside, and gripped the door frame that led back to the stairs and safety.

Uneven red and clotted-cream stripes with black veins scarred the mountain walls. An aircraft had crashed not far away, one wing pointing upwards, the other stuck in the ground. The remains of three helicopters smoldered. In the distance, the Dome disappeared behind a thick cloud of gray smoke. And in front of her, around, everywhere, the vermilion immensity shuddered at intervals, producing puffs of dust, its undulating movement reminding her of ochre waves.

Rubbing her bare arms to warm up, she savored this moment of aloneness. Her forced lack of privacy with the Face Changers and Xë in Pit 3 had been unbearable. As well as the lies. The violence of pretending to be someone else.

A wind gust slapped sand in her face and she sneezed.

"So, you found my terrace!"

One of the riders who had come to her rescue, the younger one, smiled as he emerged from the staircase. He unfolded two deck chairs. She sat near the wall.

"I thought you'd sleep longer." He settled into the other deck chair and raised his hand. "I'm Erlend MacRae, and you are …?"

He had a direct look, a lean face she instantly liked. It irked her to build this new relationship on a lie. Yet how could she not follow the Master Face Changer's orders?

"Aslone. My name is Aslone."

"Your friends are in the greenhouses where there's lots of humidity. They're looking for you. Do you want me to take you there?"

"I prefer staying here. Is that possible?"

"The sandstorm is gathering strength, and the wind will soon blow hard. But we can stay on the terrace a little longer."

"How long will it last?"

He shrugged. "It depends. With a big one like this, three or four days. Maybe more. Summer storms are unpredictable."

"So we can't go out?"

"No. We avoid being outside when the swazzi turn into a habook. That's the name for this kind of thick dust storm."

"How often do they happen?"

"The swazzi blow every night. Sandstorms are much more impressive. They blow night and day, and cover us with sand."

"So you never see stars."

"Early morning, sometimes. When I was a kid, I tried hard to catch sight of more than the three morning stars, but it never happened." A long gust of wind twirled around them, dusting their faces. She coughed. He folded his deck chair. "We'd better go back inside."

"Too bad." She got up and nearly lost her balance, surprised by the strength of the wind. "I miss stars, and night. What happened down there?" She folded her own seat with his help.

"You didn't hear anything?"

She shook her head.

"It was some battle." His eyes twinkled. "I saw everything

from headquarters, underneath the terrace, over there to the right. The small aircraft belongs to the Guild Observer. He tried to leave the valley. The biggest chopper, down there, attacked it. It crashed. Then Dag, who stood on the platform up there"—he pointed towards the top of the mountain—"shot the choppers down one after the other with an R-Laun. It was amazing. He's such a good shot …"

"Dag?"

"Farren Megan? Dag's his Redlander nickname. Follow me. Be careful; it's steep. He was with you under the Dome." Erlend walked down the steps. "He's Jack's brawan. Cowan—my brother—and he are good friends." Inside the bedroom, he locked the door and turned on a big egg-shaped lamp in a corner. "I was with Malcolm and Livia when Farren shot down the choppers. I didn't want to miss her reaction … She's so prejudiced against people like her brother and me."

"Prejudiced about what?"

"You know, druskas. Are you thirsty?"

She nodded.

"Water, whiskey, spacebooze. Or limilli? It's a spicy non-alcoholic drink."

"Water is fine." She sat in the armchair near the window. Outside, it was already dark. "What are druskas?"

"It's an insult for two men or two women who love each other."

"It's forbidden here?"

Erlend cracked up. His laughter reflected a surprise as big as her own. He handed her a glass brimming with water.

"Let's say it isn't accepted. Those of us who reveal our preferences or who are in love live hidden or find refuge within certain clans, like my brother's."

He sat in an armchair opposite hers, holding a flute glass filled with a yellow liquid.

"So, you prefer men?" she asked.

He gazed at her. A mixture of excitement and circumspection. Erlend was both open and on his guard.

"What about you? Whom do you prefer?" he asked.

When she negotiated Ashta's defection aboard the prison ship, Nand's first sexual experience was as a man with one of the female guards. She hadn't enjoyed herself. Probably because she wasn't attracted to women, and despite her appearance, she remained a woman with a woman's desires. She needed a man's body to satisfy her.

"This is complicated." She gripped the chair's arms.

"Are you so sure?"

"Yes." But the more she looked at him, the more his beautiful eyes and his athletic body stirred her longing. She pointed to her glass. "Is this water or alcohol?"

"Water."

"It's making me light-headed."

"Good." He smiled. "You need it." He stood up, unbuttoned his shirt and peeled it off. "Are you coming?"

Fascinated, she watched him. He offered his smooth golden body to her. Her head emptied: she forgot what was permitted and what wasn't. Her appearance, Aslone's body, had become hers by the force of destiny and now aroused this stranger's excitement. This handsome Redlander whom she, Nand, the young woman of another time, another place, could become— would certainly become; already was—in love with.

"It's complicated," she repeated, standing up. "I'm not …"

A truth impossible to reveal. The Master Face Changer

ordered her to stay as Aslone. But what about the need to love and to be loved?

"You're hot."

Heat invaded her cheeks. She tried again, showing her body.

"It's not me …"

Erlend didn't hear her; maybe she had only whispered it. His tanned fingers freed the buttons of the simple shirt she wore. They undressed her. Warmth spread inside of her. He took his time removing his clothes. She caught his face, brought it to hers and kissed his mouth, aroused by his soft hands on her skin. She touched him. His smooth skin. Hers belonged to another, a man. A man whom another man found attractive. Erlend, whom she liked; she, the woman dispossessed of her own body.

"Erlend," she cried to forget she was a mere shadow, a memory, a being poised between immateriality and reality. "Erlend …"

Madness.

Love at first sight.

CHAPTER 187

Quiet Day

1 May 3077, Standard Time (ST), Sixth Federal Era
Redland—Esk Strath

Nand slowly pulled herself from her dream-deprived sleep. Sitting at a table, bare-chested, Erlend was drawing.

"Are you the one who did the paintings on the wall?" she asked, her bent arm holding her head up.

"Aslone!" He put down his piece of charcoal and perched on the edge of the bed. "You're finally awake." He kissed her. "I thought you'd never wake up."

"Did I sleep long? What time is it? Is the storm over?"

"You slept a little less than twenty-four hours. The wind blew all day long, and the sandstorm has spread over a huge area. Mogud is under arrest. And everybody is getting more and more worried about Theo and the Guild pilot."

"Why? What happened?" She sat up and pulled on a shirt.

"After we rescued you, Ashta and Farren both had a vision of the Guild ship that Theo boarded to leave the Dome. It crashed somewhere."

"Farren had a vision?"

He handed her a glass of water. "He said he felt what she felt, particularly her terror, until she lost consciousness."

"It's not a vision, then." She sipped the cold water. "He must have an empathic mind like Ashta. She feels what others feel."

"Not all of you are like this?"

Erlend stretched out on the bed beside her, his hand resting on her lower back.

"No. It's a rare gift. Do you know if Ashta is in touch with Theo?"

"Not anymore, apparently. The Guild chief, someone called Clobb, is unable to reach the pilot. And because of the sandstorm, all ships are grounded. Even those in orbit can't see a thing. In some areas, the sandstorm is over two kilometers high. Can you imagine that?"

"And Farren can't reach her either?"

"No. Livia is furious. She's so mean to him. You wouldn't think they are siblings."

"They're brother and sister?"

"Yes. And Malcolm MacDougal, her husband, is also Theo's cousin."

"How's Jack?"

Concern coated Erlend's voice. "Not well. The Suni Sisters—they are our doctors—stay with him all the time. He hasn't improved yet."

She slipped out of bed and stood in front of the window.

"You don't want to know about your friends?"

Swirls of dust blurred the view. She gazed back at her lover lying on the sheets. She liked the way his white hair haloed his head, the wrinkles that gave his gray eyes a twinkle when he grinned, his skin's perfect softness.

"Axonna is dying," she said. "He contacts me off and on. I should be near him because he has always supported me, but …" she fisted her hands, "… watching him die is more than I can take right now. For Declan, it's different. He's doing the same thing I am. Closing his mind up so he can rest. Ashta's only concern is Theo. And the others aren't friends. If something happens to them, Declan will inform me."

"Mentally?"

She nodded. "It's our usual way of communication."

He sat on the bed, his arms around his knees.

"You can read the minds of others?"

"It's forbidden."

"But can you do it?"

He watched her intently. She hesitated, unsure what to divulge. She opted for the truth.

"If I wanted to, I could, but I won't."

"Why not?"

"Because I'm not interested."

"Could you read my mind?"

"If necessary, probably," she admitted.

"And you all possess this skill?"

"What skill?"

"To read other people's minds!"

"Our talent is that we communicate mentally. Instead of talking, we think messages. Reading another person's mind is against the law in Eridan."

He joined her by the window.

"There have been rumors coming from the Dome for years.

Stories about a man who uses his mind to enslave others. Who tortures them."

"This man's name was Beruk Xë. He was an Eridani. He's dead."

"An Eridani like you?"

"Yes."

"He tortured you?"

She closed her eyes as shudders shook her.

Erlend embraced her. His warm hands stroked her arms, her back. "You're not taught to defend yourself?"

The terror she had endured at Xë's mercy still drilled into her mind.

"You're the youngest. None of the others could help you?"

She brushed his mouth with her fingertips. "It's complicated …"

"Did he hurt them, too?"

"His goal was to destroy Declan. I was a decoy."

"So nobody took your side."

"There was no other choice. We had to beat him at his own game to win." She wet her dry lips. "And we succeeded."

"At your expense."

She held him tight, marveling at how peaceful his heartbeat sounded against her ear. "Declan has always supported me. Without him, I wouldn't be here talking to you."

"Why were you sent to Gambling Nova? And don't tell me again that it's complicated."

She chuckled and stepped back. "Everything about us is complicated."

"Why?"

"Because the world we live in is complex and because I'm not allowed to say anything about it."

"Not even about yourself? Your family? Your life?"

She pointed at the artworks on the wall.

"You painted these?"

"Yes. Several months ago, during a habook that lasted a whole week."

She crossed the room to examine them. Erlend followed her.

"Your paintings display Eridan's main colors." She smiled at him. "Blue, black and green. We have three words to describe our ocean's depths: clearwater at the surface, where the colors of corals and fish are seen thanks to the sun. Deeper, there's bluewater, which is the middle territory. When you swim there, you sometimes meet big mammals—we call them kidadakh—and further down, there is coldnight. A dark, cold place. My father's family lives there. Almost all Abyss people sport white hair like you. And light skin because we rarely see the sun. In my family we have black hair."

"Do you have siblings?"

"A younger brother. His name is Terri. And there's my cousin Davin. He's a gardener."

"What do they look like, the kidadakh?"

She sat at the table. "May I?" She took a pencil. He pushed a sheet of paper in front of her.

Drawing Kaipekak opened a memory dam: it somewhat restored their bond. "There, and here's my size beside it."

Erlend whistled his appreciation. "It's huge."

She drew fiskiorps jumping out of the water, ippinis sunning themselves on a shore, and a garden-island.

"We have the ocean, and some islands. Eridooneen, our capital, is in Kerven, the main archipelago. Declan lives there. He heads the university."

"Do you study there?"

She shook her head. "I travel …"

A loud bell disrupted the silence.

"What's that noise?"

"It's the dinner bell for the people who don't own personal lodgings in Esk Strath. Are you ready to face the world?"

"Can we eat here?"

"Sure. I'll get us a platter."

"You don't mind?"

"Not at all. I like having you all to myself."

CHAPTER 188

Rory

1–2 May 3077, Standard Time (ST), Sixth Federal Era
Redland—Sky Cradle

H it in its tail and wings, the Guild ship caught fire not far from the ground.

Flames flashed inside the cockpit in front of Theo. The emergency capsule where she had burrowed was ejected. It landed hard on a dune, bobbing up and down, cutting Rory's voice short. It rolled over for several long minutes and then bumped to a stop.

She gasped and blinked as a tremulous light flickered inside the capsule, now lying sideways; she called Rory. Her head pounded. Her fingers shook too hard to unfasten the security harness.

A thunderous crackling hammered the coating of the capsule, which tipped over first one way and then the other. An endless rattle. Heat suffocated her. Surfaces closed in.

She choked. She sought air.

She only found dry heat.

And a shrouding darkness.

The capsule was well insulated, meant to protect Guild agents from the worst, and when she woke up, the secondary oxygen circuit had taken over and cooled the cramped space.

A gentle humming buzzed inside the capsule. She waited a long time before summoning the courage to move. The capsule reclined in a stable position. When she slowly unlatched the upper safety lock, the capsule shuddered. She barely had time to lock the latch again before it tipped over. A deafening sound erupted outside.

After a series of shudders, the capsule rolled backwards. Theo screamed as she failed to catch the dangling harness. The capsule rotated, and she rolled with it, unable to secure herself. She lost consciousness the fourth time her head slammed against a compartment.

She woke up. She tried to move and dizziness assaulted her. She closed her eyes. The dizziness persisted. She breathed slowly. Her body ached everywhere. At least the capsule was no longer in motion. Her forehead throbbed. She found a swelling bump. She sat up, fighting nausea and fear.

A ringing replaced the dizziness. She took stock of her condition: bruises and scratches, two head bumps, nothing life-threatening.

She opened the emergency door latch. Sand poured inside.

She crawled out of the capsule. It was midday; the suns shone bleak against a pinkish sky. She gulped fresh, smoke-scented air. She couldn't make anything out. She called to Rory. Her hoarse voice made a disturbingly puny sound. She forced herself to stand up. The wind slapped her. Caught unawares, she nearly fell off the capsule and clung to the surface until the wind abated enough for her to retreat to safety.

Eyes gritty, shivering, angry at her helplessness, she dived back inside. She latched the door, insulating herself. Hunger gnawed at her. She scrounged the locker marked "Food" and found a stack of protein bars. She munched on one, drank some still water, then snuggled under a light emergency blanket and went to sleep.

When the second sun rose the following morning, she took advantage of a lull in the sandstorm to drag herself across the dunes to the Guild ship's skeleton. Distance in the desert was deceptive: it took her the best part of the morning to reach the debris.

She found Rory immediately. Alive. Barely. On his back, stuck under a large piece of wing from the waist down. Wounded in both arms, in his chest, covered with caked blood, blisters on his skin.

She knelt beside him, afraid to touch his singed face.

"Rory," she whispered. "Rory, it's me. It's Theo."

He opened his eyes at once. They were startlingly clear. They gazed at each other for a long moment.

"Theo, sweetheart …" he wheezed. "I'm happy … you're alive. You must hide … They'll come back."

A shudder rippled through him and he winced. His eyelids fluttered.

"What can I do? Tell me what to do to help you. Explain how to use the radio."

"It's too late."

"It's never too late."

He smiled. "You're sweet … Never told you, did I? Drove me nuts. But …" He coughed. Blood dripped from the corner of his mouth.

"Don't talk." She caressed the unsinged side of his face.

"In my pocket … stockey … Take it. For Jack."

"I don't want to hurt you."

"Do … it … when I'm … dead."

Hearing his labored breathing hurt.

"You can't die, Rory."

He chuckled and moved the fingers of his left hand. She grabbed them with both of hers.

"Rory …"

He opened his mouth. No sound came out. She leaned over.

"My necklace …" he whispered. "Take it. I want you to have it."

"I will. Rory, I …"

"I know. I love you too … Don't cry …"

"I'm not crying!"

"Tell Farren … best man … Jack." He closed his eyes; pain hissed through his parched lips. He looked at her and smiled. "Jethro, you came …"

His hand turned slack in hers. Silence replaced his wheezing. He was gone.

Kneeling back on her heels, she caressed his strong, bruised hand between hers, unable to think.

Rory was gone. Tears blurred her sight as she closed his lusterless eyes. She unfastened his sooty necklace and clasped it around her own neck. She cringed as she counted to three. Could she search his corpse for this stockey? He had asked her to; it was for Jack, a dying man's last request. She must. She gagged, forced bile down, and went through his clothes. He'd stuck it in one of his inside pockets, and she retrieved it fast. She sat cross-legged in the sand, her knees touching his chest, watching him. This dear friend … she remembered the day they had skipped rope together, how stubborn he was, sweat running down his face, not wanting to give up, to concede defeat; and then how he had given in and applauded her victory, inviting her to listen to music in a pub in the Barrios and share one of those gross meaty sandwiches he was so fond of.

Still crying, she walked away from the ship to take in her surroundings.

Dune hills stretched to the horizon on two sides, dazzling her with shiny spider-like threads of light. Towards her left, a pebbled stretch of desert led to Canyon Maze. The sky combined heat and fiery fuzziness: the sandstorm remained a threat. She gripped her upper arms with frozen fingers. Her legs shook so hard that she sat down in the sand.

How would she bury her friend? She couldn't move him. A huge piece of aircraft nailed him to the ground. She half-crawled, half-shuffled back to the broken ship. She knelt beside Rory, sniffling.

She couldn't possibly leave him alone.

CHAPTER 189

Sandstorm

2–4 May 3077, Standard Time (ST), Sixth Federal Era
Redland—Sky Cradle

An aircraft flew through the storm. Friend or enemy? Better not tempt fate. Theo squeezed herself under the Guild ship's broken wing. She hunkered down while the white plane circled the crash site several times before gunning it down. It disappeared in the sand clouds.

As she squirmed out of her cramped hiding place, three ships burst from above. She retreated beneath the wing. They flew low. Were they searching for her? Or Rory? They set fire to the hull. The temperature escalated and she buried herself in the sand, worried about the flames.

She cowered there all night, while the swazzi howled and screeched through the aircraft pieces stuck in the salt desert and repeatedly rekindled the embers.

She hurried back to the emergency capsule as soon as she could discern her whereabouts. The air was thick with sand and smoke. Exhausted, emotionally spent, she reached the capsule around noon. The wind blew hard and slowed her down, but she figured it was protecting her from her enemies.

She spent another day and night inside the capsule. In between fretful naps, she tried twice to reach Ashta's mind. Each time, she experienced an excruciating headache followed by frightening bouts of tachycardia. So she tended to her bruises and organized her backpack. And the following morning she braved the billowing red swazzi and headed across a narrow stretch of salt desert towards Canyon Maze.

Inwardly she thanked her parents, and particularly her father, who had introduced her to Redland's geological wonders through week-long expeditions every month during her childhood and adolescence before they moved to live under the Dome. Those lessons in Reddish geography resurfaced after the crash while she kept a vigil by Rory's side and examined the landscape: she needed no technology to tell her that until she reached Canyon Maze's qanat-side, she was on her own.

Crossing Sky Cradle—the salt desert—would lead her to certain death. With no shelter, she would be an easy target for Mogud's Fudrons, and if she survived an attack she would die of thirst before she had got halfway. Once the storm abated, Malcolm would send out people to find her and Rory, but Sky Cradle was huge, seldom visited, and far from Nomadic routes or City-Dweller abodes.

Jack and Farren, and Lonetom, and probably also the Guild would look for them. But when? Habooks stymied everybody, everything.

In her early teens, she had once trekked for twelve hours in Sky Cradle. Her father had taken her and Malcolm to the salt desert for a ten-day spring hike. They had penetrated its immensity from another vantage point. She remembered how awed she had been when she first viewed the flat and pristine expanse, and her vivid discussion with Malcolm about the mirage they had both seen after a brief rain shower.

Since she couldn't even contemplate waiting for rescue in the claustrophobic emergency capsule, she would walk her way back.

So, her shoulders weighed down by her backpack, she began her journey by striding over the white, crunchy ground for two hours until she reached the moist, oozy surface of the wide shore cupping the desert. She didn't stop to admire the landscape. Just a quick glance behind her to survey the distance she had covered before she took the trail that looped through the rugged terrain rising towards Canyon Maze's entrance.

The sandstorm enveloped her as she trudged along the rough path, bent over, head down: pebbles and uprooted spiky shrubs smacked her legs. Sand-packed gales whipped her as she gripped her backpack harness, scraping her knuckles raw. Thankful for the goggles found in the emergency capsule locker, she pushed on, one halting step after the other, breathing dust despite the cloth swaddling her face.

The winds swept through the entry canyon. Where could she hide? She found an opening, a cave two meters above the ground. After several harrowing minutes, she hauled her backpack and herself up the mountain wall and into the smelly cave. Huddled as far as she could under the narrow overhang, she wrapped the safety blanket around her body to keep warm.

The maze grumbled, its mineral noises reminding her of relentless waves crashing on a shore. Afraid she would roll out of her shelter and break a limb if she slept, she only allowed herself to doze, never letting her guard down.

She dug into far-away memories to remember everything her father had taught her about this red-rock wilderness. The next morning, the sandstorm had abated a bit, at least inside the canyon. She looked for the landmarks her father had mentioned and rejoiced when she found them, optimistic despite her exhaustion and itchy shoulder.

At dusk, she came upon a dead-end canyon in Canyon Maze, and worry seeped through. It was too late to head back and sleep in the cave, so she stayed where she was, concealing herself between two boulders. Minutes went by slowly while the swazzi hollered cold gusts. It was wiser to return to the place where she had entered the canyon and think things through. As she walked back, she congratulated herself for leaving traces of her passage.

The winds blew sand in her face throughout the day.

During this two-day hike, she did her best to counter the rising sense of defeat and alarm that embraced her each time she thought she might be lost among ramified routes that all looked alike. She finally reached Canyon Maze's Sky Cradle entry and shook with relief. The sandstorm's intensity had diminished. As she searched for a place to set up her camp, she slipped on a stone and fell heavily onto the rough ground, twisting her left ankle.

This sudden agony woke her up. It propelled her out of the trance-like bubble she realized she had been caught in since the crash. Violent shudders jolted her as she massaged her swollen ankle. Her teeth chattered; longing tightened her stomach. Loneliness gripped her throat when, to her right, she identified the Dome through a red mist, an appallingly short structure. Could it be a mirage? Beyond the Dome, the Djerrani ridge crest sparkled.

The Guild ship had covered an amazing distance before being shot down. As she took stock of both landscape and distance, she remembered Reddish geography. She was down east, not far from a vast and isolated territory where Sky Cradle and similar salt deserts alternated with sharp, spiky rocks.

Canyon Maze, which loomed behind her, was the shortest route to inhabited land. As her father had explained when he took her to Painted-Caves, which was nestled at the heart of Canyon Maze, three convoluted routes joined up there. He had mapped part of this labyrinth when he was younger. So when they traveled together, he chose a rugged trail to reach the caves and an easier path for their return trip. She recalled hearing an underwater river's gurgle as she dozed at the entrance of Flower Cave.

Canyon Maze provided shelter. She slept not far from its entry path, once again wrapped in her safety blanket. The next day, after changing the elastic compress around her ankle and squeezing her foot into her hiking boot, she inspected the nearest boulders: a detail that her father had once told her about orientation and compass points resurfaced. Even though Canyon Maze was a remote, rough and risky place, it attracted several dozen trekkers each year, so sketchy itineraries with landmarks and directions were carved at every labyrinth access point.

The map corresponding to the entry where she stood was gouged into a boulder: to reach Painted-Caves she needed to follow a route marked by several cairns that crossed the two

major interconnecting canyons and three smaller side canyons.

A long hike. How long would it take her? Fifteen days? Or
more. If her fear of heights thwarted her, the distance would
increase, as some trails might be impossible for her to take.

She copied the sketchy cairn route, committing to memory
its main landmarks—Mhuol Pillar, Stairway Arches, Horse
Ears and Red Cliffs. Once she reached the pictograph caves she
would have access to water, as two qanats started there. Before
that, she was on her own. She carried with her every water reserve found in the emergency capsule as well as water-
purifying tablets. The map indicated several water-filled potholes along the trail.

With determined hope, she began her journey.

CHAPTER 190

A Face Changer's Death

4 May 3077, Standard Time (ST), Sixth Federal Era
Redland—Esk Strath

Nand emerged from behind the partition curtain. A handsome young man trailed behind her. He reminded Axonna a bit of the real Nand with his clear eyes and his mane of white hair. The Suni nurse, who was sitting beside the bed on which he was propped up, smiled, and dimples appeared in her cheeks.

"You're Aslone, aren't you?" She stood up and invited Nand to take her place. "Axonna said you would come. I'll leave you together. If you need anything, send Erlend. I'll be in the greenhouse next door."

Somewhere, restless waterdrops fell.

"Should I leave?" the young man asked, and his voice was like a caress.

"No, stay. I'll introduce you." Nand sat on the edge of the bed, her weight pulling on the light sheet.

"Axonna, it's Aslone. And I brought you my friend Erlend."

He had always liked her voice. Its grave softness resonated beneath Aslone's more mature one.

"So, you're the one who stole Aslone away from us." He envied their dazzling youth's beauty. "Are you aware of the nature of the paradox that put you in his arms?"

He doesn't know. He only loves men.

I know.

"Not nice to think instead of talking, Aslone. We have a guest." Gripping the sheet, Axonna hated himself for sounding peeved.

"Aslone is still exhausted," Erlend said in a protective tone, his hands on Aslone's shoulders.

"What he needs more than anything—what we all need— is love, and that's what you're giving him. I won't have this luck before I die."

"Axonna …" Nand caught his hands. Her fingers were warm, dry, strong.

"When you return to Eridan," he pulled her closer to him, "I want you to tell Astriv that he was the great love of my life." The memory of their final battle in the cavern entwined with underwater embraces and the heated arguments that had peppered their tumultuous relationship. "And … I want you to tell him … to tell him …" His thoughts shredded as he pronounced them, so many words had already sunk into the abyss. He blinked: Aslone's eyes reflected a fear of being, a mirror of his own fear.

"What else do you want me to tell Astriv?" Nand gently pressed his fingers.

"That he … that he …"

After Astriv, all the men he knew, all the men he had loved, had never lived up to him. He had never loved any of them the way he adored Astriv. And Astriv had attacked him. Because of him, Axonna would sink far from Mocean.

She stroked his hands.

He opened his eyes; he couldn't stop opening his eyes, waking up every minute to avoid the ultimate moment, the moment that gobbled up his thoughts, that devoured each remaining minute.

A disciple. Aslone was his last disciple. A dam against death. He remembered why he had called Nand to his side.

"I give you my *Book of Changes*. You'll need it." She shook her head. He ground her fingers. Too much insubordination. Clive had known right away that he should trust her, and so had Declan. His own disciples—the five talented actresses who were the Miring sisters—would have helped him give a joyful air to the face-changing art. Together, they would have abandoned introspection's morose path and explored novel ways. Their deaths at noon, under the bright sun, on the white beach, had been a foretaste of his own. "You will need it." He searched Aslone's eyes, Nand's eyes, but the vacuum gnawed his optic nerves, and even if he tried his best to open, to widen his eyes, he could hardly distinguish anything anymore. "Aslone …"

I'm here.

"Whoever you are, you are you. This is the first lesson." The only one he remembered. What were the others? What had he learned? To face-change to please himself, to seduce men, and he was dying in his miserable first appearance? Supreme irony. "Afterwards choose your life. But you remain the same. At the core. At the heart of your being. We all do."

Is there something I can do to help?

There was. He didn't remember what it was, though. Something important. He must open his eyes. His eyelids weighed so much. And when he gazed around him, everything blurred. Emptiness allied itself to exhaustion; one kneaded his limbs so the other could feed on them with unwavering gusto.

An undisciplined disciple whose responsibility even Declan didn't want anymore.

Axonna …

You must heal Declan.

But—

It's too late for me. I can't do it. I thought I'd be able to once I was better. It won't happen. However, there is still hope for him. You are the only one who can push him out of the dark into the light.

She caressed his cheek. *I have no idea how to do it.* She smiled wistfully. *Even if I had the gift, how could I do that? He would hate me.*

If you don't do it, he'll die.

This mental conversation pulled him downwards. Declan's inner light had faded. He had felt it when they had talked earlier in the day.

Agony shook his breast.

Nand …

He opened his eyes, opened them again: all around him, only darkness.

"Declan!"

The terror of losing everything, of not being able to leave any memories to Mocean flooded him as pain gushed through his body wherever the vacuum hadn't finished nibbling.

"Axonna …"

She wasn't the right person.

He needed Declan. The Master Face Changer was a Ring of Sea. He had acted as resh for Clive. He could save him from the void.

Declan!

"I love you," she said, and she embraced him.

Her mind was clear and strong. So different.

He breathed fire. His heart accelerated.

On the brink of emptiness, he hesitated. Fear decided him. As water submerged him, he clutched her translucid mind, sealing inside of it his memories and his healing gift.

Cruel bite.

He carried Nand's scream with him as he sunk.

CHAPTER 191

Sorrow

4 May 3077, Standard Time (ST), Sixth Federal Era
Redland—Esk Strath

"What happened when your friend died? Why did you scream?" Erlend repeated for the third time.

They had rushed out of the greenhouse and sought refuge in a mountain recess to escape the swazzi gusts.

"I need to be alone. Completely."

Erlend searched her eyes. "Follow me."

Wind howled through round openings in the ochre mountain rock wall as they climbed the steps inside a turret. Pinpoints of light lined the spiral staircase. At the top, they stood on a landing, circled by a roof-covered, medium-high parapet.

"Nobody will bother you here."

She turned towards Erlend, barely discerning his sinewy, elegant figure in the darkness. "Thank you."

She stood, hands flat on the parapet, and watched the night. She kept her mind blank, her breathing steady. At one point, Erlend covered her shoulders with a blanket.

Purple filled the sky sooner than expected. The swazzi's trailing veils swept the dunes and masked dawn. Sand tumbled, choking the air, even where she stood. She inhaled sand, hating how it prickled her throat.

If only she was this landscape: a dune modeled by the wind. Or if she were Heris, she could cry and her tears would become an ocean in which she could melt. Evaporate. Simply go. And abandon to others the burden of living with the memory of the dead.

Her mother, Aslone, Clive, and now Axonna and so many Face Changers whose features were welded into her memory. The sunk ones demanded tears. These tears had gathered for many seasons behind her eyelids without spilling out. She had not mourned her dead. Only struggled to survive their absence. She had watched them die, she had seen how death marked their faces. Their dull eyes. Her dead had left her, taking with them secrets about her that nobody else knew.

She had never accompanied her dead ones on their last journey, kissed their cheeks one last time, braided a seaweed wreath. For her mother, for Aslone, for Clive, she was forced to postpone her bereavement until later. Until never.

Tears pushed against the dam of her eyelids; countless tears drowning her from within. Tears she wanted to shed. If she did, though, wouldn't she definitely lose the dead, forget them?

She was sinking. Like Eridan, devastated by a wall of water. She had had the vision in Pit 3, and she dreamed about it each time she slept. The water wall hid the sun, replaced day with night, left fish and underwater creatures gasping and twitching. And when it stopped rising, it crashed, flooding islands and the Shallow Seas, destroying bubflats, seaweed fields and shellfish farms.

Many Eridanis had sunk.

And Mocean … Mocean drifted; Mocean cooled.

Erlend showed up on the landing whistling, a loose basket slung over his shoulder. He carried two mugs. "I brought some hot choctea. You must be freezing, even with the blanket."

"I'd love to drink something hot, you're right." She cleared her voice as she leaned her back against the parapet to face him.

He gave her a mug. "They're burying your friend at the end of the afternoon or tomorrow morning."

She wrapped her hands around the scalding mug. "Because of the storm?"

"Yes. Everybody is so worried. The storm still covers an enormous portion of the desert. All our instruments are totally useless to locate Theo and Rory, the pilot."

Declan and Ashta had to be united in a common concern about Theo.

"Do you want to attend the burial? I'll go with you."

She shrugged. "In Eridan, we immerse people, we don't bury them." She sipped the scalding beverage. "The dead person is swathed in a woven seaweed fabric with pebbles sewn in. We put an immersion ring around the person's neck. Then the body is laid in deep water."

"So you don't have cemeteries?"

Erlend straddled the parapet, his back resting against one of the poles that supported the roof. He placed in front of him a round candle jar, poked with holes, inside which a flame shivered. He helped her hoist herself up onto the parapet.

After so many lonely days, the need to talk overwhelmed her.

"Eridan is a planet covered by an ocean called Mocean. When we die, our minds join this ocean, which is both our womb and our collective consciousness. That's why we are not afraid of dying. Or sinking as we call it. We know we return to the original water and our life memories become part of the whole. Our life in Eridan is a pathway from one state to another state."

"I can't imagine not being afraid of dying. It keeps me awake a lot. A few Redlanders believe in Sharm, the great god, but I don't."

"Sometimes, people don't die this way. In the Abyss, where I come from, death by accident happens, and in that case, the resh—he's the person who collects a dying person's memories—isn't around."

"So …?"

"The dead one is lost to our world." She caressed the warm mug. Sadness hovered as she remembered the massacre.

"Why were you sent here?"

She shook her head. He pushed the lantern towards her and sat closer, their knees touching. "You need to talk."

She sipped the sweet beverage. "I have visions. My mind contains shards of other people's lives. They rain inside of me when the outside world closes up on me."

"What do you mean?" Erlend lit a cigarette. He offered it to her and she waved a refusal. "You've been imprisoned before?"

"I stopped talking after my mother died. I physically couldn't. For a long time, I thought it was my way of punishing my brother Davin. You see, I held him responsible for her death. I was confused because I created a mental bond with a kidadakh."

"A kidadakh …" He frowned. "You mean the underwater creature that you drew the other morning? You communicate with these animals?"

"One of them. His name's Kaipekak." Saying his name warmed her. "We communicate by image-thought. I'm what our people call a hlyk, because of this bond with the kidadakh, and I live most of the time in the ocean with Kaipekak. Before me, my mother was the hlyk. When she died, it was my turn. We were together when a zuglan attacked us in bluewater. It's one of the most ferocious marine predators. My mother fought him to protect me, and … she sunk."

He placed the candle jar behind him and sat close enough to embrace her. "Why did you think your brother was responsible for your mother's death?" He rearranged the blanket around them.

"It was his harpoon that killed my mother's kidadakh during a hunt."

"Did he know this kidadakh had bonded with your mother?"

"No. My brother and I didn't know anything."

"You said the other day that you had one brother and that his name was Terri. And now you say Davin is your brother. So, who is your brother and who is your cousin?"

Heat spread over her face, and she looked towards the awakening desert.

"Aslone?"

She was fed up with her lies.

"Explain to me."

Clutching the blanket, she faced him. "I shouldn't have said anything to you. When I speak about myself, I forget what I look like."

"What are you talking about?"

She remembered his question, her answer: no mention whatsoever about a sister, about herself. Perhaps she didn't need to reveal all the details, or her gender. Having sex with him thrilled her too much.

"I am—we all are, except for Ashta—Face Changers. It means that we can give ourselves different bodies and faces." She framed her face with her hands. "This face is not mine; it's my cousin Aslone's. We took each other's appearance for fun. A silly prank. He was murdered with many Face Changers before we were sent here."

Head bent to the side, Erlend watched her as he blew smoke from his cigarette.

"What do you look like?"

"My hair is as white as yours. Straight. And my eyes are blue. I am thinner. My skin is light. It burns easily in the sun."

"And what's your name?"

"Nand. But please don't use it otherwise Declan will be angry with me, and ..."

"I'll only use it when we are alone together." He tested the name. "Nand. I like it. It's short and soft at the same time." He lit another cigarette.

She watched pink and orange cirrus invade the sky and thought of Terri. She missed him even more than she missed Kaipekak.

"You said earlier that you stopped speaking when your mother died. For how long?"

"Almost two seasons. That makes five months."

"It's a long time." He jumped from the parapet to retrieve the basket. He poured more choctea from a pitcher into their mugs and handed her a thick slice of honey-bread.

"Thank you." Her throat was so tight that she barely heard herself, and repeated her thanks. He settled once again in front of her.

"Did something special happen for you to talk again?"

The mug warmed her frozen fingers. "I don't like those memories."

"Share them with me. It will help."

She ate some honey-bread. "I talked in my sleep. Our community chief and my father found out. They thought I had lied to them, that I was only pretending I couldn't speak. They didn't understand that it wasn't a choice. I couldn't. I couldn't tell them about the hlyk either. Davin wasn't around, and …"

"And …?"

"They punished me because they thought I was feigning being mute. I was condemned to silence, and forced to stay in our underwater city in the deep. I wasn't allowed to go out, I wasn't allowed to speak, and nobody could talk to me either. It's around that time that I had the first visions I really remember. Two men appeared in them: Declan and Farren."

"Farren? You mean Dag? You dreamed of him? How is that possible?"

"That's the mystery I want to solve." The topic change relieved her. "I had visions of him during my stay below the ocean, and later, at another time when Mocean became hot and uncontrollable."

"What kind of visions?"

"Personal memories. I want to find out why I had them. There has to be a reason."

"How long did you stay in the deep?"

"Three months. One day I escaped."

He grinned. "Good for you. Did you make peace with your brother?"

"Yes. We don't see each other often, but we stay in mental touch. I'm closer to my cousin Terri, Aslone's younger brother."

"When you became mute, could you still communicate mentally?"

"Only with Kaipekak."

"This is so strange. I love my horse, but sharing thoughts with it?" He wrinkled his nose.

"I don't share thoughts. It's like a mental representation that I interpret. I can try to show you if you want."

"For real?"

"It depends if you're receptive or not …" She slid off the parapet. "Come over here. It's safer since we don't know how you'll react." She covered Erlend's forehead with her hands and pressed her face against them. "Close your eyes. Relax, and let's try."

Erlend grabbed her around the waist, hip to hip.

"If it doesn't work we should dance together."

"Shhhh …"

"You're so hot."

"Hush."

For the first time since arriving in Gambling Nova, Nand indulged in the joy of Mocean, which had helped her so much at first: slowly swimming in coldnight; the phosphorescence of gigantic shellfish with thick and pointy carapaces; lava fountains vanishing in chilled bubbles that popped hot. Undulating movement upwards; salt water pouring into her; shell-decorated, brown-seaweed-strewn rocks. Warm bluewater; big yellow-and-blue-striped fish with inquisitive globular eyes emerging from black corals. A sandy sea bottom with an enormous brown-and-white-dotted ray hedge-hopping.

Swimming through dark blue, icy waters, layers of green seaweed pressing at the surface. Terri sat on a raft imprisoned by ice-crystal water hills. She emerged from the deep. Bright sky, bleak horizon. Thick air. Her throat stung. Her skin numbed. Slow, slushy waves surrounded her, waves freezing into rolls. The silence was broken by a rumbling echo from beneath: a pod of kidadakh surged from the deep and crashed, skidding on the ice waves' solid and uneven surface. Their bellows wove the white atmosphere with death.

From coldnight to clearwater, Mocean froze.

Moaning, Nand opened her eyes. She stumbled away from Erlend, yet stroked his arm, her hand sliding to his hand, which she gripped.

"Sorry … I shouldn't have. I'm so sorry," she whispered as she collapsed on the paved floor, covering her head with her arms.

"Can you explain?" Erlend sat beside her. "It was so beautiful at first. I loved it! But then …"

Leaning against the parapet wall, she locked her hands around her knees.

"You saw the frozen waves, didn't you?"

He nodded.

"I can't explain why I have visions like this about Eridan. In one of them, a white and sterile desert replaces Mocean. Twice I saw enormous waves that devastated everything. And now it's ice."

"They might just reflect your worry at being far from your home."

"Maybe."

"What about your visions with Dag?"

"They're different. Like memories of things he has seen or done. Sometimes he's young; sometimes he's as old as he is now."

"How strange!"

"Yes. I met him for the first time the day we escaped. Until then, I wasn't sure he even existed." She stretched her legs.

"Visions about your home, that I can understand. But Farren Megan ..."

"I want to question him about a place where he went when he was young. He travelled with an old woman who told him a myth mentioning Heris. Heris is an entity linked to Eridan's origins. But with Jack sick, I don't want to bother him."

"There might be another way of getting information." Erlend stood up. "I'll see what I can do."

She got to her feet as well. Desert and sky mirrored the same orange.

"Can you stay with me a little while longer?"

"Let's watch the second sunrise together."

CHAPTER 192

Mhuol Treatment

4 May 3077, Standard Time (ST), Sixth Federal Era
Redland—Esk Strath

Whenever Farren left Jack's side, he talked with Malcolm and Cowan about Theo and Rory. The sandstorm progressed so slowly that no aircraft had yet ventured to the crash site. Everybody speculated and worried about Theo and Rory. Waiting for the sandstorm to abate, not knowing if they were hurt, hoping that they could handle the situation rattled each one of them.

Farren slept two or three hours at a time in a hammock installed in Jack's bedroom, while Kilu or another Suni Sister kept a vigil.

A few days after initiating the mhuol treatment, Kilu asked him if Jack had been in a serious accident when he was young. Even if most of the scars marring his brawan's body had faded away, some were too deeply ingrained to disappear entirely. Farren resented Kilu for alluding to them, was already thinking that she should stop caring for Jack, when her next words made him realize how paranoid he was.

Jack was overloaded with pain, she explained, and it would take time for him to react positively to the treatment. When she examined his body, she noticed many marks. X-rays confirmed that bones in his limbs, his shoulders, had been broken, some two or three times. Hence the question about the accident.

He told her there was none, leaving her to guess the truth—that Jack had been physically abused.

The way she saw it, hardened layers of hurt needed to be reduced. They had to work together on freeing Jack from this burden. He was quieter when Farren held his hand. From now on they would strive to ease him away from past nightmares and bring him into the light.

Kilu encouraged Farren to talk to Jack. One of mhuol's unexpected side-effects was to sharpen a sick person's awareness of things, particularly in cases of delirium. The Suni Sister wanted to lean on this acute awareness to modify Jack's perceptions. "Dig up the past," she said. "Tell him what you know of his life, the subjects you never broach. I suppose he didn't confide much. And you didn't ask out of respect. You thought you would embarrass him. I think you were wrong. Your prince is now walled in by bricks of ugly memories. Replace each brick with a good memory; open windows for him. He needs love right now."

So they worked in parallel: she alleviated the trauma of broken bones and torn ligaments, while he brought the wall down and found new bricks.

A voice like a safety line.

Farren spoke to Jack in the Suni Sisters' absence. Ashta and Smanul visited several times a day, bringing food, tea or stronger drinks, friendship and support. Smanul found Farren a flute. He liked the wooden instrument's suave, mellow sound. When he played the flute, forgotten moments resurfaced. He told Jack about the singing mountain where his father used to take him when he was a kid. A plateau high up where the swazzi blew through holes in rocks. They would sit, side by side, cuddled under a blanket, his father's arm around his shoulders, and listen to the wind melodies.

There was also the dented saxophone Smanul had bargained for him on Gambling Nova's black market, which he had left behind. These too-fresh memories he kept to himself. Yet what had happened to his treasured sax back home? Was it stolen when the Metropolice ransacked their home? He hoped not. This precious instrument had once belonged to Crazy Moon.

Each day, he practised the vivacious descant he had heard in Yelun the last time he had traveled there, before their lives unraveled. He recounted this trip to Jack, interlacing words with music.

Farren wished he had inherited his mother's storytelling talent. Crazy Moon had possessed the gift too, effortlessly spinning tales about the Th'ans. The old woman had loved music, and they had invented songs and tunes together. He had to dig deep to remember them. He tried each day, cringing when he croaked wrong notes.

He wiped Jack's dry body with a wet cloth. Kilu insisted that the knots were loosening, yet his brawan remained out of reach. He tried telling Jack what he knew of his childhood and youth, things he had unearthed a long time ago and never shared. The few words he pronounced turned his hands clammy. Wasn't he betraying his brawan by telling him what he knew?

Those ugly bricks proved too hard for him to dislodge in such a manner. So he recounted his own youth, his childhood in Redland, his close relationship with his dad, and his nine-month stay in Yelun. Jack knew some stories, but not all of them, and none of Farren's reflections that followed from his last trip to Yelun.

Farren told him again how he had worked for nearly three years in an Omniliner's cooking brigade to earn money to pay for the SpaceSS Academy, and how he had escaped a mining company in Yelun, a danger-filled facility where his youthful gullibility had thrust him, and met Crazy Moon.

When he had asked the old woman how she knew he intended to escape the morning they met, she had shrugged off his question.

He had learned the truth from Silver Blue, her brother, when he had gone back to Yelun the year before: the Th'ans kept an eye on the mining facility, now closed. They had insiders gathering evidence about wrongdoings, such as hiring youngsters. As it was, the men who had helped him out of the barracks were Th'an agents.

Silver Blue acknowledged the manipulation. He disclosed that his sister had had a pre-cog dream about Farren. She wanted to travel with him, live her last months in his company.

Silver Blue had given in, a decision that still rankled. She was fighting a blood disease. If she had stayed at home and accepted her treatment she could have lived longer.

"But you made my sister happy," he admitted. "You were the son she never had. You allowed her to teach what she knew, and to cross our beautiful land from north to south one last time. So, even if I resent you because you kept her away from us, I thank you today, because I now know how intense and exhilarating her last months were. You see, she left me a notebook."

Farren pinned sheets of paper on the walls of Jack's bedroom and tried to outline the places he remembered. Drawing frustrated him, so Smanul took over. Each memory occupied a square card.

Smanul's questions forced Farren to delve further into his past for details.

In standard time, a Yelun year lasted ten months. Six cold months—the Silent Waters—and four not-so-cold months—the Singing Seas. During the not-so-cold months, ice melted and, in some places, uncovered a dark fertile earth. Red, purple and yellow flowers blossomed close to the ground, grass grew thick and sharp, and there was a flurry of insect and animal activity.

Farren stayed about nine months with Crazy Moon.

She rescued him in the middle of Silent Waters. She fed him and took care of him, always reserved. She sometimes left him alone for a morning or an afternoon. One day, she returned with a second wadda. She informed him she would teach him how to bring the white—sometimes blue or green—immensity surrounding them into his heart.

Some emotions, such as fear, Farren couldn't share with his brawan.

He believed he had lived up to Crazy Moon's expectations for many years, but the hardships he had recently faced since Donatella Simpson had forced him to go to Gambling Nova had changed him.

CHAPTER 193

Devastation

*6 May 3077, Standard Time (ST), Sixth Federal Era
Eridan (207th Cycle, Cuttlefish Season, Whirlpools' Blue
Year)—Oniraveen*

The day after the water wall, fetid seaweed appeared on Mocean's whole surface and on the beaches. Experts said that it was torn from the sea bottom during the big wave, and not to worry, just burn it.

The same tenen, mental snapshots relayed by thought-twisters contacted by Joos pictured the devastation across Eridan, from the garden-islands to the Shallow Seas, from Kerven to the Northern Abyss. The people who knew about the Face Changers' fate, those who were questioned and others, sent pictures that showed seaweed clusters resting on sandless beaches or cluttering open waters; stranded kidadakh and thousands of dead fish. Snapshots soon showed that throughout Eridan clearwater and bluewater were growing darker. They showed surface waves rolling stronger and taller. They showed Eridooneen inhabitants hounding Keith each time he set foot out of The Towers. The audio snapshots proved the most damaging for the kwirimok, with his stutters and bellows, his denials and refusals to comment on the changes Mocean was undergoing.

Carmen and Terri coordinated the mental snapshot network in Oniraveen, while Joos and Cass headed the Eridooneen group, and Mona and Kij handled the Shallow Seas one. They organized themselves the day Keith of Rain Forest announced that the water wall had originated from an underwater earthquake.

Free Mocean was the banner under which Eridanis from every region rallied, a movement that challenged Keith of Rain Forest's legitimacy as kwirimok. Questions were asked about Declan. And then snapshots of Bibiana's drawings of the Vatatui massacre circulated widely.

Carmen, who was waiting for Terri on a bench by the cliff path overlooking Oniraveen Bay, not far from the Savalwomen Fortress, was worried about everybody's safety. She waved at him as he walked towards her.

They hugged, and sat side by side. They both skirted around the first words, those that expressed concern for their dear ones. After the water wall crashed, engulfing their world, they thought and shared their sympathy with each other and all the others.

Carmen and Terri found themselves to be kindred spirits. Dependable was Sofini's way of describing their quiet ways. He gave his friend a box containing a pastry; she offered him a pot of wapui preserve.

"You look tired," he said. "Still not sleeping?"

"Look at you! You've lost weight since a tenen ago."

They smiled. She opened the box and took out the orange cake.

"Sofini baked it." He pointed at his backpack. "You can eat this one right away. There are plenty more for later, or to share."

"Thank you. Thank Sofini. How is she?"

He shrugged. "Her mother's arm is not healing well … Fortunately, the others are fine, at least the adults. The children …"

"I know. We must do something about the nightmares. Bibiana?"

"She left the hospital, and she's moved in with us. But she won't stay at home. She's working part-time in Ollie's fish farm. What about Sheer?"

Carmen shrugged. "She's worried. Like you. The same deep worry you won't share with us. Her mind is closed around a secret. Yours is too. I know it; I see it, Terri. What's going on? Have you found out something? Is it related to Mindrule?"

"She's still in the Shallow Seas?"

"That's where she is most needed right now. Half of the Savalwomen have joined her there. About a quarter are in Kerven helping with the collapsed aquatrain tracks, and the others, the youngest, they stay with me. But they all want to leave!"

She nibbled the cake, watching him sideways, waiting.

He sat cross-legged beside her, his elbows on his knees, watching the view.

The dead were few, the wounded many. Most bubflats had already been put together again. However, the farms—fish, shellfish, seaweed, as well as most vegetable and fruit boxes—

had suffered massive destruction, particularly in the Shallow Seas and almost all the garden-islands. Their owners said that it would take at least four seasons, maybe longer, for their crops and their cultures to grow again.

"What is eating at you, Terri?"

"Keith." He looked at her squarely. "He was happy when Xë sunk. I … I saw him. I felt what he felt. Mindrule isn't an idea anymore. He controls Mocean and Whitecur."

"How so?"

"The water wall … It had nothing to do with the Master Face Changer, Evetha and Xë. It started before they fought. Didn't you feel it? The pull?"

She shook her head. She was too busy getting the Saval-women into safety on the fortress's upper esplanade.

"I did. I felt as if I was drawn into the water wall. That I became this wall. I was awake, not asleep, but my mind wasn't my own anymore."

He returned to the contemplation of the bay.

She put her hand on his knee. "What aren't you telling me?"

"He enjoyed the thrill. He'll do it again. Soon." He faced her, his expression grim. "He must be stopped."

CHAPTER 194

Burial

7 May 3077, Standard Time (ST), Sixth Federal Era
Redland—Esk Strath

Many people attended Axonna's burial: Kilu, Alk, and Fern Maddiogga, Theo's formidable mother; Malcolm and Livia, Cowan and Erlend MacRae, Farren and Smanul, nimble on his crutches despite the leg wound received during the Xen4 attack; Lonetom, the Guild Observer with mournful eyes; and almost all the people who had escaped the Dome at the same time as the Eridanis. Nand met the friendly Captain Kirby, who manned the ship that would get them back to Eridan.

The ceremony took place during a morning lull in the sandstorm, two days after Axonna died. He was buried in the Esk Strath cemetery, off the main valley—a red stone garden. Each Face Changer and Ashta spoke for him. Afterwards, a choir composed of women, mostly Suni Sisters, and a few men, including Erlend's brother Cowan, sang in memory of their friend.

The songs and music soothed her soul.

After the ceremony, Declan nodded to Ashta and to his Half-Masters.

Before leaving them alone, the Savalwoman drew Nand aside, out of Declan's earshot.

"You two must talk," she said. "That's why we're leaving."

"I know."

"He's upset."

Nand shrugged.

"Remember what Keith did to him."

"Don't worry."

Ashta gripped her arm, searching her eyes. "I'm aware he's been unfair to you, but please bear with him."

"I'll try."

Ashta smiled that little smile of hers that meant that she wasn't fooled and, waving at Declan, she left the cemetery.

Nand followed the pebble path that circled each tomb—a roundabout way to join the Master Face Changer. Dusty wind brushed her face. She adjusted her light blue shawl around her head the way Erlend had taught her.

"Where have you been all this time?" Declan asked, from the bench where he sat. "I was worried about you. Why didn't you answer my mental prompts?"

Some exhaustion had vanished from his face even though his eyes remained clouded.

"I needed to be alone."

"With that Redlander?"

"We're friends."

"Only?"

"It's none of your business."

"You are the hlyk, so everything you do is my concern. You have no future here."

His mouth's harsh downward lines struck her.

"I don't intend to stay, not with Mocean in full metamorphosis."

"What do you mean?"

"What happened in Yelun has befallen Eridan. The cold is coming and it is freezing Mocean."

"Yelun?" He frowned. "What are you talking about?"

"*The Tales of Zodostar*! You know: Eridan's creation myth, the story of the twins Yelun and Heris."

"These are myths, Nand. Nothing else. But what's this about Mocean? You had a vision?"

She picked up a few pebbles and rolled them between her hands. "I have all sorts of visions. End-of-the-world visions. Frost; drying up. We must go back home. The sooner the better."

"Not before we find Evetha. You heard about the crash?"

"Erlend keeps me informed."

"You are the hlyk, don't you forget it."

"And you, don't forget you are the Master Face Changer!"

He straightened up, his hands flat on his knees. "Meaning?"

"That you must heal yourself before we go home."

He touched his cheeks self-consciously. "You don't know what you're talking about."

She stepped closer. "Don't I? Why haven't you worked on your scars since we escaped? If you face-changed, you could get everything to disappear, even your arm wound."

"Don't you remember your lessons?" Anger strained his voice. "An original appearance can't be modified. It stays the way it is, or you lose yourself when you face-change."

The wind blew stronger. She tucked her shawl in. "Axonna told me he explained the healing process to you. Have you tried?"

"That is none of your concern."

"Before he sunk, Axonna said that if you didn't heal yourself, I should do it."

"He wasn't thinking straight in the end." Declan stood up. A muscle twitched in his cheek.

"How would you know? You weren't there!"

"I didn't need to be around."

"Axonna was concerned about you, about your future. He believed in you. That's what kept him alive. He wanted to heal you but he didn't have the strength to do it." Her heartbeat quickened. "I will do it."

"No."

She smiled, drawing fortitude from the kindness, the love she'd always felt for him. "I helped Terri bring you back to the surface when you were sinking. I can't let you suffer any longer." She folded her arms against her breasts in the face of his ire. "I like you too much not to get involved."

He stepped back, putting the stone bench between them.

"Don't do it!"

"Then heal yourself."

"No. Leave it."

She struggled to get her words out. "If I help you, I lose you. If I don't, I lose you too. We all do. I know it. The same way I know Eridan is in danger." She softened her voice. "Our home's only hope of returning to normal rests on your shoulders, Master Face Changer."

He shook his head. "It doesn't."

"You're the only one left!"

"Many others can take my place."

"You have responsibilities towards the Face Changers, towards all those who remained behind in Eridan." She hesitated. "Responsibilities towards the dead."

His fists whitened. "You saw nothing of what happened that day."

"Actually, much more than you think."

"You're too young to understand. Is it your new friend who gives you these bad ideas? The Nand I know respects me and would never dare address me in this manner."

She stepped forward until her shaky legs rested against the bench. "That girl is gone." She met his keen eyes. "You know nothing about me because we never met during the tenens preceding the massacre. You have no idea about the questions I ask myself. I'm not Sharra." She raised a hand. "Let me speak. I don't have a husband, or children, or a family structure to support me. I was never prepared to be a hlyk, the way my grandmother prepared my mother. I am the hlyk because when my mother sunk, I was with her. I experienced her death and my birth as hlyk simultaneously. I lost her and I gained Kaipekak. If I hadn't wanted to hunt that day, she would still be alive. Without Krilli, but alive."

"Nand …" A soft, entreating voice.

She shook her head. "I don't reproach you for anything. You are the Master Face Changer. We know our fates are linked. You hadn't even met me, and yet you went out of your way to protect me from the yeold. You protected me again from Xë. Without you I would've surely gone mad in Pit 3. If I am here, today, alive and not buried in this cemetery next to Axonna, it's thanks to you. I owe you, and it's my duty to return the favor now."

"You have no idea how to proceed," he whispered.

Putting one foot on the bench, she leaned forward and placed a hand over his. "I don't, but Axonna did."

Declan's purple eyes turned blue in the sand-hazy light. "He gave you the gift before he died?" When she nodded, he pulled his hand away from beneath hers. "You mean you collected his memories? That in addition to being a hlyk, and possessing a rock mind, you are a resh? Congratulations! I'm relieved to learn his memories live in Mocean thanks to you."

His resentment and envy wounded her more deeply than any words he had said so far.

"I'm not a resh! He explained how the healing process works …"

He wrapped his shawl brusquely around his head. "The Redlanders have prepared a meal. It's a tradition here after a burial. They're expecting us."

"Go. I'll join you in a little while."

"I won't let it be said that Eridanis don't have manners."

"In … a … moment."

She sat on the dry ground beside Axonna's tomb, her back to him. He hovered behind her for a moment. Then he hurled his thought-voice at her so hard she put her hands over her head: *YOU CAN TURN YOUR BACK ON ME, BUT YOU CAN'T CHANGE ME AGAINST MY WILL!*

CHAPTER 195

Elder

8 May 3077, Standard Time (ST), Sixth Federal Era
Redland—Esk Strath

Snuggled beside Erlend, Nand couldn't sleep. She was re-membering Axonna. The first time they met, he had impersonated a tall woman with compelling eyes and a spar-kling grin: a buoyant, unusual silhouette, high cheekbones, abundant curly hair as red as a cooked lobster with matching finger- and toenails, and a throaty, mesmerizing, self-mock-ing voice. Even though she had only just begun her face-changing initiation, she had felt instantly at ease with the woman Axonna was.

So, you liked me in this appearance.

She heard Axonna's lilting voice as if he stood next to her. Fear slithered like an eel up her spine.

You're not imagining things, Nand.

Removing Erlend's arm from around her waist, she sat up. Her heart pounded loud in her ears.

I'm here.

What was happening? A dead friend's voice resounded clearly in her head.

Dead, indeed. An elder now, sweetheart. I am your elder.

She pressed her hands over her ears.

You welcomed me when I sunk. And now I am with you.

No. She shook her head. This couldn't be. Only kwirimoks had elders who spoke in their heads. She left the bed. Cold seeped from the soles of her feet to her fingertips.

She shut herself into the bathroom.

She opened the half-window.

What are you doing?

A sand-filled gust of wind whipped her face.

She didn't have the guts, the will, to face this new hurdle. She was too tired, too desperate.

I'm sorry. I didn't realize what this meant for you. Forgive me. I'll disappear. Never bother you again.

The windowsill was a perch, and she a bird. She pulled herself up and squatted on the edge, her talon-like toes curled over for balance as she hunched, her arms holding her knees tightly against her chest. The wind stroked her, softly ruffling her feathers. It lulled her gently; it encouraged her to let go; the swazzi would fly her far from the valley and its sorrow.

Far from her grief.

"Nand!" Erlend caught her by the waist and pulled her back into the room. "Are you out of your mind?"

She wished she was. Literally out of her mind. She sagged against Erlend. He embraced her, he half-carried half-dragged her back to the bed. He held her tight against his bare, warm chest. She pressed her ear against it, reassured by his steady heartbeat.

"What happened? If I hadn't woken up to piss, you …" He pulled her closer. "Is it because of your friend who died? Sometimes, sorrow makes us want to die too."

"My life doesn't belong to me anymore," she whispered against his hot skin. "It belongs to me less and less." She gazed at his beautiful face. "You don't know who I am, really. If you did, you wouldn't love me. My body is an illusion. And my mind a sponge. Don't love me. It will only hurt you."

He pulled her closer; his hand caressed her back up and down. "It's normal to be sad. Talk to me about your friend."

"Not now."

"Let's go for a trek. There are friends I want you to meet. Would you like that?"

"Very much."

They snuggled under the sheet.

"We need to talk," she said.

"We're talking." His smile lit his voice. He nuzzled her.

"I can't explain what happened. I was dozing, and then I heard Axonna's voice in my head. It terrified me. I wanted to escape. I wanted to fly away." She shrugged. "I wasn't myself."

"You dreamed about him because you miss him."

She laid a hand against his prickly cheek, recalling how envious he was that Eridani men didn't have to shave. "He heard me thinking."

"That's impossible. Even on your weird planet."

"Actually, it is. It's the kwirimok's privilege. He's our spiritual leader. When the kwirimok becomes a kwirimok, some"—she hesitated—"dead people become his counselors. We call them elders. They are part of him; they never leave. They have the memory of the past, and they guide him. They bind him to … our collective consciousness."

He held his head up with a hand. She did the same. The bathroom light barely enabled them to distinguish each other's features.

"The dead become counselors?"

His bafflement mirrored her own.

"Very few do. The kwirimok is always a resh. He welcomes the minds of important people who die. I already told you. In Eridan, the souls of the dead join Mocean. And at night, we unite with Mocean during the death of sleep."

"And so you think Axonna became one of those talking dead?"

"Either that or I'm turning mad."

"You're not."

"I can't be sure."

He caressed her face. "You're afraid."

"I'm terrified."

If this worries you so much, I'll leave.

She moaned, closing her eyes.

"What's happening? Did he say something?"

She nodded. Erlend embraced her.

"What did he say?"

"That if I was worried that much, he'd leave."

"Perfect!"

"No."

"Why not?"

"Axonna is my friend. I have no right to tell him to remain silent."

"Make a pact with him. Tell him you will solicit him when you feel at ease with the idea that he's part of you. And in the meantime, he must keep silent."

Let me get used to you.

As you wish. I'll wait.

Nand perceived vast relief, then Axonna's presence vanished and she was alone with herself. "I don't hear him anymore." She frowned. "It's strange."

He stroked her body. "I don't understand your Eridani stuff. I don't understand how the mind of a man who died could be inside of your head. I'm not saying that you're fibbing or that you're crazy. It's so unbelievable that it's probably true. But there must be a way to render this presence less invasive. Don't you have a little box in your mind where you could keep him?"

She laced her fingers into his. "No …"

"Really?" He kissed her. "If you can communicate with Kaipekak, it seems to me that could create another canal for Axonna."

She held him tightly. "Maybe."

CHAPTER 196

High Trail

8 May 3077, Standard Time (ST), Sixth Federal Era
Redland—Canyon Maze

Theo wiped her face and squelched back a spark of fear. "Don't look" was her mantra. She must stick to it.

She had walked a good distance towards Stairway Arches since the middle of the afternoon. Thirst dried her mouth. She tried to swallow. A glance down. Her heart filled her ears with its loud beats. The distance to the bottom leapt up at her, too huge for comfort. Her legs wobbled. Not far behind her, wild thyme crept. Sitting on her buttocks, she scrambled to grab a handful of the woody, gnarled stems and wrapped them around her fingers, anchoring herself.

The thyme was sturdy, the prostrate kind, deeply rooted between rocks and earth.

It held her.

She squeezed her eyes tight shut, unable to fight her sense of defeat.

She had believed that she would succeed this time, even

after three failed attempts to take this short cut. Her fear of heights had stymied her once again.

Wasn't there any way to tame her uncontrollable fear? She had forced herself to hike a bit higher each day on this trail. Draining, pointless efforts for such bitter results.

How would she cross Canyon Maze if she couldn't walk higher than four or five meters?

She held on to the gnarled stems.

She wouldn't make it. She couldn't. Too much of a coward.

She opened her eyes. Her body temperature had dropped so low that her teeth chattered. She needed to retrace her steps.

And admit defeat.

She was not a Savalwoman.

She was nothing.

Tears rushed out hard and fast. She buried her face in the scented leaves, her body so tense it hurt.

She must get down.

Tomorrow, she would choose the safer, longer route that meandered around the empty river bottom.

If she could reach the ground without falling.

Right now, she was stuck, her legs too shaky for her to move.

She examined the path she had climbed earlier. A side glance confirmed her fear. If she moved, she would fall.

The void beseeched her to let go. Break her neck. Die alone.

She shook her head.

Her mind played against her reason.

To beat her mind, she would occupy it with something else. Eradicate the heart-beating thoughts that jarred her body. Distance herself from the void licking her reason.

She could go down on her buttocks from bush to bush. She had already done it twice.

Not from so high up.

She must try.

She straightened the straps of her rucksack with one hand and focused on the bush twenty steps away.

She snapped one of the thyme sprigs in two and counted. Each sprig had one, two, three, four, five, six smaller stems, and each stem had fifteen—no, some had sixteen, some had seventeen—narrow leaves, so to find out the exact number of leaves on the sprig she held, she needed to multiply. As she counted in her head, she let go of the bush and scrambled down the path, not minding the ache springing from her sprained ankle, until she reached the next bush.

There was an incredible number of spikes on this new stem, over 108. She repeated the number out loud. She couldn't just multiply it by six or seven. A few more steps and she would reach the next bush. She crouched her way down and grabbed it with both hands, forcing herself to look up at the red cliff, at the blue sky whitened by the suns' glare. She waited until her heartbeat returned to normal.

A dozen steps and she would reach the bend. She clutched the sprig of thyme. How many leaves had she counted so far? She couldn't remember.

Sweat drops fell into her eyes, burning them.

She must count again.

Bent forward, unsteady, she hurried further down. Numbers jumped inside her brain. On the first stem, 108 leaves, 97 on the second and 75 on the third, but how many did that add up to? She reached the bend. Where was the shrub? Alarms rang in her ears as her shaky legs collapsed. Huddled on her knees, she pressed her body against the boulder for safety. She hooked a finger into a nook by the ground. And closed her eyes.

She was half-way down, wasn't she?

If she walked instead of crouching, she would get down faster.

Could she do it without looking down?

In the distance, she recognized the spindle-shaped rock beside which she had slept the night before.

One hundred and eighty-one leaves for three stems? What a dimwit! She added the numbers again as she hurried down, forcing herself to stare at the sprig in her clammy hand, at the tiny silver-green leaves growing on the stem, noting their shape. This time, she found 282.

Her legs shook; her ankle hurt.

The void lapped louder at her side. It implored her.

She stared at the stems. Which ones had she counted? The fourth one had 63 leaves. How was that possible? It was longer than the first one with its 108.

The leaves danced in front of her gritty eyes.

She reached the point where she had stopped the day before and marched on, half bent, her legs tense and shaky. Yesterday's panic still tasted foul.

She re-counted the leaves on the first stem, her sluggish mind unable to process the simplest addition. The figures popped in and out of her brain.

Something nudged her, encouraged her to glance down over the edge.

She focused on the stems she gripped, her nails biting into her palm. She recognized a pair of shrubs, a black, sharp-edged rock that reminded her of a rabbit.

There were 62 leaves on the first stem, not 108. And the second one had 64, and the third 64 too. So their numbers were basically the same. All she needed to do now was to add or multiply.

She raised her head. She was further down than she had thought.

Hot shivers and cold sweat used her body as their battleground.

Focused on her counting, she increased her stride.

A minute later, she stumbled over the rock pile that she had carefully avoided earlier, and lost her balance.

News from E-Met

8 May 3077, Standard Time (ST), Sixth Federal Era
Redland—Esk Strath

Farren typed a series of secure codes to access hypernet from Kirby's ship, and waited as his first one-to-one call to Jered went through. After a restless hour, his friend's face appeared on the screen.

"Ah, my dear friend, finally! We stayed up until two, and then we dozed on the bed, waiting. We thought your call would never come through." Jered smiled as he put his glasses on. "It's so good to see you alive. How's Jack? Is he any better?"

Farren hunched over, his eyes blurring upon hearing his friend's voice. "The same." He cleared his throat. "I followed your advice, and so, with Lonetom's help, I put Elimar in hypernet contact with the doctors here. From what they all figured, the Xplo-bullet poison has entirely entered his blood. Mhuol might save him, but it's too soon to know."

"Have faith. If this drug worked on Theo, it will work on Jack." Jered turned aside and yelled towards the background.

"It's Farren!" He moved to one side and Roger's face appeared on the screen.

"Farren!" Roger grinned. "I'm so happy to see you. Any news about Theo and Rory since yesterday's message?"

"No. The monstrous sandstorm is still blowing. Even the Guild ship that orbits Redland can't trace them."

"That I find hard to believe," Jered said.

Worry about Theo and Rory, about Jack, gnawed at Farren day and night, and his attempts to diffuse it failed. "What about you two? How are you? How's life?" he asked.

"We're fine with lots to do. Roger finished repainting the house. Any progress about knowing when you'll head back?"

"It depends on Jack."

Roger reacted to the catch in his voice. "He's strong, and even stronger now that he's found you again."

Jered and Roger counted among their best friends. He needed to know.

"But he did give up, didn't he? When you thought I died."

Jered frowned and pressed his lips together in that familiar way that generally expressed embarrassment. "He did. But in truth he didn't."

"Tell me what happened. He hardly said anything to me."

Jered and Roger shared a glance. Jered adjusted his glasses. "Not now. He's alive; you're alive. Leave it at that for the moment."

"How bad was it? How could he be discharged from SpaceSS?"

"I'll send you the trial minutes." Jered hesitated. "It was a personal vendetta. Donatella Simpson went after Jack deliberately. He was her target from the outset."

"Why would she do that?"

"Does the name Bahg Yn Poal' mean anything to you?"

"No. What is it?"

"It's her real name. It turns out that she's a Symb and belongs to one of the Families who lived on lands acquired by Kanner Talmand. From what we've gathered, the rejects of one of the components used in his factories modified the Symbs' DNA. Their symbionts die when they turn twenty. No matter what is done, they can't be saved."

"A Symb? How did you find that out?"

"From Max Simpson. He's her brother and a dangerous sociopath. I don't know if Jack ever told you. He helped me with this case. He found proof that she covered up every single murder perpetrated by her brother. He murdered many women. We found pictures of Theo and Annie at his home."

"Sue's little daughter?"

"Yes. She and Theo are close friends," Roger said.

"Annie is such a brave girl," Jered said. "You can be proud of your goddaughter. She served as bait so that Max Simpson could be arrested. Once they removed the chip in his head, the Metropolice got him to talk. Can you imagine that? Putting a chip in your brother's brain to stop him from blabbing about you?"

"Still no news from the Spylady?"

"Nothing. It seems that she left with a Metropolice officer, Cyand Emmett, who might be involved in Valenta's death. Sycal Veld arrived yesterday, and she's probably going to take over the running of SpaceSS from Morning."

"When did she leave exactly?"

"Not long after Theo crashed her orgacomp. Hackers are investigating the personal files she hid inside of it. She went

AWOL after she sent Jack to the Ring of Whalience on April 23 ST."

Another layer of fear deepened Farren's distress: each day brought new horrific details about Jack's fate after Farren's forced disappearance. "He never said anything about the Ring of Whalience."

"Probably because he never got there. The Guild extracted him and sent him to Gambling Nova."

"What aren't you telling me?"

Jered scowled at he cleaned his glasses. "The official investigation is underway, but I've put my team on it. We're building a strong case against her. Two cases, actually, or even more. One concerns you, and I will question you about your life in Gambling Nova." He pressed the bridge of his nose. "The other case … What you said earlier, that the Xplo-bullet's poison has poured entirely into Jack's blood? I went to Iglölü with Lonetom and Dr. Remesh when he was released, and I spoke with Elimar after she told us about the Xplo-bullet. She said it would take at least six months for the poison to drip entirely into Jack's blood."

Anger ripped through him like a bullet. "Go on."

"I saw images taken aboard the prison ship, the one headed for the Ring of Whalience. We're still working on sound."

"She tortured him, didn't she?"

"The Metropolice will find her and we'll sue her, and win the case, I promise," Jered said.

Farren thought of Kilu's words concerning Jack's pain, about discussing the matter with Ashta. If Axonna hadn't died, he could have alleviated Jack's hurt mentally, since he was a healer. Even perhaps root it out as if it were a splinter.

"She won't be easy to find," he said.

"I'll talk to the Families if need be."

"How are things with Lonetom?" Roger asked.

"Not easy." Delving into emotions exhausted him. He sat back in his swivel chair. "He tries to make amends, but … I can't forgive him."

"He was framed."

"You're right … Still, how could he believe for one second that Jack would harm me in any way?"

Jered nodded. Beside him, Roger snorted. "Blame Simpson, that's what I keep telling Jered," he said. "She's the one who did the most damage. Not Lonetom."

He had a point. Yet …

"Talk to Clobb. Get information. Get him to speak about Simpson," Jered said. "The Guild is after her as well. He knows more than any of us."

And undoubtedly what had happened between Jack and Simpson on that prison ship.

"I'll do that. Right now, he's busy with Mogud." Farren checked the time. "I must leave you, guys. I don't like staying away from Jack for too long."

"Hug him for us. Tell him we love him and want him back home. And let's organize another session after-tomorrow at the same time. We'll have Annie and Sue over."

CHAPTER 198

Addiction

*9 May 3077, Standard Time (ST), Sixth Federal Era
Eridan (207th Cycle, Cuttlefish Season, Whirlpools' Blue
Year)—Eridooneen*

"We need to talk." Donatella Simpson erupted into the large, beautifully decorated hall where Keith now lived. She hobbled in, leaning on a crutch, leaving her faithful cyborg at the door.

The bedraggled SpaceSS leader's voice, her attitude, her demands, everything about her irked him. The headache beating in his temples increased.

"Later."

"Now!" She planted herself behind him. She breathed noisily. She tapped the ground with her crutch.

Keith pressed his fingers against his forehead. He needed to rid himself of this migraine. He faced her. The panic she had experienced when the water wall—his first attempt at Mindrule—crashed over The Towers, creating a small underwater tsunami that felled a few stone walls and turrets and the safe-room where she hid, still hollowed her shrewd eyes. It turned her voice brittle; it erased her manners. She had survived thanks to her cyborg, who had helped her with her oxygen bottle and swam her out of harm's way.

"You're here about the news?" He forced a smile through his rebellious migraine. "Mogud is fighting against the Guild. And the girl who caused all our problems is dead. She died in a crash when she escaped the Dome. But you already know this, don't you?"

She nodded, leaning on her crutch. "The hounds are hunting me. I must leave Eridan. But before I do, tell me. Does our deal still stand? My Families. Can I tell them to pack?"

"Don't you want to stay and be part of Mindrule?"

"Didn't you fail?"

He chuckled. "No. That big wave was a mere try-out. I'll launch Mindrule as soon as I get rid of my headache."

"It's too dangerous for me if it involves Mocean. I nearly died a week ago."

"Mindrule is mental." He held her gaze, searched and easily found her sharp and plump mind. He infused it with the light she craved. She moaned and shook as if she had had an orgasm, her face free of wrinkles. He gripped her arms, keeping the light bright and strong. Xë had told him he had addicted her to light in mere seconds.

The Kresdan had convinced Keith of her utility. As SpaceSS leader, she was an asset they could not afford to lose, with invaluable experience in Federal matters. Her addiction to light gave them leverage.

So Keith gave her light for long minutes. She was powerless and malleable. Trembling so hard her legs folded. He laid her on the floor, then he straddled her, locking her arms against her sides. He diminished the light.

She opened her eyes, vacant eyes. "Please," she whispered. "More, please. I need it."

He increased the light, brightened it. She squirmed, she writhed. He intensified it even more.

"What are you doing to her?"

Startled, Keith withdrew his light. Donatella jerked and lay still. Astriv stood beside them, his eyes burning with anger.

"Making her happy." The SpaceSS leader lay unconscious. He stood up and embraced his lover. "Nothing to worry yourself about. She's a light addict. I gave her what she craved, and more." He liked Astriv's cloudy expression, the jealousy whitening his thin lips. "It was only light. I'm ensuring that she'll never leave us. We need her."

"Sorry, it's just that … I saw Face Changers near The Towers."

Keith walked his lover to the door. "Tell The Kresdan and he'll handle them. Right now, I need to be alone. I have work to do."

Astriv caressed his neck beneath his ear, tickling him. "Your headache?"

"It's almost gone." He kissed his lover to placate him, his mind on the woman. "That's why I must work. I haven't done anything in days. Go now. I'll see you later."

He locked the door behind the younger man and returned to where Donatella Simpson lay.

Giving her the light she lusted after had erased most of his headache. Could he rid himself of it entirely if he gave her more?

He straddled her again and slapped her face to wake her up.

Her eyelids fluttered. They opened wide when she realized he was sitting on her stomach.

"What are you doing?"

She wriggled, trying to free her hands, which were held tight against her sides by his knees. "Get off me!"

He leaned forward. "Don't you want more light?"

"No! I've had enough."

"Are you sure?"

"Yes …" She nearly succeeded in unseating him, so he infused her mind with a gentle, continuous light.

"Don't …" She quivered, shaking her head. "Keith, you must stop. I'm fine. You gave me a good dose already …"

She fought with herself, with the need and fulfilment he kindled inside of her. He increased the flow.

"But you like it, don't you?"

"Not like this. Stop it!"

She was a fit woman and, bracing herself, she bucked once.

He laughed and tightened his hold on her. He leaned forward and held her shoulders in place. His migraine still pulsed in his head: he wasn't finished with Donatella Simpson yet.

"What are you doing?"

He heightened the stream of light.

She was an intelligent woman, quick to understand.

"No!"

She squirmed, she writhed, she tried to dislodge him, but he weighed too much, and the light weakened her will.

He steadily brightened it. "You like it, don't you? You've wanted this since you lost your symbiont. Why are you fighting me? I only want to make you happy, Donatella."

"Not this way."

She was stronger and more willful than he had imagined. She refused to give in to pleasure.

So he saturated every part of her pudgy mind with light.

She moaned. She shuddered.

"What do you want of me?" she whispered after long minutes of inner struggle.

She was weakening.

"Everything."

Her mouth quivered as she endeavored not to surrender to the pleasure she ached for. Sweat covered her face.

"What …?"

"I want you to stay in Eridan and tell me everything about SpaceSS, the senators in Nuong, the Federal government, Mogud, the Guild … everything."

When she didn't answer, he escalated the brilliance another notch. This time, she cried out. Her legs twitched. She no longer controlled the spasms crossing her body.

"I …" Tears glistened on her red cheeks. "All … all right. I'll answer all your questions."

"Your word is not enough. You're a professional liar. You want our light for your Families. I want your knowledge to rule the worlds."

He severed the light beam and sat back. Had he successfully hooked her?

She took deep breaths. She squeezed her eyelids tight.

Would she be strong enough to master the loss of light, the immense need he had sown in her, and pull herself together? She quivered from head to foot. Had he vanquished her? Impatience drove him to nudge her mind with vivid flashes.

She twitched. "Stop! That hurts," she said in a hoarse voice.

Defeat and humiliation darkened her eyes as well as the vulnerability of need. "I'll tell you everything you want, but first give me more bright light. I need it now." She opened and closed her mouth, and shuddered like a fish out of water. "Please. I'll tell you everything you ask. I swear I will." Her mouth quivered; tears wet her cheeks. "Keith …" She gasped for air. "Please, Keith!"

Her defeat eliminated the last remnants of his migraine.

He leaned forward. "You want this for five minutes?" He filled her whole mind with a bright and warm light that lasted the forty seconds she needed to reach the jolting orgasmic rush that only he could give her. He stopped the flow just before she attained pleasure. She widened her eyes.

"What are you doing? I told you … I need it. I need it now …"

"Then earn it." He stood up. "Talk to The Kresdan. If he tells me that you did a good job, I'll give you five full minutes of light, and the contentment that goes with it." He winked. "Not before. You've already had a lot. Now hurry up and leave me alone. I've work to do."

He was ready to launch Mindrule.

CHAPTER 199

Bibiana

9 May 3077, 22:00 Standard Time (ST), Sixth Federal Era Eridan (207th Cycle, Cuttlefish Season, Whirlpools' Blue Year)—Oniraveen

Ashta often told Bibiana about the dreams she had when she traveled away from Eridan after Norwen's death. The strange, ephemeral worlds depicted by her lover beckoned to her, and her paintings reflected her attempts to represent them.

At first, those dreams tormented Ashta with their vast array of sensations, colors, places, people she had met, or not. Bibiana reflected on and toyed with the idea of what it meant to be free of Mocean. She spent hours examining her own dreams, so dull compared to Ashta's. She wrote them in her notebook; sometimes she drew them. She had kept a diary of dreams long before she met Ashta. It was her secret garden.

It all started as a game played with Sofini to prove to Mona, Aïlin and their parents that the bond they shared as twins generated the same dreams. A far from perfect demonstration. Her sister soon lost interest, but Bibiana kept writing down her dreams every morning. She noted the wave and color shifts that iterated depending on the seasons.

Nand knew about her book of dreams. Bibiana had told her friend about it not long after the young woman began traveling in the deep with Kaipekak. Nand voiced her concerns about Mocean. She spoke of the ocean's unrest, its irregular tides; she spoke of putrid seaweed and schools of dead fish, their silver bodies catching the sun.

Bibiana painted her friend's concerns because they resonated with the patterns she noticed in her own dreams. Subtle changes in the color prism and in the waves, their height and movement, outside seasonal patterns.

When Declan nearly sunk after the mindblinder blast, Mocean's red waves created messy twirls in Bibiana's dreams, and gradually the peace and smoothness produced by Mocean morphed into permanent unrest.

The change was subtle. In her artwork, it followed a rising tide's motions: it flowed and retreated for a few nights, and flowed again, deeper, sharper, once, twice, overlapping, and then it became shy, soft, almost gentle.

The limpidity of her childhood dreams had not returned, even after Declan recovered.

For many seasons now, Mocean had fluctuated. And Bibiana's sleep, her dreams, as well as everybody else's, had altered as well. Or she thought they had. What impact did this have on people? Most of them let themselves be carried away by Whitecur, unable to step back and watch the stream.

Ashta once admitted preferring her own dreams to those produced by Mocean. They suited her better, she said; they gave substance to her moods.

Amid Mocean's unrest, Whitecur flowed. Its icy-white, flimsy presence meandered through Bibiana's dreams. During a few seasons, it expanded, becoming a large river; later, it trickled back to a mere nudge at the ocean bottom. She had noticed that the river-like Whitecur only existed when Evetha was there.

Since Evetha's departure, Mocean had evolved. Twirling seaweed ribbons, jellyfish crowds and moaning kidadakh intruded upon her dreams.

Ribbons floated; jellyfish lit her conscience, beautiful, loving and deadly. She felt endless ripples during the days—she later realized—that followed the kwirimok's death, and the moment Keith became the new kwirimok.

Ribbons of seaweed and jellyfish. After the massacre, those smooth green and brown ribbons floated everywhere.

Sorrow submerged her then. She remembered linking it to Ashta's absence. Yet when she painted her melancholy, she felt that it was not hers entirely. A similar grief blanched Mocean's dark blues, as well as its greens and grays or her dreams' turquoise waters.

Her canvases showed that Mocean's chalky-white sadness spread over more of its surface each day. The deep blues she enjoyed had lightened, as if covered by a constant haze. Fishermen had noticed this faded coloring and so had shellfish farmers in the Shallow Seas.

Scientists studied Mocean's whitening and concluded that it was harmless, since no side-effects had been noted and fish remained plentiful.

After the water wall destroyed her sailing-boat and drawings, Bibiana moved her work to a bubflat far out in Oniraveen

Bay. She sealed her dream-painting series in waterproof frames, and as she worked, driven by an urgency she could neither explain nor understand, new patterns emerged.

The pull on her mind slashed at her: a gathering flow that seemed to suck her from her very pores. Colorful bubbles popped in her mind, dazing her. It was as if thousands of crabs' sharp mandibles tore at her, gorging on her soul, her self.

She crashed to the ground. Blindly, she groped and gripped the tableside. She forced herself to her knees.

She would not give in.

And yet who was she to say no to Mocean?

The flow rose, pulling her into its fold. She was one among swarms of others, caught in a net, most of them asleep, unaware, having a strange Mocean dream.

Powerful, luminous Mocean. A reminder of the water wall.

Mocean surged like a splendid wave towards the sun, and beyond it, into the deep, dark sky. The crabs nibbled at her, but Bibiana hardened her self-protection.

She was not asleep. She was awake; she perceived in her mind some red beyond Mocean's blue.

Red and black.

Like a coldnight geyser, Mocean rose.

She stood in her studio. She perceived millions of lullabies, gentle minds, soft, strange, alien.

They weren't Eridanis!

She screamed when these gentle minds burst like bubbles.

She screamed as she wriggled to shake free from the net.

She was not a destroyer, a conqueror, a killer.

She screamed in her mind to rouse the Eridanis.

Wake up! Wake up!

She fought the mandibles.

She screamed aloud because of the pain she—caught up in Mocean's folly—had inflicted on foreign souls.

She screamed as she cut through the net, as she freed others who awakened.

She screamed because she was one moment baring her soul, the next closing it.

She screamed, and heard faint echoing screams that she recognized: Sofini, Terri, Carmen, Mona, Sheer, and many others she did not know.

She screamed herself out.

CHAPTER 200

Mindrule

*9 May 3077, Standard Time (ST), Sixth Federal Era
Eridan (207th Cycle, Cuttlefish Season, Whirlpools' Blue
Year)—Eridooneen*

Keith went to his den at the bottom of The Towers, the place where he interacted directly with Mocean. He sat on the edge of the square mosaic basin and watched whirlpools playing in the depths. He tested his expanded mind's glossiness, admiring its fascinating plasticity now that his migraine had vanished. He completely undressed and went down the steps straight into the cold water, down to his private seaweed garden where Whitecur streamed. He walked through the ruffled fronds of circular-shaped rose-purple and black-green seaweed, untangling himself from the thick red blades of dulse ribbons that wrapped around his waist and legs. He still wasn't used to the garden's freezing waters.

He stepped into the middle of the white current, laughing when its coldness slapped his body and mind with an equal sting. He waded against the flow until he reached a stone arch where he had secured metal rings. He clasped the buckles over his ankles; he secured one wrist after the other. He clenched his fingers around the rings, his back flat against the arch's uniform surface. Even though he had been controlling Whitecur for numerous tenens, it remained a powerful force from which he had learned to protect himself. Anchoring himself allowed him to experience the current's full onslaught without being hurled against the rocks.

He consigned to memory the details precluding his moment of triumph: black seaweed spinning around him, his body numbing, his fingers tightening around the rings.

Whitecur rushed by, teasing his mind into joining its stream.

Keith closed his eyes, and opened his mind's eyes. He skimmed Mocean's surface, black-blue near the abysses, turquoise-blue in the Shallow Seas, transparent around the garden-islands. Whitecur lifted its whirlpools to meet him. Keith encompassed Eridan, his mind swelling. Froth crested the rolling waves where Whitecur's eddies sizzled.

Grinning, poised between past and present, Keith waited a few moments before hooking himself into Whitecur. As usual, he battled the white current for supremacy. The water wall had left frailties which Keith clogged. He wormed his way inside the white current and latched onto the Eridanis' collective consciousness. Most Eridanis slept; some dozed; a few were still awake. He smiled, thrilled by the irradiating force their minds produced.

Simultaneously, Mocean's waves unleashed their considerable energy.

He embraced their movement, their unity. He surged and swelled. He glided on the surface of this aggregation of spirits, as he had done with the water wall. He gathered it within his own mind and expanded across Eridan.

He encompassed the whole world. He was all Eridan, planet and people, at once. He burst with pride, his body warming the white current now bubbling around him.

One with Mocean's momentum, he propelled the collective consciousness towards Eridan's closest neighbor, a sparsely inhabited planet.

He ignored the minute tears in the collective consciousness that surfaced when he clamped upon the foreigners' soft and malleable minds. Identical imperfections had developed here and there during the rise of the water wall: probably Major Rings busy protecting Minor Rings, or the Free Mocean do-gooders who were determined to bring him down.

He sucked dry each foreign mind and popped them into the whole.

Strident fissures appeared. They reminded him of wind screeching through sails.

He pushed Whitecur further, faster, stronger.

The fissures widened into gashes. They slowed him down; they tore apart the collective consciousness.

Fury galvanized him. He was Whitecur. Mindrule, his will.

He tightened his grip on the multitude as he attempted to suck the minds that had escaped back inside.

They eluded him; they swam back to poke at him, to widen cracks in the collective consciousness. More fled. He burned some rebellious minds off his path to mend the gaps.

He was engaged so far in the Mindrule dimension that when his breathing became labored, he did not notice.

A few minutes later, a debilitating energy loss stiffened his mind.

What was going on?

He couldn't open his eyes.

He wriggled his toes. He couldn't feel them.

Hyperventilating, he detached his fingers from the rings above his head. He tried to bring his arms down. They bounced and burned against a frozen surface all around.

Cold seeped inside him.

Ice pushed against his face, his torso.

Terror replaced bliss.

Astriv!

He scratched ice with his fingers.

His nails hurt.

Why didn't Astriv answer?

His eyes were glued shut. He retreated against the sharp rock. His back chilled.

He opened his mouth. His lips, his tongue, stuck to ice.

Cold gripped his throat and slithered down to his stomach, firing his entrails.

His lungs filled with crystal flakes.

Icicles gutted his body.

He screamed. His voice crystallized.

Whitecur submerged him with acute grief.

Its sorrow solidified inside his shrinking mind.

He whimpered.

His body was so numb, he no longer felt it.

Whitecur cleaved itself out of his mental grip, leaving him bereft.

Alone.

CHAPTER 201

Concussion

10 May 3077, Standard Time (ST), Sixth Federal Era
Redland—Canyon Maze

"Althea! Althea!"

Theo jerked awake, her nose stuck in a shrub, and groaned. She blinked. She touched her forehead beneath her cap and cried out. She lay sideways, a rock jutting into her side, her backpack pushing against her shoulders. She raised her head and dizziness blinded her, instantly followed by a surge of nausea; she closed her eyes, feeling faint, and breathed deeply.

Memory returned. The trail, fear, scrambling from bush to bush to get down, missing the rock pile, falling. What time was it? How long had she been unconscious?

She opened her eyes with care and tried to move her head. The pounding dizziness returned. She relented. A concussion, probably.

The suns still shone, burning the side of her face that wasn't resting against the leaves from the bush. Fortunately, the ledge above her offered some shade.

"Althea! You must drink!"

She groaned. Her father's stern voice struck a powerful alarm, bringing back faraway advice. "Go wherever you want, but go prepared," he had often repeated. "If you are hurt and can't reach anybody, take care of yourself. Get fluids inside your body. Protect your skin. Eat."

For now, she must lie still. She could nevertheless obey her father's order. Her right arm was stuck beneath her, so she slowly extended her left one to grope behind her. She fingered her backpack and fumbled with the side pocket strap. She opened it and her fingers brushed the small gourd. It took her long, irritating minutes to extract it, and longer to remove the lid. She smelled water even before she raised the gourd to her parched lips. She savored each mouthful. She had to be careful. Not drink too much.

Her efforts exhausted her. She closed her eyes and slept.

———◆———

Cold woke her up. Night covered the sky, and the swazzi gusts sprayed sand. Her face—the cheek not lying in the shrub—burned. She tested a head move. No lightheadedness. None when she wriggled out of the backpack straps and slowly eased herself onto her back.

Panting, she rested while her heartbeat returned to normal.

She needed to protect herself from the cold and wind. She drew her backpack close to her, thankful again for one of her father's lessons: pack your stuff, and unpack it with your eyes closed. You must always know where everything is. Pack the most useful stuff on top, where you can reach it fast. She found the emergency blanket, the goggles, the sun lotion, medicine. She had no recollection of the landscape surrounding her. She wanted to sit up but a massive headache drummed like a warning bell. She swallowed a painkiller and creamed her face. Fatigue slowed her movements. She wrapped herself in the blanket, tucked Rory's cap over her face and gave in to sleep.

Both suns were shining when she emerged from her deep slumber. She tested her head, raising it a bit. The pain bubbled hard beneath her skull, but the dizziness had vanished. She sat up and examined the cliff above her. She was amazed at how high she had gone up the trail. She considered the distance, the rock pile. She had still been far up when she had tumbled down. If she hadn't learned during her Thumo training how to fall properly she could have been dead or stuck with a broken leg or arm. As it was, she had scraped hands and knees, a sunburnt cheek and a big bump on her head.

The boulder against which she sat provided some shelter now that she was leaning against it and not beside it.

She pulled out her map to evaluate the situation.

CHAPTER 202

Healing

10 May 3077, Standard Time (ST), Sixth Federal Era
Redland—Esk Strath

Axonna, I'm about to heal Declan.
Nand ...

The relief coating the former Half-Master's mental voice brought tears. She smashed them with her knuckles.

How long ... since my death?

Does it matter? Evetha is still missing. Declan has already drunk himself into oblivion twice. He's totally wiped out, so I'll do it now. I need you to monitor me.

I am at your disposal.

Nand stood at the door of the large hospital room to which the Master Face Changer had been transported. Feyn and Ashta were whispering not far away, and she glanced their way, still apprehensive about her decision, yet relieved that they supported her.

Kilu entered the room with Fern, whose stern personality Nand appreciated, and she followed them inside. The Suni Sisters had questioned her about this mental healing process. Kilu wanted to know if it could be learned and applied to non-Eridanis.

After closing the door, they set to work. Fern cleaned Declan's wounds and scars, and Kilu evaluated his unconscious state. Once they were done, Nand sat beside the elevated table where Declan was stretched out on his stomach. It was the first time that she had viewed the horror Keith had wrought on his back. More tears wetted her eyes. How could the Master Face Changer endure this pain, this constant reminder of the massacre? The raw state of his wounds reinforced her decision. Yet would she succeed?

We will. Have no fear.

She had retained Declan's mental imprint from the time she had visited his nightmares. Coughing to clear her throat, she told Fern and Kilu not to mind her if she mumbled.

Then she closed her mind to the outside world.

The pathway to Declan's nightmares led nowhere. His mind reflected such complexity that she sat for a while at multiple crossroads to ponder. Axonna advised her to choose the protruding dusty layer; it had to be the one related to change. She slid into a tunnel of lusterless mirrors fitting into each other. She carefully pushed them aside one after the other. The last one hid a winding staircase; she reached a door which collapsed on its hinges when she touched it.

She stepped onto gray sand and embraced a desolate expanse of barren, slashed-open land. No perspective in this bleak, colorless landscape. She walked a short distance. When she turned around, she noticed that she left no imprint.

A thick fog rose from the ground and wrapped around her. A cool, fluffy whiteness. Hail riddled her face: if there was water, no matter how icy, hope prevailed.

This is the right place. Heal the land, and you will heal the man.

Drawing upon the knowledge Axonna had bequeathed to her and the experiments made upon herself over the last few days, she launched into the slow process of tissue reconstruction. At the end of three hours, grass was once again growing on the land. She left Declan's mind. She checked his state in the Suni Sisters' company. The minute progressive healing of his back, arm and face, which left no traces of the wounds, had them in awe.

The Suni Sisters made her eat and drink before she left the room. Erlend waited for her with Ashta and Feyn. He embraced her and kissed her in front of everybody.

She told Ashta and Feyn that Erlend was taking her for a two-day horse trip. "Good idea," Ashta said. "It will leave us enough time to pacify him if he makes a fuss. We'll explain that it was a decision we took together. So enjoy yourself."

Feyn nodded, his expression so condemnatory that she nearly pulled him aside to ask what was bothering him. But she was exhausted, so she left with Erlend, ignoring this sliver of worry.

CHAPTER 203

Wind Followers

10–11 May 3077, Standard Time (ST), Sixth Federal Era
Redland—Esk Strath

They rode from Esk Strath to the Cairndearg canyon, and this journey took them a day and a half. They camped in the mountains and reached their destination before the second sunset. Throughout, Nand admired the arid landscape's warm hues and jagged outlines. Keeping her balance on horseback proved strenuous, and soon her thighs chafed beneath the hide pants Erlend had lent her. She didn't mind; she smiled whenever he checked on her progress. The wind flapped without pause, enveloping them in a sandy mist that stung her eyes.

On the afternoon of the second day, they followed a trail at the bottom of some narrow canyons protected by vertiginous black rocks streaked with red. Sometimes, mhuol trees dangled from the mountainside like gigantic spiders.

Dusk had enclosed the landscape when they attained a sheltered plateau on the upper part of a canyon. Vivid yellow and orange flames danced against the mountain wall. Voices and laughter crossed the air.

They walked the last stretch, leading their horses to a sheltered meadow.

"Is this grass?" Nand asked as she helped him unsaddle their mounts.

"Good grass. There's an underground river running in the caves."

"A river? I thought there was no water in Redland."

"The path we took in the canyon is a riverbed. It's dry right now, but after heavy rains a river flows in it."

As she took off the indigo cloth protecting her head, dust fell off. She combed her hair with her fingers. He grabbed her by the shoulders and kissed her. Barking erupted, and two dogs bounded out of the cavern.

Nand stepped back.

"Don't be afraid! They won't hurt you," Erlend said.

The big dog jumped at him, its paws on his chest, and licked his face; the smallest wagged its tail. Nand squatted to scratch behind its ears the way Erlend had taught her. The dogs, Berry and Juniper, frolicked and barked, and led the way.

Nand followed Erlend into a vast cavern that reminded her of Abuion's main hall. No pungent iodine and salty seawater here, though; instead a spicy and soft fragrance. Three people sat around a crackling fire that sent sparks up into the air.

"Here you are! We weren't sure you'd make it tonight!" The man who greeted them wore a bright red sweater. White strands streaked his carrot hair and beard. "How are you? How's my friend Cowan?"

"Fine. Busy. You'll see him in Esk Strath."

"With Nemi's death and the Dome's spaceport explosion, Livia must be driving all of you crazy." The second man stood up. He wore a hat decorated with feathers that threw shadows onto the mountain wall behind him. The way he held out both hands to Erlend, as well as his size and crinkling smile, reminded Nand of Terri. An older version of her cousin.

"Any news about Theo?" the woman asked. She must be in her sixties. Her braid of hair, long and black with a few locks of white, rested against a blue-and-orange shawl wrapped loosely around her shoulders.

"No. With the sandstorm the ships are grounded."

"She and the pilot must be hiking back here. He's lucky to have her with him. She trekked a lot in that area with her dad," said Terri's lookalike.

"How's Jack?" The woman waved at Erlend to sit beside her.

"There's no change. High fever, despite the mhuol treatment. He screams a lot." Erlend hugged her. "I'm sure Farren will be relieved when you arrive."

"He must be so worried."

"It's not only that. Malcolm and Livia hold him responsible for what happened to Theo. They say he should have forced her to leave the Dome with the rest of them."

"That's ridiculous," the woman said. "They know Theo would never have left Fern behind."

"Livia's prejudice is strong. She's settling scores."

"I hope Farren's wise enough not to give in to her baiting," the woman said, rearranging her shawl.

"He tries …"

"Erlend, will you introduce us to your friend?" the man in the red sweater asked. "I see that the dogs take to you, young man."

Erlend turned her way. His love's warmth enveloped her.

"This is Aslone. He's one of the Eridanis that were imprisoned in the Dome and escaped." Smiling to overcome her shyness, Nand stepped away from her lover's side. Berry, the tall dog, settled beside her. She placed her right hand over her heart in the direction of each person he introduced. "Aslone, this is Yussu Johnston." The man in the red sweater raised a hand. "He's the leader of the Wind Followers, the storytellers' clan. On Yussu's right, that's Ethelwin Gorani, who left my brother's clan to join Yussu's. He's, among other things, a poet and an artist. He paints his visions on rocks in the mountains." A keen knowledge of life, so like Terri's, filled this man's eyes. Had he already guessed that she was fake? "And I'm sure you recognized Nujise." Nand shook her head. "She's Farren and Livia's mother."

"You're Farren's mother?" Nand searched the slightly wrinkled face for reminders of her children's features.

"I'm told my children don't take after me." She grinned. Juniper, the curly-haired dog, lay in front of her, head on its paws. "Let's eat. Are you thirsty, Aslone?"

"Always." She sat between Erlend and Ethelwin. "I'm always thirsty."

"Aslone comes from a planet entirely covered with water, and he lives underwater most of the time," Erlend explained.

"Underwater?" Yussu chuckled. "I have a hard time imagining a pond, so a planet ..."

"Imagine a surface like your desert, except that it's water instead of sand." Nand caressed the soft blanket where she sat. "Our mountains and plains, hidden valleys and rivers, lie beneath the water."

"Does this mean you breathe underwater?" Yussu asked.

"No, but we can hold our breath up to three hours. It's a sport for some Eridanis."

"Amazing." Nujise handed bowls of soup to everyone.

"You must hate it here with all the dust." Ethelwin stirred his spoon in his bowl. "What's the weather like?"

"It depends where you live. Hot, cold, humid. Rain, wind."

"Wind? Like we have here?"

"No. Nothing like swazzi or sandstorms."

"We are the Wind Followers." Yussu held his bowl of soup between his hands and blew softly on its surface. "Those who tell stories about the Red Land."

"Besides storytelling, the Wind Followers are famous because they build all sorts of wind-powered vehicles," Erlend said.

"Your generation does that. Children fly kites," Ethelwin said. "And old people like us tell stories."

Erlend elbowed Nand. "Ethelwin is a former desert-yacht champion. How many prototypes did you build? Ten, twenty?"

"Thirty-two. But the young ones are catching up. The speed of those kite buggies …"

"The sandstorm prevented us from getting to Esk Strath by desert-yacht. Otherwise we would already be there," Yussu said.

"I'm learning to drive one," Nujise said with some pride. "I like my horse, but for long distances, the desert-yacht is so much quicker."

"That's because you think time flies too fast," Yussu teased, and Farren's mother shrugged, not disputing his assertion.

Ethelwin kindled the fire. "When you're a story-collector, your perspective on time changes." New flames shot up, sending yellow sparks into the night.

"You're right. I fear I won't have enough of my life for my myths' and tales' tapestry. It's frustrating."

"Nujise's project is to create a database that contains the founding myths of as many civilizations as possible," Yussu explained.

Farren's mother stretched out her hands towards the flames. "I collect stories and I compare them. Thanks to Farren and Jack, I'm in touch with other story-gatherers through hypernet."

"It's particularly useful for other languages," Ethelwin said. "We search words and their etymology. It's amazing how close other people's worlds are to ours. The sky, the wind, the desert. And the mountains …"

Nand felt content for the first time in many days. How had Erlend guessed that meeting these interesting people was what she needed?

"Did Erlend tell you the meaning of Esk Strath, Aslone?" Yussu asked as he handed out a plate of honey-and-seed delicacies.

She shook her head.

"The water valley. Surprising, isn't it? And yet not really. Several years ago, Nujise and three other Suni Sisters discovered an ancient tumulus at the end of a path nobody uses anymore in mountains west of Esk Strath. This tumulus is made of red and black rocks piled up in an elaborate diamond design. It was erected high above the edge of a crater that used to be a lake. Inside the tumulus, drawings showed the existence of a cellar. It took time, but the Suni Sisters found its entrance. This air-tight, oven-like cavern housed thousands of scrolls stacked inside glass tubes. We've been studying the contents of these sheets of paper ever since."

"Do you know where they come from?"

"Nujise, this story is yours to tell." Ethelwin bowed her way.

"It's more fact than fiction," she said. "But yes, I will tell it."

Yussu and Erlend gathered more wood for the fire. Ethelwin filled everybody's mug with hot choctea. Sweaters and blankets were handed out.

Nujise sat on the storyteller's stool by the fire and began her story.

"A long time ago, long before Nomads travelled across this land, it was inhabited by small people with dark-gold skin who were called the Smenns. They were gardeners and vegetarians. Redland's name was Teek'neg, which meant Circle of Trees. Forests, flowers and grass covered the land. When the first Nomads arrived, the Smenns were extinct, but traces of their presence remained. We recently discovered ceramics and jewelry. We believe it is desertification coupled with several years of hot and dry weather that caused the Smenns' disappearance. In one of the scrolls, it's written that red sands gulped green grass and uprooted trees. Water evaporated from the surface and dived underground, far from the suns. The new inhabitants, our ancestors, who loved the desert's heat and beauty, are those who called it Redland. We knew next to nothing about the Smenns until their secrets were uncovered in the tumulus. Research is now being conducted throughout the planet. Inside one of the glass tubes we found a sacred scroll. This thick and beautiful paper contained seeds. The ferns in Esk Strath greenhouses originate from these seeds."

"I remember when the scrolls were found," Erlend said. "Every kid wanted to be the one who broke the alphabet code. It kept me awake for nights …"

"We'd still be having headaches if your brother hadn't found that solid burl in the Dilli riverbed. It's a huge piece of wood, apparently sawn from the middle of a giant redwood tree. And the alphabet, a tree alphabet, is sculpted in it."

"Our cracked-dry land hides its story well." Yussu added a log to the fire, sending sparks into the air. "Trees everywhere?" He smiled at his companions. "Sometimes, with closed eyes, I open my mind's ears to the sounds of dawn and, believe or not, I hear a breeze rustling through leaves."

"This is fascinating," Nand said. "Thank you for sharing this story with me."

"I don't think we've ever come across tales about Eridan," Ethelwin said.

"No, we haven't." Nujise smiled apologetically. "But as soon as I can, I'll search hypernet."

"You won't find anything. Our planet is not referenced."

"Too bad …"

"But Aslone, I'm sure you know stories about Eridan, don't you?" Erlend asked.

Nand nodded.

"Can you share one with us?" Yussu handed out more delicacies.

"Why don't you sit on the storyteller's stool?" Nujise suggested. "You'll understand why I like telling stories. It's comfortable."

Nand had to admit that she was right: the stool, a short-backed chair, brought relief to her tired muscles. She snuggled into the blanket covering her shoulders and spread her hands on her knees.

"I work on this with my cousin Terri. We believe there are

two stories at the origin of Eridan. The first is the creation myth. It's part of a book called *The Tales of Zodostar*. These tales are written in Tlelgow, an old language spoken by scholars. I managed to translate most of it. Not long before we were sent to Gambling Nova, I became aware of a myth about another water planet. And it shares some names with our own creation myth." She shrugged. "Maybe the place our ancestors came from. It's called Yelun."

"Yelun?" Nujise leaned forward. "I know that name! Farren stayed on a planet called like that."

"So it's true … it's real." Nand sat back. "Both myths mention an entity called Heris and they begin the same way."

"Heris? Spelled h–e–r–i–s? I know it too." Excitement reddened Nujise's cheeks. "Before I say anything, tell us Eridan's creation myth."

CHAPTER 204

A Creation Myth

10 May 3077, Standard Time (ST), Sixth Federal Era
Redland—in the mountains

N and gathered her thoughts. "It's long, so I'll shorten it, and I'll tell you the long version another time."

"That's a good idea."

"Heris was movement. On the water planet where he lived with his mother and sisters, his wild energy caused him lots of problems. After an accident that seriously wounded one of his sisters, his mother told him to leave. So Heris created his own world elsewhere. He carried in his heart the light that his twin sister Yelun," she smiled at Nujise, "gave him as a farewell gift. He traveled long and far and one day he arrived in a red land." She sipped some choctea. "Heris had never seen such a vast and empty territory. This red land fueled his own energy. He skipped and twirled and somersaulted, and he created clouds of dust that darkened the sky. Each night, sadness overcame him because he had no one to talk to."

Yussu chuckled. "Ah, these lonely creators ..." Nujise

shushed him.

"He longed to hear the sound of waves rolling on shores," she continued. "He sat on a hill and stared at the immensity, pitying his own fate. A breeze blew. The earth's dust gripped his throat, hurt his eyes. He blinked; he coughed. He was thirsty. Tears pricked at his eyelids. His tears fell. They soon gushed from his eyes into a cascade and splashed onto the land. Water sizzled. Tears kept pouring from Heris's eyes. The cascade turned into a stream. The stream became a pond. The pond grew into a lake. The lake spread into an ocean." Nand drank more choctea. "When Heris stopped crying, the red land had disappeared under the sky's blue coat. The water was cold, so he took a little bit of Yelun's light to warm it up."

"And that's when he began working, didn't he?" Ethelwin asked.

"Yes. He liked the blue surface, but it was too calm. He shook his feet and bubbles popped up. He walked into the clear water. When it reached his waist, he plunged his hands into the water and searched the bottom. He mixed and kneaded the silt. He remembered the smooth and amiable fiskiorps he used to play with and he sculpted one. In memory of the warm earth colors hiding beneath his ocean of tears, he traced orange and black lines on the blue-gray fiskiorp. Once it took shape between his fingers, Heris blew a breath of Yelun's light into the mammal's nose. The fiskiorp jumped out of his hands and dove into the ocean. Delighted, Heris used the alluvium encircling his ankles to create other beings for his world: fish, frightened like him by loneliness, that swam only in large numbers; huge forests of leafy green and ribbon-like brown seaweed clinging to rocks; and shy mammals that enjoyed the great deep's cold night. Heris was tireless. His creatures became more and more colorful.

"They spluttered and jumped and flew; they crawled; they
walked and swam. However, the water surrounding him
stayed still. He wanted movement, and at the end of the day,
when most of his creatures went to sleep, he squatted underwater. Eyes open, he blew what was left of Yelun's light into the
ocean, bringing life to its immensity. The ocean was his mirror.
He melted into it.

"Once liquid, Heris invented tides. A perpetual movement;
a pleasure of being. His waves carried him forward, a renewed
and eternal reunion with the land. Heris became a mobile entity, whose liquidity changed in time: airborne when foam flew
away, earthly where silt was deposited, ethereal when sun
evaporated him."

Nand stopped and finished her mug of choctea, which
Ethelwin immediately refilled. "Movement and change. The
themes of your world aren't far from ours," he said.

Nujise clapped her hands. "What a wonderful story. You
can't imagine how happy it makes me." She wiped her eyes. "I'll
need to record you, Aslone. Because the myth you told us is
the missing tale in an ensemble that I've been working on for
years. Your myth has a sequel, and I have it at home."

"A sequel?" Surprise choked Nand.

"Yes. Tomorrow, on our way to Esk Strath, we can go by my
home and I'll give it to you to read."

"Where did you find it?"

Nujise put her hands closer to the fire. "The stories about
Heris belong to Farren's past."

"They're related to Yelun, aren't they?" Nand asked.

"Yes. Unfortunately, I know next to nothing about this period of his life." Longing filled her eyes. "Kane, my husband, was murdered by Skodraks a long time ago. Farren turned wild when it happened. They were very close. He was sixteen, and he went after those killers. I have no idea what he did, but he came home one day, dirty and disheveled, his rage spent. He said he would take the Skodraks to court in Nuong, and that he had to study abroad to do that. I needed to heal my wounds on my own. I've always been like that, even when Kane was alive. Livia was four years old. I encouraged my son to leave. It hurt to let him go, though. I survived, like mothers do. At first, I got news often. But during the white year, nothing."

"The white year?" Nand queried.

"That's what I call it. It's a year that contains no memory of Farren. Nothing." She raised her hands. "It was only after he enrolled in the SpaceSS Academy that he contacted me again. He never said much about that year. Only that he got shanghaied by a seedy mining company. He found himself stuck on the frozen continent of a small moon with other buggers. Drilling and digging ice-fields to reach pockets of minerals below."

"How did he leave?" Erlend asked.

"An old woman helped him."

"Really?" Yussu's face expressed as much doubt as his words. "What was she doing there?"

"Her name was Crazy Moon." Nand sat closer to Nujise. "She took care of him and taught him everything she knew about her world."

"How do you know this?" Nujise asked. "Farren told you?"

"No. I met him for the first time the day we escaped the Dome. We haven't spoken to each other yet."

"That's why I brought Aslone to you," Erlend cut in, his arm over Nand's shoulders. "He's had numerous visions that stem from Farren's past."

"His past?"

"Only episodes that took place in Yelun. I had these visions during a period when our ocean was very hot. I was frightened and they soothed me. I wrote each of them down and I called them *The Chronicles of the Frozen Land*. In one of them, Crazy Moon tells him the myth of the origins of the ..."

"Th'ans."

"Yes. The Th'ans," Nand confirmed, surprised by Farren's mother's knowledge. "Your son told you?"

"He sent me a text which might be the transcription of what you heard. But to confirm this, I need to hear you say it," Nujise said. "Come here, next to me, so they can also hear you."

Nand sat cross-legged beside Farren's mother. "It's the second myth I talked about earlier. The one that made me want to dig some more.

"Before ice, there was Mawat, the water. She had four children: Yelun the light, Heris the movement, Shandar the earth and Shalee the forest. Mawat loved calm and quiet. She often fought with Heris, who was the only boy. She found him too agitated, too independent. He didn't know how to measure his energy. The world was devastated by his storms, lands were flooded, trees fell. One day, Shandar and Shalee nearly drowned and Mawat told Heris that he had to leave.

"He asked his twin sister Yelun to go with him. She hesitated, yet in the end stayed with her mother and sisters. But she gave him half of her light. Soon after Heris left, the cold came. Happy Shalee wilted, snow buried splendid Shandar, and Mawat froze, a prisoner of herself.

"Heris was too far away to help them. He had used the light Yelun had given him to create his own world, a world that depended on him and that he couldn't abandon. So Yelun faced the cold alone. She wanted to understand why her world had changed, who was this cold that separated her from her mother and sisters. She wanted to hear her mother's crystal voice again, now muted by frost; she wanted to uncover the secrets of Shandar's forest; she wanted to hear birds chirping again and see them fly above the flowers and fields that had once covered Shalee.

"It took time for Yelun to realize that the cold had come to stay and that she was powerless to make it leave. However, once a year, after a long sleep in her husband the wind's embrace, she warmed enough to melt ice. Sounds and color erupted; her mother's songs mingled with Shalee's gurgles and Shandar's flutters. Too soon, though, Yelun's light diminished, cold regained power, and water turned to ice. So, with her children, the Th'ans, born of her union with the wind, she devoted her life to probing the memory of ice, seeking its secrets."

Yussu turned towards Nujise.

"You already told me this myth."

"Yes. It's a longer, more detailed version of the text that Farren sent me. It's Yelun's myth of origin, the Th'ans' land."

"I'm sorry to ask again. But is Yelun a real name?" Nand asked.

"Yes. I checked on hypernet. It was easy to find because there was a scandal with the mining company. It's been closed down, and the Th'ans live peacefully in their cold land."

"So when Crazy Moon revealed Yelun's creation myth to Farren, she was talking about her homeland," Nand mused aloud.

What did this mean with regards to Eridan? "And you found other stories?"

"Yes. Information about Yelun and the Th'ans is easily accessible. These stories shed light on the bond between Yelun and Heris, and explain how Heris's world was peopled with humans."

"This is so surprising …" Nand said.

"Aslone …" Nujise's voice sounded different, almost hesitant. "What can you tell me about Farren's life over there?"

"I …" She hesitated, not wanting to crush the other woman's feelings. "I'm sorry, but these visions are not mine to share. They're his. I can't reveal secrets that were transmitted to me without asking his permission."

"Your words honor you, Aslone." Her voice implied the contrary.

"Yes, they do," Yussu added. "Nujise, I know how hard it's been, but you can't ask this from Aslone. You'll see Farren in a couple days. Ask him yourself."

Nujise rearranged her shawl around her shoulders. Nand gave in to her sadness.

"What your son experienced with Crazy Moon was an initiation," she explained. "She showed him that Yelun's white landscape held mysteries. They journeyed on foot. One of the first things she told him was that the name of his totem animal was engraved in ice, and that he had to find it. And he succeeded because she told him Yelun's creation myth the day he was admitted among the Th'ans."

Nujise patted his arm. "Thank you, Aslone. You're a good man—a brave one, too. Your words bring me peace." She smiled. "I now know that Farren's reserve about his stay over there isn't due to some hurt he must hide from me, but is linked to a special learning that demands secrecy."

Nand buried her flushed face in the choctea mug.

"Do you know why you had these visions?" Ethelwin asked.

She shook her head. "Besides cooling our ocean, no."

"You need to talk to Farren," Yussu said.

"I intend to."

"It's not with Farren that you need to talk, but with Nujise," Ethelwin said. "She's the one who has the answers."

Farren's mother nodded. Nand looked from one to the other. "I don't understand."

"The meaning of an event is not always clear at first glance," the man who reminded her of Terri explained. "Evidence suggests a meeting between Farren and Aslone, since one has visions about the other. What bonds link Farren the Redlander to Aslone the Eridani? Behind the obvious, other keys exist. Erlend grasped this by bringing you to us."

Erlend shook his head, his lopsided smile showing that he had no idea what the older man meant.

"Nujise, will you tell them?" Ethelwin asked.

"Yes. Ethelwin is interested in the ways tales and legends meander. What motivates heroes and heroines."

"Farren might help you decipher part of the mystery, but it is Nujise who will lead you down the good path." Ethelwin paused. "Do you want to know why?" Nand nodded. "Because she corresponds with the Th'ans' kwisimok. Their spiritual leader."

"Kwisimok? In Eridan, our spiritual leader is called a kwirimok."

"See?" Ethelwin chuckled as he poked at the glowing embers.

"As soon as we reach Esk Strath, I'll write to him through hypernet."

"Thank you," Nand said.

"No, thank you, young man," Yussu said. "I feel a creative spirit blowing through this assembly. You have galvanized our minds, and we needed it, didn't we, my friends?"

"What about your world?" Nujise asked. "Can you tell us about it?"

"It's blue. And …" Nand hesitated. "And it's sick …"

"The ocean in Eridan is alive," Erlend explained.

"A living being? Like in the creation myth?" Ethelwin scrutinized her with even more intensity.

"Yes. We call it Mocean. We share an intimate bond with it."

"Which snapped when you and your friends left."

"Yes." The deep trust she felt in this rugged, inquisitive man puzzled her. "We discovered our mortality and our individuality."

"And this saddens you?"

She clenched her fingers in her lap. "Until a week ago, my only concern was to survive. I feel better now. Less tired. I haven't begun to reflect on the consequences yet."

"Why were you sent to Gambling Nova?" Yussu gathered the mugs and teapot.

"Rivalry and revenge between Declan Reel, who is the Master Face Changer, and Keith of Rain Forest, his cousin, who is the new kwirimok."

"What's a Face Changer?" Nujise inquired.

"A person who has the gift of the ability to change his body's physical appearance."

"Are you a Face Changer?" Something in the way Ethelwin eyed her worried her.

"Not a good one."

"A Face Changer … What a strange notion!" Yussu said. "Is this something you can all do?"

Nand shook her head. "It's a talent some are born with. You study for a long time. You learn not to lose yourself, to forget yourself. It's hard."

"And you don't like it," Nujise said. "Can you tell us why?"

"I prefer working with words."

"Do you have many old writings in Eridan?" Ethelwin asked.

"Yes. I studied them extensively when I was younger. There is *The Memory of Ice*, the *Waves of Eridan*, Sorja'u's poems, and the *Tales of Zodostar*."

"Do you write stories yourself?" Nujise asked.

"Not yet. I'm still studying."

Beside her, Erlend yawned. "Sorry …"

"It is late." Yussu gave a hand to Nujise to help her stand up. "We should all turn in. We have a long journey tomorrow. Come with me, Erlend. I'll show you where you and Aslone will sleep."

CHAPTER 205

Caring for Jack

12 May 3077, Standard Time (ST), Sixth Federal Era
Redland—Esk Strath

Ashta spent most of her time with Smanul and Farren in Jack's room. Farren enjoyed her company. She answered his questions about Eridan, about how their society was structured. She told him about her relationship with Theo, how her feelings of love had transformed into a close friendship, and about their mind connection, which had ended ten days before, after the Guild ship crashed. She mentioned her lover, Bibiana, who was an artist; she described the book they were working on together before the massacre and her deportation to Gambling Nova. She recounted the time Jack came to Eridan to get Theo, the water rising in the sewer. She said that Theo and Declan had been close; that their story was over now and had been since Theo left Eridan.

They talked about Theo every day, speculating like everybody else about her whereabouts. Once the Dome was secured, and even before the sandstorm ended, Lonetom and other Guild pilots flew to the crash site. Rory's body was found. His remains were buried in the cemetery.

Traces of Theo's presence were apparent in the emergency capsule and, more importantly, at the Sky Cradle entry to Canyon Maze. They surmised that she had been inside the emergency capsule when it was shot, and had probably been hiding each time a rescue aircraft circulated the maze.

She remained invisible.

Convincing Malcolm to send trekkers to meet Theo turned into an unforeseen hardship. Once the Redlanders agreed that she was crossing Canyon Maze, they decided that she was finally doing her Long Walk, and that she should be allowed to pursue it without interference.

This interpretation infuriated Farren because it didn't allow for the fact that Theo hadn't asked to trek through the maze. She did it because she had to, not because she wanted to.

"And because she's a Savalwoman," Ashta repeated. "We taught her well about finding the courage to go on."

So, in the beginning, and once the storm abated, Malcolm's only answer to Farren's daily request to get to Theo was to send an aircraft to fly over Canyon Maze. In Malcolm's opinion, if his cousin needed help she would show herself.

Farren was torn between staying with Jack and heading to Canyon Maze himself to find Theo. Fern, Malcolm, Cowan and even his own mother repeated that Theo would be fine. She had trekked in Canyon Maze many times with her father; she knew where to go, how to orient herself, how to find food and water.

His worry wore Malcolm down—or perhaps the man finally saw reason—because he announced a week after the crash that he had rallied canyon-savvy trekkers.

Unfortunately, except for two who were resting at home because of torn ligaments, the others were participating in an annual three-week-long trekking competition along the Djerrani Ridge. The race organizers were able to reach a couple who often took groups hiking in Canyon Maze, and they agreed to withdraw from the race.

"I really like this drawing," Asha said one evening. It portrayed Farren sitting cross-legged at the entrance of a tent. He was looking up at a starlit night sky. "Where were you?"

They were sitting together beside Jack's bed.

"In Yelun, when I returned for a visit a little over a year ago. I couldn't sleep. So I watched the sky. I was happy because I could remember the star configuration of the not-so-cold season." He chuckled. "That's what Crazy Moon called the Singing Seas when the ice melted."

"I miss the stars. When Norwen and I were children, we often paddled our raft far from the shore. We lay on our backs and stargazed. During the hot season, which we call the jellyfish season, many shooting stars would zip through the sky. We talked all night."

Farren took a drawing from the wall. "I like this one too. I told Jack and Smanul last night about growing up in Redland, with no stars in our sky. One of my father's fondest wishes was to see one. When I was ten years old I decided to learn to fly a ship and take my parents into space to view the stars."

"Did you?"

"No, but when I met Jack he had already designed two small aircraft."

"He's such a gifted man."

"Yep. His grandfather owned a spaceship factory. Jack learned to pilot at twelve. He took part in many competitions."

"I'm impressed. Does he still?"

"He had to give it up."

"Why?"

"It wasn't his decision."

"What do you mean?"

"It was for the best."

She frowned. "But he gave up something he liked."

"He pilots choppers occasionally." Farren remembered Faircrest, how Jack had fearlessly hedge-hopped the buildings to get to him. "You can't imagine how mean his family was. His mother died when he was six, he doesn't know who his father is, his aunt abandoned him. So his grandfather took him in. That man …" Farren stood up. "That man hated Jack. He was beaten, starved, locked up in dark places. Sometimes he slept with the chickens or the pigs. Other times, they left him outside in the cold. His older cousins sexually abused him. And no one in that big family, no one who worked there, not one of the people who visited—and there were many—no one ever said a thing, not even an anonymous tip. Nothing at all. So …" He faced Ashta. "One day, he refused to fly for them anymore. His grandfather took him to court. The judge was a friend. Jack lost the right to pilot the family aircraft. Thankfully, by then he belonged to SpaceSS, and this judgment could not be enforced within SpaceSS." Farren watched Jack's drawn face, willing him to open his eyes. "So, if he wanted to, he could fly aircraft. But besides helicopters, he won't."

He sat beside the bed and took one of his brawan's hands between his.

Ashta rustled behind him and slipped out of the room. He pressed Jack's fingers against his lips. He kissed them.

"I still can't bear it that you've been hurt so much."

———◆———

"You need to go outside and breathe sun into your body," Ashta told him the next day. "So, Smanul will keep Kilu company this morning, and I'm taking you out. If anything changes with Jack, Smanul will call me on this cell. We'll walk, or even jog a bit, and afterwards I'll take you to the greenhouse. You'll lie down on my bed and sleep."

———◆———

Kilu confirmed that she saw an improvement: knots had loosened; older pains were receding, some faded altogether. Could it be true? Jack was so thin, his skin stretched tight over his bones.

Farren gripped his hand and ordered Jack to squeeze it back. He was sure Jack heard him, that the cobwebs of delirium were becoming more transparent and would soon wear away. Now that he had voiced Jack's abuse, he repeated the words and told Jack that he no longer had to carry that burden alone. He wanted to inhale some of Jack's hurt into himself, to mingle it with his own, and to throw it far away from them.

Jack needed to remember.

So did he.

Memories flooded his mind.

His father's murder in the mountains.

That morning, his father had gone hunting on foot before dawn. Farren remembered waking up with a bad feeling, which his mother shared. As they finished breakfast, their dog Pebble appeared in the yard, whimpering and limping, her coat smeared with blood. He went to search for his father, riding his stallion, and found him a few hours later in the mountain above their home. His father had been caught in an ambush, trampled by hooves and left to die.

Farren arrived too late.

And the Gold Mines.

Noise, voices barking, the loss of his identity. They shaved his head; they stripped him of his clothes, his shoes. They tattooed a barcode on his wrist. They shackled his ankles and wrists. Hot dust, sand, thirst. Hour after hour of hard labor, snatches of sleep; fights for food, for tepid water, for the right to stay alive. Men dying each day. The gurgling sounds of cut throats. Each day resembled a slippery, rough slope he had to climb up on his knees. No thought.

He forgot music, love, silence, rain pattering against a window pane, cooking, being clean, smelling nice, laziness.

Suffocating heat, drinking water once a day, washing once a week. His solitary confinement in the cage. Impossible to stand up. Time stilling, playing silent tunes in his mind.

He stared at Jack's beloved face.

Did they still have a future together?

———◆———

"First there was ice …"

Jack breathed quietly beside him for the first time in many days.

Farren took one of Smanul's pencils, wrote the entire poem that Crazy Moon had taught him on a sheet of paper, and hung it beside the drawing his friend had made of the old woman laughing beside her wadda.

He often discussed what took place in Pit 3 with Ashta and Smanul.

He remembered how ice blocks ground in the background, and how he had grinned at the man with the eerie gray eyes. He realized in retrospect that he had put into practice Crazy Moon's lessons. She had taught him how to laugh himself out of any situation.

Crazy Moon had him practise blind sight to sharpen his intuitive mind during the weeks that preceded her death. In Pit 3, physically blinded, Farren explained to Ashta that Crazy Moon had crouched beside him. She had murmured in his ear, "Brain Warrior." And her teachings had returned to him in a flash. He had shielded himself from the bear; he had lured the mean beast into curls of spiraling vitality and drawn his enemy's mind into endless ripples of laughter.

CHAPTER 206

Walking

12 May 3077, Standard Time (ST), Sixth Federal Era
Redland—Canyon Maze

Theo was driven by two needs each day: finding water and hiding from Mogud's ships that regularly circled the canyons. She forced herself to stay hidden when an aircraft flew overhead. Sometimes, however, after she had stumbled and tripped along for hours, her hands and knees a mess, when she worried that she would not get to Painted-Caves because she was so exhausted, she showed herself. She didn't wave, just stood and watched. Afraid the pilot would spot her, and yet hoping he would.

After her failed attempt to take the highest and shortest trail to Painted-Caves, which meant escalating Stairway Arches, she opted for the trek through dried-out riverbeds. She bypassed Horse Ears and aimed for Eagle Nests instead.

Her walking day began two hours before dawn. Throughout the day, she remained wary of where she placed her feet, as the many rocks and holes easily trapped her weak ankles. She stopped to sleep when the two suns shone bright in the sky. If she could not find a place in the shade, she rested under the safety blanket. Dehydration was her enemy, so she covered herself entirely to reduce water loss. She generally found cover between boulders and tall shrubs. As soon as the sunrays no longer drilled heat into her body, once they joined the other side of the canyon, she walked another two to three hours in search of water to replenish her ever-dwindling stock. The creeks-and-potholes map aided her, but quite often she foraged off course to find her daily supply.

Recollecting another of her father's lessons, she treated the water she found. Filter and purify. During the first week, she relied on purifying tablets found in the first-aid kit. Their supply diminished too fast, though, so she boiled the water, which enabled her to eat hot soup.

She enjoyed lighting her fire before night fell with the swazzi in tow, replacing dry air with cold wind. During the short hour between dusk and night, she took care of herself.

Food was as vital as water. The Guild emergency kit was packed with hundreds of portions of lyophilized soups and high-energy bars. She had taken everything with her. At first, afraid of not having enough, she ate half-portions. Exhaustion swiftly caught up with her, so she augmented the portions.

She kept in mind a discussion between her mother and father about a group of teenagers who survived a perilous trek on the Djerrani ridge. It gave her hope of surviving her own ordeal. She clung to the memory of her parents promising that, should she go hiking and get lost, they would never give up on her; they knew she would find her way home.

Theo hoped her mother would recall the lost teenagers'

story, that she would trust her to prevail, that she would convince others. She never reflected long about Jack and Farren, or Ashta. Particularly Jack. She couldn't afford to become emotional. Not in this empty, mineral landscape. If she thought about her friends, loneliness kicked in, with its trail of insecurity, solitude, loss, and fear of being lost.

She forced herself to counter her anxiety by forging on, despite her aching feet.

She sucked on a pebble each day to keep her mouth moist—another piece of advice from her father. When her hunger took over, she exchanged the pebble for mhuol root. Mhuol was integral to every Redlander's pharmacopeia. Her mother used it to cure all sorts of infections, even as a toothbrush when she traveled.

So, the day Theo laid eyes on a mhuol bush, she cut several thick twigs, peeled off the bark with her knife and prepared a stack. Mhuol roots had a powerful effect that energized her. The plant boosted her spirits and lessened her hunger.

Thirst remained another matter. To her surprise, the handbook in the Guild pilot's emergency kit provided various methods of finding water. She discarded the first one, which meant digging a deep hole in the ground and staying around all day. The easiest method, which she practised daily after two unsuccessful trials, was plant condensation.

Some days, it took several hours to produce water, but in the end, she had enough to get by. Each afternoon, she searched for a place to set up camp near shrubs, or trees when she was lucky. She wrapped the end of a plant or a small tree branch in a plastic bag and sealed it tightly. The plant or leaves transpired water; water vapor condensed in the bag. She then filtered the water with coffee filters and poured it into her gourd. After the first two days, she set up five bags during her daytime sleeping hours and another five at night.

One day she came upon prickly pear cacti. She hesitated a long time before deciding not to pick them. She had gloves, but she remembered her mother's warning. The fruit was good to eat; she could even grill it. The problem rested in getting to it. The prickly pear cactus was associated with one of her most painful childhood memories, when she had grabbed one of the stacked fruits before it had been peeled. Her palms and face were scorched by the prickly spines, and it took much of her parents' patience to remove them.

She couldn't take the risk of renewing such a distressing experience on her own, with nobody to help.

So she kept clear of the cacti and moved on.

CHAPTER 207

Betrayed

13 May 3077, Standard Time (ST), Sixth Federal Era
Redland—Esk Strath

The Wind Followers and their friends skipped the stop at Nujise's home and camped in the desert instead. They traveled at a good pace and reached Esk Strath in the middle of the afternoon. They parted at the valley's entrance, promising to meet again later for dinner. Nujise barely acknowledged Ashta as she hurried out of the stable to find Farren. Yussu and Ethelwin introduced themselves and, aided by a group of chirping children who carried their bags, went to meet friends.

Nand and Erlend unsaddled the horses, and Ashta helped them.

"How's Declan?" Nand asked. "He's not too angry, is he?"

Ashta shrugged. "He's a bit upset, but he'll get over it." She did not sound overly concerned. "He joked this morning with Korund. He wants to see both of you."

"Why Erlend?"

"I've no idea. Maybe he'd like to be properly introduced. Just humor him."

Nand patted Erlend's stallion. "Good boy. You're so beautiful." She winked at Ashta. "Erlend is going to let me ride his horse tomorrow."

"I'm taking Aslone to New Islay. Would you like to join us? It's a stunning city."

The Savalwoman chuckled. "On a horse all day in Redland's heat? No, thanks."

———

Nand and Erlend entered the greenhouse. The three Half-Masters who were talking to Declan left. On his way out, Feyn gave Nand an encouraging smile.

The Master Face Changer had worked on his face, adding harshness.

"How was it?" he asked, his voice mild, his stance firm.

"Great. I met three Wind Followers," she said. "They're the storytellers. You'll never believe it! I found out Yelun is a real planet. And Nujise—she's Farren's mother—she knows about Heris and Yelun. Can you imagine that? She invited me to her home to see her collection of stories and to give me the sequel to one of our own myths ..."

"There's no time. We're leaving after-tomorrow."

Erlend moved closer to her.

"After-tomorrow? But—"

"Captain Kirby is taking us to Nuong. There, he'll help us board a ship for Eridan. You do remember that we must go home?"

She swallowed. "Of course. I didn't think it would be so soon."

Declan turned towards Erlend.

"You'll have to say your farewells to Aslone. He can't stay here. And you can't come with us. Not that I think you would want to if you knew the real identity of the Face Changer you've been sleeping with."

Alarmed, Nand stepped in front of the Master Face Changer. "Don't!"

She stumbled back at his glare.

"I know Aslone's real name is Nand," Erlend said quietly. "And that his hair is white like mine, not black."

Declan scowled at her. "You told him your name?" Disbelief clipped his voice. "You told this man about us? Despite my orders?"

"Erlend won't say anything to anybody."

"You're right. He won't. And you want to know why? Because he'll feel too ashamed after being wronged by a Face Changer. Won't he?"

"What do you mean?" Erlend's gaze switched from Declan to Nand. "Nand, what does he mean?"

Don't do this.

You shouldn't have healed me.

The Master Face Changer smiled at Erlend. "What I mean is that Nand is not a man. She's a young woman."

Erlend shook his head. "I don't believe you."

"It's the truth," Declan said. "Ask her."

"Nand?" Erlend stared at her. "Is it true? You're a girl?"

Her world crumbled in slow/fast motion.

She looked at her feet.

"Your lover took the appearance of her cousin Aslone as a prank the day our order was massacred in Eridan. She's been stuck with it ever since. If she was a good student, she would've changed back to her original appearance a long time ago." Declan's scathing tone and words scraped her raw. She forced herself to face Erlend's hurt eyes, his shocked expression. "But she doesn't know how to do it because she forgot." He folded his arms. "She never studied much. Which is fine, because she's not meant to be a Face Changer. I suppose she also failed to tell you her crucial role in our planet's wellbeing? That's why she must leave." He showed his teeth when he smiled. "But let's be frank. Would you want her to stay now that you know the truth?"

Erlend stood still. His face had paled.

"He's telling the truth?" He questioned her harshly. "You're not male?"

"No. I'm a woman. But Erlend …" She tried to catch his arm. He sidestepped her. "I was going to tell you. I wouldn't have left without doing it. I …" Her mouth was so dry she could hardly get her words out. "I … I didn't want to lose you. I never lied about loving you. I love you, Erlend." She caught his hand.

He pushed her away from him. "Don't!"

She staggered back, and lost her balance as she collided with a fern-tree trunk.

"When were you going to say something?"

"I waited because …" She locked eyes with him. He was the only man who mattered, the only one she needed to convince. "I knew it would be over between us when I told you the truth. You love men, and I, even if my current body says the contrary and gets along so well with yours, am a woman. And I love men, like you do."

"You never wanted to be a man."

"No. I like myself as I am. The Master Face Changer's right—I'm not a good Face Changer. I apologize, Erlend. I never wanted to hurt you. I love you. Can you forgive me?"

Shaking his head, hands fisted, Erlend swiveled towards Declan—watcher, listener, judge—and searched his face.

"When Aslone spoke about you, he always said nice things." He coughed to clear his voice. "How thanks to your support, he survived the ordeal in Pit 3. He holds you in great esteem. Healing you wasn't an easy decision. He talked about it with Ashta and Feyn. Aslone knew—or should I say, he thought he knew—how you would react. We discussed it together. He feared your anger. He never envisioned humiliation."

Declan opened his mouth. Erlend raised a hand to cut him off.

"When you are like me, a man who loves men, and you don't hide, here, in Redland, being demeaned by others is something you expect. But after learning about the way of life in Eridan, I never thought I would be shamed by one of you." He stepped back. "Did you have good fun at my expense? The Winds help me!"

He strode towards the exit.

Nand ran after him. "Don't go! We need to talk."

"I don't think so."

"Erlend …"

He glanced over his shoulder. She sucked in her breath at his ravaged expression. "Goodbye."

He stalked out of the greenhouse.

"How could you do this to him?" Nand demanded as she walked back to where Declan stood with a satisfied smile on his face.

"You're no longer part of the Face Changers' order," he stated in a curt, emotionless voice. "I won't forgive you. I trusted you, and you betrayed me. How dare you enter my mind against my will? I told you not to do anything. And yet you did, and you convinced Ashta and Feyn that it was for the best. Who are you to decide what's good for me?"

"I didn't betray you. I made you strong to face Keith when we get back home. My visions convinced me. I did the right thing even if you don't think so." She hugged herself against the grief rooting itself inside of her heavy body.

"What visions?"

"I have nothing to say to you."

"Tell me."

"Don't demand anything from me. We aren't friends anymore. You made sure of it." She clasped her hands together for strength. "I did what I did because I loved you, because I thought the torment you've been enduring clouded your judgement. Erlend is right. I expected your hate, your anger. I never imagined that you would go after him because you wanted me to suffer. Erlend is a fine man. He didn't deserve this."

"Nand!"

"Leave me alone!"

She fled the greenhouse.

CHAPTER 208

Nand

13 May 3077, Standard Time (ST), Sixth Federal Era
Redland—Desert

Erlend refused to let her into his flat. How could she blame him?

Where could she hide and cry? Nand hesitated. She didn't want to see anyone. On her way to the stables, she waved at the tall, bearded man who had come to their rescue in Pit 3. He stopped hobbling on his crutches to wave back. She had no recollection of his name, only his confidence.

In its stall, Erlend's stallion neighed and pressed its brown head against her hand for a caress. She entered the stall and laid her cheek against the horse's neck.

Her anguish, her sorrow, grew as she tried to contain her sobs.

She saddled the horse the way Erlend had taught her, hoisted herself onto its back after three attempts, and left. Boys were playing an elaborate stone game by the entrance to the tunnel. She met nobody else.

On the other side, the dune-ribbed desert beckoned to her. In the distance, dusk's orange tints rose from the horizon to lap at the sky. Between the desert and the mountains, she chose the safest path, and trotted towards the southern canyons.

The first swazzi gust surprised her as she rode between two boulders. She pushed her horse forward, towards the narrow entrance to Buzzard canyon, which Erlend had pointed out on their way to meet the Wind Followers—when he still loved her.

This canyon belonged to the sophisticated qanat irrigation system implemented in the surrounding mountains that provided water to Esk Strath. In Buzzard canyon, rivulets irrigated mhuol shrubs, cacti and good grass for goats and horses.

She slid off the horse, grabbed the reins and ventured into the canyon. She shivered in the chilly air, surprised by the gloom. After a long walk, she reached a wide area. An intricate design of pools and deep-green grass filled its center while leafy shrubs huddled against the stone wall to her right. She unsaddled the horse and tied its reins around a mhuol branch. She squatted by a pool to drink. Afterwards, carrying the saddle with her, she climbed five steps dug into the mountainside to a large and smooth red stone protected by an overhanging rock.

The swazzi howled. Unfazed, Erlend's stallion munched on the bushes and swished its tail. She hugged her knees close to her chest and gave in to her grief.

Her tears wrung her body. They cut her breath.

How could she live without Erlend?

She cried, she hiccupped, she wreathed herself with the agony of loss until darkness drowned all sounds except the swazzi.

The powerful winds fueled her decision.

There was no turning back.

Axonna … You must help me recover my original appearance. Now.

What happened? You're so sad! What's going on?

Don't you know already? Can't you hear everything that goes on in my life?

No, sweetheart, I can't. You've found out how to cut me off. I can't listen in unless you let me.

She gave him access to her immediate memories.

He's jealous. He didn't mean what he said. Of course he'll help you.

When? When we get back to Eridan? I need to face-change now. But I can't do it alone. You must guide me.

Are you sure?

Yes.

Then let's do it.

She shivered. *I'm afraid.*

So am I. What happens if you panic?

I won't, because you're with me.

Ah! Let's remember the fundamentals and go through each step. If the Miring sisters could do it, so can you, hlyk!

———◆———

Nand woke up. Daylight brightened the sky above her. Heat warmed her bare feet. She sat up and examined her small hands. She ran her fingers through her straight, thin hair; she brushed her hollow cheeks, her smooth throat. She wriggled her feet, the middle toe no longer bigger than the thumb toe;

she tested her calves, hard and smooth, her knees. She checked her sexual organs; the transition from penis back to vagina no longer tingled. She felt her trim lower stomach, her breasts still small but soft and hers.

She had been Aslone for so long, she had to see herself. She searched the saddle for the bag of amenities and pulled out a square mirror.

Blue eyes stared back at her instead of black. Their red-rimmed sadness remained, though. Her wind-mussed hair was white. She pushed it behind her ears. She licked her lips, rosy and feminine, liking their delicate feel.

Happy?

Relieved. Thank you, Axonna. Without you, I don't think I …

You did it all by yourself, and you can be proud, dear friend.

She hugged Axonna's mind, keeping hers half-open, like a window-shade which allowed sun rays through.

She washed in a large pool, rediscovering her body's dips and curves. Her stomach growled. In one of the saddle bags, she found hard, spicy biscuits, which she munched and washed down with water.

When she emerged from the canyon an hour later, saddle over her shoulder and in search of her mount, she found horse droppings, but the stallion had disappeared.

Shading her eyes, she examined the landscape: boulders and cacti were scattered over the deep-orange desert. Where was the horse? She left the saddle by the entrance and took the water gourd. Her head and shoulders wrapped in Erlend's wind shawl, she scaled the closest boulder for a better view.

The ascent proved a tougher feat than anticipated, so she gave up and walked around the massive rock in search of an easier way up. She found a trail among cacti and rubble, relieved that it led up a slope. Her loose sandals were not hiking material, and she tripped often. She followed the winding trail, wiping her face, while heat settled over her body. She drank often, sips, wishing she had sunglasses.

The suns blazed in the sky.

She stopped to evaluate the distance she had covered, surprised not to see the boulder anymore, only the moving, singing dunes in the distance. Their sound enveloped her; she even felt it resonate inside her stomach.

The sky darkened; thunder rumbled. She lay on shaky ground and rain brushed her skin. A cold, comforting humidity. Her head rested on hard water. Under her fingers, ice crystals melted. She brought her fingers to her lips. This cold seawater told her the narrative of a dead person. She turned over onto her stomach, onto all fours. She licked the crystal flakes; she tasted frozen and melted moments.

She heard a distressed grumbling.

"Kaipekak!" she screamed, standing up. "Kaipekak!"

She ran towards the source of the noise, slipping on the frozen ocean's hard surface. Thunder boomed again. She raised her head: the sky mirrored the frozen ocean.

Everywhere, sky and sea blended, slate-blue, stretching to the horizon.

"Kaipekak!"

Her kidadakh's moan spiraled.

She ran, she fell, banging her knees, her palms smarting.

As she tried to stand up, she felt his presence beneath her, under the thick ice.

"Kaipekak."

She distinguished his mass.

Her kidadakh was choking.

She dug at the ice. Her fingers barely scratched the surface.

"Kaipekak."

She called his name out loud and in her mind.

The ice-field shook. Big blows knocked against the thick ocean surface from below.

She keel-hauled and slipped again as mounds of ice rose around her. Blows banged hollow. The frozen ocean striated and burst. Crystals, thousands of crystals, exploded as a huge black body surged from an equally huge hole in the ocean.

The kidadakh fell hard on the ice; his body bounced once, twice; it rolled over, then slid over it without breaking it.

She ran towards Kaipekak. His breath burnt her like a geyser.

He was cut in several places. His oozing blood froze on his skin.

She pressed his shuddering body; she tried to reach him mentally. In vain. She couldn't communicate with her kidadakh; she only perceived a rumbling with meaningless image-thoughts.

She knelt beside him.

Ice hardened, enveloping the mammal in a frozen blanket.

"Kaipekak."

Nand blinked. She removed Erlend's shawl. She was too hot. Thirst thickened her tongue. She hated the ice that surrounded her. She trudged, she slipped, she crashed. She screamed, her mouth full of sand. Her knees hurt. She pushed herself up.

Above her, the sky shone blue. Around her, the mountains stood red. Huge cacti broke apart. And, before her, an abyss she knew, that she had once explored. An abyss opening in Mocean. She scrutinized this gaping wound in the frozen ocean.

Terri walked out of the ocean and she called to him. Anguish suffused his eyes.

He took her by the arm. "Come," he said.

She walked with him. He seemed taller.

Relief warmed her.

"I know what to do," she said.

"So do I," he said, and he smiled tenderly as he squeezed her arm.

"Declan doesn't know anymore. Will you tell him?"

"I will," he promised.

"Kaipekak's dead," she said.

Sorrow suffused her. He was gone. He had abandoned her.

The suns shone and she loved watching them chase each other across the sky. But she longed to see stars.

"I'm afraid."

She wiped off the sweat running down her forehead and dripping along her nose. She sucked her fingers, tasting their acrid saltiness.

The trail was easier to climb now. She walked fast. Erlend would be proud of her.

"You'll remember me when you become the new kwirimok?" she asked, and Terri hugged her hard. "I love Erlend, but he hates me now."

Terri wiped her face. "I love you," he said.

"I love you too, Terri. Always have, always will."

The light sent back by the mirror blinded her. She kept her eyes open. She shuffled up the slope.

The same light as the day she had merged with Kaipekak.

An explosion of noise and movement.

"Did you know that Heris cried so hard when he was alone that his tears created an ocean?" she asked.

"He fiddled with the ebb and flow," Terri said. "I wish I knew how to do that too."

She walked. The pebbles scratched her feet. Her hot body. Her own body again. Loneliness, the price of being herself. Madness to think she could be loved for who she was, beyond the physical appearance that had saved her life.

"Aslone," she said. "He died instead of me."

"I've been grieving him, and many others," Terri said. "My mother stays in Ourlane, and Issavern wants me to go there, to be their yeold."

"Keith of Rain Forest hurt Declan. I didn't."

"I know. I know everything." Terri's voice brushed her face with a sea breeze's lightness.

Thirst dug a hole in her throat, bloated her tongue. Wind threw her to the ground. She fell, somersaulted, her head banged against a rock.

"Nand …" Terri whispered in her ear. "Nand," he repeated. His voice dug into her brain. She opened an eye; dust shut it.

"You know what you must do," her cousin said.

She couldn't control her limp body. She tried to move an arm, a foot.

Coldnight welcomed her.

"Do you think I can still hold my breath underwater?" she asked.

Terri sat cross-legged beside her.

"Your body knows. Don't worry."

She worried. Would Mocean welcome her again after her transgressions?

She didn't think so. Not ever again.

"Axonna wants me to talk to Astriv. About how much he loved him."

"Come home, Nand. We need you."

"I will." It hurt to smile. "Tell me, Terri. Did I disappoint you too?"

"What are you talking about?"

"I've disappointed everybody," she said. "My mother, my father, Declan, Erlend, Aslone, Davin, Sheer, Clive. All of them."

"I love you, Nand. You could never disappoint me."

Sadness embraced softness. Sadness darkened her thoughts, made them permeable.

"Promise me you won't be sad anymore."

She didn't want him to be sad.

He promised, but he cried, his face pressed against her shoulder. He cried. Like Heris.

"You'll never be alone again."

He held her hand and stretched out on the sand beside her. They watched the stars.

"They are so pretty," she said.

"You need to rest now," he said.

Her eyes batted close. She tried to keep them open; the stars twinkled so bright, the dark so cool and nice.

CHAPTER 209

Worry

13 May 3077, Standard Time (ST), Sixth Federal Era
Redland—Esk Strath

Ashta knocked at the door of Erlend's small flat. He flung it open. His expression closed up when he recognized her.

"Erlend, sorry to disturb you. Is Aslone with you? The dinner in our honor is beginning and he hasn't arrived."

"You mean she? Nand."

She nodded. "So, she told you the truth, and you're upset. I—"

He shook his head. "She didn't say anything. Declan Reel did. That's why he wanted to see us together."

She automatically rose to defend her friend. "He wouldn't do something like that."

"Well, he did." His smile was grim. "And he enjoyed it."

"I'm so sorry."

"Why? It's for the best. You can go home now and share the joke about the fool who fell for the girl disguised as a man." His voice vibrated with quiet anger.

"You're not a fool."

"You all knew."

"No. Only three of us. Feyn only found out about Nand being Aslone the day we escaped. They're not close at all."

"Is this supposed to make me feel better?"

"No. I want to reassure you. None of us thinks you are a fool."

"Declan Reel does."

"No! He …" She was at a loss: why had Declan crossed the line?

Erlend stepped forward. "He what? He's in love with Nand?"

"No, not at all." She swallowed a nervous chuckle. "He feels responsible for her."

"And this gives him the right to interfere in her private life?"

She raised her hands. "I'm not trying to defend him. I don't understand why he told you about Nand."

He stepped back into his apartment.

"One thing … Where did you see Nand last?"

"At the greenhouse."

Hurt filled his eyes. Ashta's anger towards Declan rose, surprising her with its vigor.

"I've been looking for her. Is there a place where you think she might be?"

He hesitated, his hand on the door frame.

"You have every right to feel betrayed and I understand that you don't want to have anything to do with her or any of us. But …" she let concern enter her voice, "with what you told me, I have a bad feeling. She's prone to acting rashly."

"I know." He sighed and joined her on the landing. "There's the tower where we stayed after Axonna died. I'll take you there."

"Nand loves you and she must be devastated," Ashta said as they hurried towards the tower. The first swazzi gusts blew dust into Esk Strath.

After a few strides, he stopped, and she did the same.

"She lied to me. She used me."

"I'm sure the situation troubled her a lot. She was probably afraid of ruining everything between you, and she was right, wasn't she? The truth ruined everything."

"It's not that simple. I was wronged. You have no idea what it's like in Redland for people like me."

She placed a hand on his arm. "I've seen and heard enough to grasp what you mean. It's tough, and I wouldn't like to live here. Eridan is a much better place for people like us." She winked.

"Us?"

"I love women. I have a lover waiting for me back home, and I miss her so much, it hurts telling you. So I can relate to what's going on in your mind right now." She squeezed his arm. "Nand is honest and brave. She would have told you the truth before we left."

"I'm sure of it too. But she lied to me, she pretended to be a man, and that's unforgivable. It's up here. Many steps to climb."

Even though night securely embraced dusk and shadowed the desert, the view from the turret was grandiose. Nand wasn't there.

"She could be with Farren," Erlend said as they went down the stairs.

"Farren? Why?"

"Don't you know about her visions of him?"

"Nand is a close-lipped person. We're friends, but we're not the same age. She doesn't share her secrets with me."

Erlend's voice softened. "Well, she's had visions of Farren in Eridan, and in Pit 3. She intended to talk to him today."

"Really?" What could this mean? Had Nand shared this information with Declan? Ashta guessed not. "Let's find out."

Half an hour later, they reached Jack's room in the infirmary.

"Erlend, Ashta, what's up?" Farren opened the door. "I'm not attending the dinner. I'm sorry, but I don't want to leave Jack. It looks like he's waking up. I want to be there when he does."

"Is Aslone with you?" Ashta asked.

"No. Only Smanul and my mother."

Nujise appeared behind Farren.

"Erlend? I hoped to see you and Aslone this afternoon. I wanted to introduce him to Farren."

Farren glanced at his mother. "You've already met Aslone? Where? When? I haven't met him yet."

"Erlend brought him to us in the mountain two nights ago. We had a great storytelling session. You must talk to this young man. He knows things about you."

"About me? How? This is all so mysterious. What's going on?" He winked at Erlend. "A lovers' quarrel?"

The young Redlander shook his head. "If only ..."

Smanul emerged from the adjoining room. "What's up? Is it Jack?" He hopped on one foot towards them.

"Aslone's missing," Farren said.

"I saw him around five. He looked forlorn. He was heading

for the stables."

"Did he take one of the horses?" Erlend questioned.

"I don't think so."

"We'd better check," Erlend said. "Thank you, Smanul."

"Tell us when you find him," Farren said.

Horses neighed when Ashta and Erlend entered the vast stables. Each took a row, checking the stalls.

"Over here!" Erlend called. Ashta joined him. He stared at her with amazement. "She took my stallion."

"Do you know where she could have gone?"

"No. And we can't go after her now. It's too late; the swazzi blow. We wouldn't see a thing."

"She's traveled with you." Ashta wanted to reassure them both. "She'll keep safe."

"How could she? She doesn't know the desert. She's in great danger." He gripped the stall door.

"It's not your fault if she left."

"Isn't it?" He looked at her. "She wanted us to talk. She stayed at my door for hours, and I didn't let her in. I didn't give her a chance to explain herself."

She pressed his cold fingers. "I'm sure she found a place for the night. We'll find her tomorrow."

———◆———

While the Redlanders were organizing search parties that would leave before dawn, Ashta drew Declan aside.

"If something happens to Nand, I'll never forgive you," she said, not bothering to curb her anger.

He chuckled as he slid his hands into his over-shirt's large sleeves.

"The Redlanders' flair for drama has washed over you. The girl's tough. A night outside won't kill her."

"Have you been drinking again?"

"Open your eyes! Riding out of the valley on her own is nothing but a show of temper."

"Are you serious?"

He leaned against the wall, nodding. "It's her way of getting back at me."

"This isn't about you! It's about her love affair with Erlend. That you shattered on purpose." She got into his face, pitching her voice softer to better carry her aggravation. "How could you out her? You, the Master Face Changer?"

"She lied to Erlend. It was time for him to know the truth."

"It was her business to solve, not yours!"

"She ran away after healing me. Too much of a coward to face me."

"Well, I can't blame her. You barked at Feyn and me. She was waiting for you to calm down." Ashta waved her hand in front of his eyes. "Look at me! Why did you hurt her like that? Don't you think life has been hard enough on her since we left Eridan, or even before? Do you remember how old she is? Who she is?"

"She's the one who forgot."

"And? We're not in Eridan. You destroyed her relationship with Erlend. You humiliated them both. For what reason? De-clan! Tell me!"

He stood still, his own anger hardening his taut features. "She betrayed me. She deserved what she got."

She considered him for a long moment. "No," she said finally. "This isn't about betrayal. You're jealous."

"What are you talking about? I'm not jealous."

"You are. I know you, Declan. You couldn't let Nand be happy, not after Evetha let you down. She's not around, so you took your anger out on Nand."

"Evetha has nothing to do with Nand."

"On the contrary, she has everything to do with what you did to Nand."

He shrugged, avoiding her eyes.

"Don't think I haven't noticed how moody you've been since you talked to Theo. Long before she went missing."

"Missing?" He glanced sharply at her. "You think she's alive?"

"I trust the Redlanders. If they think she's on her way back here, I believe them. I don't feel her anymore, but I'm sure I'd know if she were dead."

"Should we postpone our departure?"

"No. We need to get home. She'll catch up with us when she can."

He stepped away from the wall. "I don't understand how you can be so … unconcerned … It's not the right word, but you get my gist."

"I agree; unconcerned isn't the right word to define how I feel about Theo, but then you don't know my feelings and how invasive her mind could be."

Surprise lit his eyes. "You're relieved that your minds aren't connected anymore."

"Yes, I am. The empathy link complicated things between us from the outset." She smiled grimly. "It nearly cost me my life. I'm free now, and I look forward to the moment we meet again as two separate entities." She straightened. "But our discussion isn't about Evetha and me. It's about your relationship with her, and how it blinded you to Nand."

He sighed. "Nand!"

"Erlend asked me if you were in love with Nand. I answered no, of course, but I understand now that you reacted like a scorned lover. Except that you confused Nand with Evetha. Nand is your disciple. She saved my life; she saved yours more than once. She may be the hlyk, but she's above all a brave young woman who fell in love. You can't blame her for that. And yet you, the Master Face Changer, the man who swore to protect her, you deliberately broke her heart." She punched her index finger into his chest to mark her words. "Your jealousy where Evetha is concerned has blinded you. It has turned into envy and you deliberately attacked this young couple."

"You've got it all wrong."

"Have I?" She considered him from head to foot. "I remember what you told me the morning of the massacre. I know how tough it can be to lose the person you cherish to another man." She met his eyes, satisfied when he reddened. "When this happens, you must be brave and face it. Not push a young woman to despair."

"You're overreacting! She'll be fine."

"I hope you're right. I really do."

CHAPTER 210

Find the River

14 May 3077, Standard Time (ST), Sixth Federal Era
Redland—Canyon Maze

A splatter of rain falling after an explosion woke Theo up. She was asleep, dreaming of Rory. He embraced her, he comforted her, telling her not to lose hope, to keep on.

It wasn't the first time she had dreamt of him. At first, her dreams made her cry. He called her to save him from the flames and she was too much of a coward to brave the fire—even in her dream—to drag him away. So she watched him die repeatedly, and spent the following hours consumed by guilt.

Those guilt-ridden dreams weighed her down. As she walked, she took to talking to herself, and to Rory. Hearing her voice kept solitude at a distance; it enabled her to retrace the events that led to the crash.

Rory's anger morphed into support. As she progressed through the canyons, he sometimes whooped in her dreams. His teasing forced her out of her melancholy, the ever-present concern that she would not succeed, that it might have been wiser to stay in the ship, to wait for Mogud's Fudrons to finish her off.

The sound came from beneath the ground: it was running water! She listened to the rumbling. She imagined herself riding this subterranean river to Painted-Caves. Instead of walking under the suns' glare, swimming through the dark. She sat up. She preferred a blazing landscape to a cavern's obscurity. But if she found access to water, she would wash and drink and rest.

She could only hear the sound if she crouched. The underground river seemed to run away from her trail. What should she do? Follow it upwards or downwards? What if she got lost and lost time? She couldn't afford to extend her trek, with water and food already stretched to the limit.

"Rory, I'm sorry," she declared. "I can't go back!" She forged on. The trail proved hard to follow, often nonexistent as it meandered around clusters of shrubs and piles of sharp boulders on an uneven riverbed filled with empty potholes. She walked slowly, sucking a mhuol root, focused on where she put her feet. She only raised her head when she found herself in front of a tall boulder, stuck in the middle of her path. She checked her map: no boulder indicated. She walked first to one side, then the other.

Impossible to squeeze past the boulder. She could only scale it. She examined its smooth surface and instantly admitted defeat. Since her fall and concussion, she had avoided any trail that rose above a few meters.

She took the mhuol root out of her mouth and drank some water. The suns filled the sky with light, and she needed to rest. She had learned the hard way, as always, that skirting away from her routine added failure to failure.

So she set camp on the boulder's right-hand side, the widest, with a shrub growing in front of it, and squeezed herself beneath it to get a modicum of shade. She was so exhausted that she went instantly to sleep.

"What if we get separated?" Malcolm asked Ian, Theo's father.

"Separated how?"

"Well, if Althea falls and gets hurt, and I can't reach you. What should I do?"

"Follow the map," she said.

"Yes, the map will help you even if it's not perfect. Remember that many rivers flow underground. If you get lost, you must find the one that runs closest to you. And if you are lucky enough to hear an underground river, find it."

"Why?"

"They're mapped. We use water to grow our crops. All brooks have entries. Each entry is marked and will contain essentials: food, water tablets, a map showing the main access points within the canyons. Remember: the water-shepherds tour each entry regularly."

"What if the river goes the wrong way? Should I still follow it?"

Her father smiled, crinkles around his sky-blue eyes.

"Yes. A river can save you. A trail can't." Her father looked at her. "Find the river." She nodded. He took her hand. "Do you remember what I said?" He squeezed her fingers. She nodded again. He squeezed harder. "Wake up. I want you to remember everything I said this time. You can't afford to forget again. You are getting tired, Althea. Get to the water."

Theo forced herself to wake. She winced at her cramped legs, her aching joints. "Find the river, find the river," she repeated out loud and went back to sleep.

CHAPTER 211

Unforgiven

17 May 3077, Standard Time (ST), Sixth Federal Era
Redland—Buzzard Canyon

The voice came and went like a lullaby.

She floated.

She enjoyed the feel of water on her skin as it spread over her parched lips, lingered on her bloated tongue, pooled inside her dry mouth, went down her gritty throat.

The voice cajoled, ordered, beseeched.

She swam.

The voice insisted.

"Nand!"

She heard a moan. Pain pierced a hole between her eyes.

"Nand! Nand! Wake up! Come on. I know you can do it."

She tried to prise her eyes open. They were so thick with sand she could hardly discern the outline of Erlend's figure looming above her. He poured water over her face.

"What are you doing?" she wanted to say, and heard a miserable croak.

The water drenched her, wet her hair, nestled beneath her head, her back.

Blurry shapes surrounded her.

She slept.

The wind was howling when she woke up. She lay on her back, her hands and feet dipping in tepid water.

She turned her head, and the figure sitting by a boxed fire stood up.

"Nand!"

Holding a lantern, Erlend knelt beside her.

"You need to drink," he said. He helped her raise her head and brought a bottle of water to her mouth.

Pain shot through her right arm. She winced.

"You broke your arm," he explained. "I set it in a sling for the time being. A Suni Sister will examine it tomorrow."

She didn't remember falling.

"Take it easy. I'll give you more later."

She licked her lips.

He tucked a folded blanket beneath her head.

She wished she could see his eyes.

"You need to eat."

He left, and loneliness slapped her.

He returned, carrying a bowl and a spoon, and sat next to her.

"I can feed myself."

He chuckled. His teasing smile warmed her: maybe it wasn't over between them; maybe they could work something out.

"Open your mouth," he ordered.

The sugary fruit mush tasted divine.

"I saw ice … Can you imagine that in the desert?" she said after several mouthfuls. "It must have been a dream. I talked to my cousin Terri."

"You have sunstroke and you're lucky to be alive. You could have died. The first rule we learn when we're kids is that you never leave without telling at least one person where you are going." He gave her another spoonful. "When you knocked at my door, I couldn't talk to you. At dinner time, your friend Ashta came looking for you. Smanul told us he saw you by the stables. By then, it was too late to go after you. We had to wait until morning. I thought you went to New Islay." He sounded grim as he continued to feed her. "When Malcolm and his search party found my horse trotting twenty miles from Esk Strath at dusk two days ago …" His voice trailed to a stop. He leaned forward, and she felt the full force of his tempestuous emotions as he stared into her eyes. "You're lucky I remembered about Buzzard Canyon. I went there on a hunch this afternoon. I found the saddle. You left an easy trail to follow. You knocked your head and fell, and during the night the winds covered you with sand. That's what saved you. The sand protected you from the suns. I found you half an hour before sunset. Too late to bring you back to Esk Strath tonight. But they know."

"You found me." She caressed his face. He drew back. How could she erase the harshness pinching his mouth? "I love you."

He sat back on his heels.

"You lied to me from the beginning."

"I wanted to tell you so many times … But I was afraid of your reaction. I've never been this happy in my whole life." She moved, jostling her arm, and winced. "I'm not a brave person. I'm sorry, Erlend, that you had to learn the truth this way."

"Maybe if you had told me before, I could have accepted it. But now …" He scowled. "I feel like I was a joke to the Eridanis."

"No …" She shook her head and closed her eyes against nausea. "Face Changers aren't like that." She forced herself to look at him. He deserved a full explanation, and even if her head throbbed and her eyesight was scrambled, she would deliver it. "Korund and Vilmar don't even know I'm not Aslone. They'll be surprised when they find out. Feyn's only concern is getting Declan back to his feet. Axonna was like you." She tried a smile. "He found you handsome. He envied me. He always face-changed into a woman, and it distressed him to die in his original form. And Ashta … She's like you too. Her lover is a friend of mine. Her name is Bibiana, and when I escaped Abuion, Bibiana and her three sisters helped me." She wet her lips. "Face Changers are loners and women Face Changers are infertile. The face-changing process has a side effect on genitals. We can go from female to male and back, but we can't bear children."

"Face Changers in Eridan, that's part of your life. I get that. But here? You say you love me. But how can I believe you?"

"I never lied about my feelings."

"Don't you think I deserved the truth?"

"I knew it would be over the moment I told you. I couldn't stand it. I fell in love with you that first evening."

He shrugged. "How could you do this? You wronged me. And I was so stupid. I believed you. I was ready to follow you to your home planet, to learn to swim and to live on an island somewhere, to be with you. I didn't want to lose you."

"You still could."

Anger whitened his face. "It's over."

"Am I that different?"

"Of course! The last time I saw you, you were a man with curly black hair, tanned skin, and a hot body. Now …"

"My body isn't hot anymore? It seems very hot to me." She touched her scorched face and tried a smile.

He answered with a fleeting one of his own.

"I don't know the face looking at me; I don't recognize the voice talking to me. Your skin, your smell … You're a different person. You're a woman. I could never love you or want to share any kind of intimacy with you."

"The core of who I am is the same. I haven't changed, Erlend. Only my body."

"Your body is you."

Hope crumbled. And she couldn't let that happen.

"Everything we shared, the things we said, the lovemaking, doesn't any of it count?"

He leaned forward to meet her eyes. "I loved Aslone. I would never have noticed Nand."

"It was only his appearance. My behavior confused the Face Changers when we were in the prison ship. They said Aslone wouldn't react the way I did."

"I wouldn't know."

"No. Of course not. It's just that you didn't meet the real Aslone. I could never be him. I never wanted to."

"What does it change?" He shrugged. "The bottom line is that I fell for a guy who turns out to be a woman. A young woman. And I'm not attracted to women, and I never will be."

A lump formed in her throat.

"So it's really over."

"Yes. I'm sorry, Nand."

She would have liked to say to him: did you notice that our hair is the same color now, that we even look a bit alike? She wanted him to hold her; she wanted to caress his body, to suggest that she could face-change into a man again if it could make things right again between them.

She didn't dare.

"Don't be." She hated this prone position that stuck her to the ground. "I guess we were wrong." She strove to keep her voice steady, to instill wry detachment, as her soul shattered. "We were wrong. It wasn't love after all. Only sex." She grinned. "Good sex." She closed her eyes. "I'll sleep now."

"With a broken arm?"

"Can't hurt more than a broken heart."

Friends

18 May 3077, Standard Time (ST), Sixth Federal Era
Redland—Esk Strath

Farren knocked at the door and entered the room, down the corridor from Jack's, where Nand had been installed.

She sat on a chair, an IV drip in her arm. A figure of sorrow. She smiled shyly, inviting him to sit opposite her.

"So, we finally meet. I've heard a lot about you. How's the arm?"

She moved a shoulder slightly. "Is Erlend all right?"

"He's with his brother. Cowan will watch out for him."

"And Jack?"

"He's awake."

"I'm happy to hear that. And you? How are you?"

Nobody had yet mentioned the intensity of Nand's eyes. Only their new color. But then, rare were those who visited her, even among the Eridanis. Erlend had done his best to protect her. Her face and hair were covered when they entered Esk Strath, each riding a horse, and Kilu and Fern had helped her to the infirmary.

Tension ran high among the Eridanis, with Ashta angry at Declan and Nand refusing to talk to any Face Changer. Off-shoots of this tension sizzled throughout the valley. Cowan reported on the gossip about Aslone turning into a freak overnight and on the insults directed against his brother. Declan came forward to explain about Face Changers, but Farren's mother said that his brittle and defensive attitude was counterproductive. The sooner these guests left the better, Malcolm had told Farren earlier that morning. Yet until Nand fully recovered from her sunstroke, the Eridanis had to wait.

"I'm tired. Like you."

She nodded. "It was stupid, what I did … Can you tell your brother-in-law that I'm sorry for the problems I caused?"

"Why don't you tell him yourself? I'll ask him to visit you."

"Do you think I should?" She sighed. "Will it make things easier or more complicated for Erlend? Your sister … she's been mean to him. I don't want to add more dislike."

"Malcolm is more open-minded than Livia. He'll appreciate that you talk to him."

"Then arrange the meeting." She scratched the red skin above the cast. "I must talk to you too, but I don't know where or how to start. It's complicated …"

"My mother mentioned visions."

"Do you remember this poem?

In the beginning
there was ice
salmon jumped
up-river
after their ocean journey

through
the liquid seasons of time.”

His chair screeched as he pulled it closer to her. “Who are you? How do you know these words?”

Her eyelids fluttered, her cheeks reddened, and he regretted his harsh tone. But she rallied and gazed at him straight in the eye.

“My name is Nand. I am the hlyk. In Eridan, it means the person who understands the kidadakh—sea mammals to you.” She visibly steeled herself. “And visions come to me. You've visited me for many seasons. You walk along shores in a white landscape, or ride a strange animal covered with long hair. Sometimes you're young. Other times, you're as old as you are now, and you tell poetry to the waves. The liquid seasons of time. So beautiful. So vivid.”

“Who knows about these visions? Declan? Ashta?”

“The Master Face Changer knows I have visions because hlyks usually do. But not their content. I wrote them down and shared them only with my cousin Terri in Eridan, and Erlend, a bit. I told him about the cold land. That's why he took me to meet your mother and the storytellers. He thought she might know about it.”

“Why not ask me?”

She made that little shoulder movement again, a mixture of embarrassment and bashfulness. “My visions about you never gave me your name and seldom showed your face. I only heard your voice. When you spoke in Pit 3, it jostled my memory. That's when I realized that you were the man from my visions. After we escaped, I didn't want to bother you and Jack. Not right away." Her voice trembled. "Your mother mentioned the white months, the year you went missing, and her research about Yelun after you told her you had lived there." She gripped her cast. "Erlend said I had visions of you. She questioned me. It wasn't for me to tell her." Her smile was apologetic. "She was so disappointed that I mentioned the old woman who cared for you. Crazy Moon."

What moments of his life with Crazy Moon had filtered into her visions?

"You were so lucky to meet someone like her." She chuckled softly. "I envy you."

"I've been remembering those days. Recounting them to Jack. It was part of Kilu's therapy."

"That's good. Do you remember the day you found your totem animal, the sense of belonging you experienced?"

"No, I don't."

"I'm sure it will come back. For me, it was more a feeling than a vision. I compared your experience to the ones I regularly have with Kaipekak, my kidadakh. The sense of belonging to a pod."

"You have a kidadakh?"

She shrugged. "That's what the hlyk is all about. But I don't have him as you would own a pet. Our minds are fused and I can understand his image-thoughts. Or at least I could before we left. I don't know if I'll retain this capacity when I get back."

Her melancholy pervaded each word.

"Do you know why you've had visions of me?"

"Ethelwin thinks it wasn't so much about you as about meeting your mother who knows so much about myths and stories. It's true; the information she gathered will help me understand my world. About Yelun and the Th'ans. There's a link with Eridan."

"You aren't convinced."

"No."

"What's your take?"

She smiled for the first time. "My visions of you when you stayed in Yelun influenced Mocean."

"How so?"

"When I had them, Mocean's waters were burning. Each time I saw Yelun, the temperature dropped." Disappointment clouded her eyes. "You don't believe me."

He raised his hands. "I am open to strange notions, but this is too farfetched for me. An ocean's temperature drops naturally. Even if your ocean obeys its own laws, the power of imagination can't modify it."

Again, her graceful one-shouldered shrug.

"Can I ask you a question?"

"Go ahead."

"It's about what happened in Pit 3 with Xë. You trapped him. You created a snowstorm in your mind."

"You saw it?"

"Xë described it and I imagined it. You changed him into a bear. Then the bear was surrounded by a curtain of snowflakes that it couldn't cross. It was so impressive. You rendered him powerless. How did you do that?"

Her genuine awe touched him. He sat back, thinking about that awful moment. "Xë terrified me. I had to stop him, and … I remembered some of Crazy Moon's lessons."

"She taught you well. It drove Xë mad. And powerless. He had no idea how to get the information Mogud wanted. I don't think any of the Face Changers ever realized how strong you are."

"I wish I could use this kind of knowledge to help Jack. You know, protect him."

"Mentally, you mean?"

"Yes."

"He doesn't need it. He's like Erlend. Their minds are harder than diamonds. Nothing can scratch them or hurt them."

"How do you know?"

"Xë tried to penetrate Jack's mind when he arrived in Pit 3. He couldn't. That's why he went after you in a rage. Jack attacked him, and Xë was powerless. He couldn't defend himself physically and couldn't defeat Jack mentally."

"You're the first one to say this."

The dainty shrug once again. "I watched."

"You mean you watched out for me, didn't you?"

Her rosy skin flushed. "I was weak. I don't know what I could have done, but yes, I kept an eye on you. It was my duty. Your laughter rescued me in a bleak period of my life. The least I could do was try to counter Xë after Mogud allowed him to pierce your mind. I couldn't let this happen to you."

"Thank you, Nand."

She smiled shyly and yawned. "In the end I didn't do anything. But you're welcome."

He stood up and leaned over to kiss her cheek.

"You need your rest. I'll come by later. I'd like you to tell me about your visions."

CHAPTER 213

Qanat

18 May 3077, Standard Time (ST), Sixth Federal Era
Redland—Canyon Maze

Theo stumbled back the way she had come the day before with a single purpose: to find the qanat's entry.

Exhaustion seeped up her limbs and lower back. She slept in the same place she had spent the night two days before, her ear pressed to the ground. She dreamed that she swam in Mocean. This dream brought back blue-green colors. In the pre-dawn hours the next day, as she trudged along slowly, concentrated on catching the river's gurgle, she remembered her anger and distrust, her discussions with Washone about her father. She longed to question her mother about how her father and the kwirimok met.

When she stopped at sunrise, she tried again to contact Ashta mentally: the resulting painful flash left her breathless. Her telepathic power—if she had ever possessed one—had evaporated in the crash. Relief mingled with disappointment. She liked it that her mind was entirely hers now, but in Canyon Maze it meant that she was on her own—utterly alone.

The river noises played hide and seek. Sometimes they totally disappeared, leaving her dismayed and afraid. She fell twice, an hour apart, her weak ankle twisting. The second time she was clambering down loose rocks, holding a shrub for support. The branch snapped and she lost her balance and fell backwards, hurting her elbow.

She felt dizzy and so tired she wondered if she would find the strength to stand up and walk some more. She pulled Rory's cap over her face.

"If I can do it, so can you!" Jack's voice rang in her ear.

He was a fighter, so much more valiant than she was.

She opened her eyes.

He stood in front of her. She touched his dear, beloved face, and he caught her fingers between his. They were firm and warm, and she felt secure.

"Don't go!" she croaked.

He grinned. His face was young, beautiful. He embraced her, held her tight. His heart beat against her ear.

"Jack!" she said, and her own voice woke her up.

"Jack!" she repeated softly to herself.

Was he alive? Was he dead?

And Farren?

Tears spilled out of her dusty eyes.

She pushed Rory's cap off her face. Above her, birds of prey circled in the sky. She watched them glide with envy.

Her elbow, her head throbbed. Rocks poked at her tender back.

She lay still. Unable to move.

Her exhaustion had won.

How could she find the river? Maybe she was hallucinating.

Maybe there was no river. Maybe she was going around and around, like the birds up there.

Maybe this was it. The end.

The glare hurt. She closed her eyes.

"Theo!"

She licked her dry lips. More fluid loss after her tears.

She inhaled deeply a few times, then braced her muscles and sat up. If Jack could do it, so could she. She assessed her bruises. Her elbow hurt when she extended her arm. She tested her ankle, wincing as she moved her foot clockwise. If she removed her boot now, it would be impossible to put it on again. Better leave it to compress her ankle.

Until she found the river.

In close vicinity, there were many more shrubs than earlier in the day, even short blades of greenish grass down to her left. The landscape had changed without her noticing.

A whiff brushed the back of her neck.

She turned around on her buttocks and searched the cliff for the origin of this cool breeze. Above the rubble, near the ground, close to where she sat, she finally discerned the large well and rain signs, gouged on a flat rock, which marked the cave's entry.

She dragged herself and her backpack to the opening. She pressed her fingers on the river sign, comforted that someone else had been in this spot before, that this location had a name on a map.

She took out her torch and fastened her backpack around her shoulders. She swung the torch beam from side to side as she crouched on a smooth surface inside a tunnel that quickly widened into a cavern where boxes were neatly piled up. A wide, round shaft lit the cave from above. On the right, a flight of clean and accessible steps went down. A rope passing through loops in the mountain wall served as a rail. Her ankle hurt too much, so she went down on her buttocks, and after long minutes reached a smooth rock. On her left it dipped into a large turquoise pool. On her right, water flowed in a tunnel high enough for a tall person to stand. A rail lined the tunnel, which seemed to stretch far away, lit even in the distance by regular light shafts.

Theo knelt by the qanat tunnel. She drank; she splashed cool water over her face, her hands, her arms. She undressed and hobbled into the tepid pool, where she sat down, sighing with pleasure as water covered her body.

A Disaster

*21 May 3077, Standard Time (ST), Sixth Federal Era
Eridan (207th Cycle, Cuttlefish Season, Whirlpools' Blue
Year)—Oniraveen*

Hunched inside a fur-lined bodysuit, Sheer stood behind the bench where Carmen used to sit on the cliff. She gripped its back with her cold, red hands as she scanned Oniraveen Bay with its ice packs and cooped-up sailing-ships.

Keith had launched Mindrule and had provoked a disaster.

New consequences erupted each day, leaving her no time to grieve. No more waves; no more energy; an ocean fragmented into ice chunks; frigid winds blowing; their economy trickling to a stop. In place of their fish diet, Eridanis hunted seagulls and ducks.

Mocean was freezing throughout Eridan, from Kerven to the Shallow Seas, from the surface downwards. The only Eridanis who still experienced mild conditions lived in the Southern and Middle Abysses, where hydrothermal vents flushed hot sea water.

Kidadakh still broke through ice floes to breathe, thus helping other sea mammals to the surface. Ice entrapment increased each day, though. Black masses were spotted beneath the ice: many fiskiorp and dwetwal pods caught beneath thick ice slabs had sunk. When such entrapments happened close to villages, people gathered to break the ice, but most pods were trapped by surprise as they swam in deep uninhabited areas. Fiskiorps, kidadakh and dwetwal populations were at risk, while ippinis and most seabirds survived.

Sheer sneezed and blew her nose. She tightened her collar. Here, away from the fortress, far from distraught and heartbroken Savalwomen, she could think.

Why had she postponed her visit to Keith? Why hadn't she listened to Carmen's concern? Or Terri's? The young man had told her of his experience, an experience she shared. She knew that Keith was serious about the Mindrule folly, and yet she had not talked to her former lover; she had remained in the Shallow Seas, and when she had finally packed her bag to return to Oniraveen, it was too late.

Keith had launched Mindrule. He twisted and tore apart their collective consciousness, sowing sorrow, grief, pain and madness, and provoking the sinking of many.

If only she had been true to her call as Savalwomen leader, Carmen, her dear, her wonderful Carmen would still be around to guide her, to share her optimism.

Her arms rigid, Sheer bowed her head. She battled with the agony of losing her double, and failed. How could she go on living without the woman who had stayed by her side for forty years, who knew of her vulnerabilities and strengths?

How could she continue?

Why hadn't she notice how sick and frail Carmen had become? Sheer pressed her lips together. Because she had no patience with ill health. Carmen had teased her about her intolerant attitude and hidden the extent of her sickness. During their years together, her double had always put Sheer before herself: for all her feebleness, she had been the genuine Savalwoman.

A nipping breeze whipped Sheer's face. In the Shallow Seas, ice floes joined fast, transforming Mocean into a uniform surface. Scientists had told her that cold storms would increase as their ocean stilled.

"Sheer!"

She shoved her hands into her pockets and faced Terri in his warm-looking Northern Abyss outfit. He pulled a box from his backpack and placed it on the bench.

"When Carmen and I met here, I brought her cakes that Sofini baked."

Were her eyes as red-rimmed and sad as his?

"Carmen enjoyed your talks." She cleared her throat. "I'm not like her. I can't sit."

"Let's walk, then." He put the box back into his backpack. "Fortress or Oniraveen?"

She stepped in the direction of the city. He joined her.

"How can I help?"

She frowned. "You don't like me. Why would you?"

"For Carmen, who tried hard to get us to work together. I want to do it for her." He gave her a half-smile. "And because you are the only person who can pull Eridan together."

She snorted, even though his words buoyed her. "If we find a way to sleep without nightmares."

He shrugged. "That too. When are you leaving for Eridooneen? I'd like to go with you."

"It's complicated getting there. No boat, no aquatrain."

"I have my kite buggy. I brought it with me from the Northern Abyss when I moved here. In this wind, it will take us less than a day to get there."

"A kite buggy?"

"It's fast and safe. There's a smooth ice sheet along the aquatrain rails where it can roll. I checked earlier."

The path brought them close to the cliff edge. Below, Oniraveen's inhabitants attended to their business as if ice and sleet were common occurrences.

"There's a rumor in Eridooneen about a foreign woman living in The Towers," Terri said. "She claims that she's the SpaceSS leader and that she must be allowed to leave. She's locked inside her room and acting up. My informer says she has an addict's mad eyes. Something happened between Keith and her."

"He has a thing for powerful women." She had stopped yearning for Keith a long time ago. Had she ever told that to Carmen?

"The bodyguard accompanying her is not human. He's a cyborg. A man, speaking in a woman's voice. The cold disrupted his functioning. He's in a cell below, at freezing temperature."

"I heard about him from Savalwomen in Eridooneen. They are questioning The Kresdan and the new so-called Master Face Changer. Astriv." She blew on her fingers to warm them. "We must find Keith."

"He sunk. Those of us who were awake, aware, we know."

The path went inland, and they walked between rusty ferns. "We can't be sure until we find his body," she said. "People need to be reassured that there won't be any new attempt at Mindrule."

"Astriv says Keith sunk. Don't your Savalwomen believe him?" He peered at her sideways. "So … he didn't say anything to them, did he?"

Terri was too astute for her liking.

"How do you know what Astriv said?"

"He contacted a former friend of his. A Face Changer."

"When?"

"In the hours that followed Mindrule. My Face Changer friend says Mindrule opened Astriv's eyes. He's frightened and full of grief. He's beginning to measure the full extent of his responsibility." He appraised her. "He'll only speak to Face Changers, though. He knows where to find Keith's body."

"Rotweed!" She pointed a finger at him. "I don't like this! Who does Astriv think he is? Why haven't I been informed of this before? Why didn't you tell me?"

"I'm telling you now."

"I don't like this," she repeated.

Terri smiled. "Can I attend the Council meeting?"

"Why you …?" She stepped forward.

He raised both hands. "I support you, and you need all the support you can gather."

"What do you want? Power?"

He shook his head: "No. I want you to take charge of Eridan."

Carmen used to say that Sheer could glare a zuglan down. Would this puny man be intimidated? "So this is all about sedition? Savalwomen don't govern. They support the kwirimok."

He stood his ground. "They do. But where is he? In any case, Keith can't be kwirimok any longer. Look around. Open your eyes. Eridan is dying. He destroyed Mocean! He killed Washone!"

Sheer grabbed his arm. "How do you know?"

"Nassour told me. Nassour tried to sink himself, and friends of mine stopped him. He's blabbing now. His nightmares terrify him. He's the one who poisoned Washone and left Niumi with students for Keith to finish the job. One student was concerned that Washone had stayed alone. She returned. In time to see Keith leave Niumi. She's the one who found Washone."

"Nassour? He and Washone were friends."

"Whatever Keith promised him, it changed his mind. He isolated Washone. Every Council member is compromised."

"Issavern included?"

"Yes. I don't know to what extent."

Carmen had been right all along: Terri had insight, and he compensated for his small height by an indomitable presence and acute intelligence.

"What Ring are you?" she asked.

"I've no idea. Does it matter?"

"Only Major Rings attend."

He removed his gloves and scarf and stuffed them into his backpack. "Don't tell them anything. Nobody needs to know, and nobody cares right now. You can change the rules. That's what leaders do."

She faltered. "Until we know otherwise, Keith remains the kwirimok."

"How can he still be after what he did to us? To others?"

Her heart skipped a beat. "What do you mean, others?"

"So it's true what some say." He gripped the straps of his backpack. "Not everybody experienced the dying." He pinned her with his penetrating eyes. "We killed hundreds of people. We are collectively responsible for mass murder. The nightmares, that's what they are telling us. We murdered them."

"What are you talking about? We didn't do any such thing!"

But as the words came out of her mouth, Sheer remembered, and her body froze.

"Didn't you hear Bibiana's screams? Many people I know did. Even in Eridooneen, even in the Shallow Seas, they heard her." He stepped closer. "And you're telling me that you didn't?"

She had been awake, watching the stars as she lay on a beach, imagining ways to repair the wreckage caused by the water wall. Unable to sleep after mentally yelling at Carmen who had demanded to know why she hadn't talked to Keith. Sheer had simmered in her own anger, not heeding the mental pull, the young woman's screams, until it was too late.

She hurried down the path until it neared the cliff edge again, winding around three benches. She stood on hard, brown earth at the tip of the land.

Carmen had been the first Major Ring to respond to Bibiana's screams. She had sacrificed herself to wake Eridanis from their sleep, using her flailing energy to wrench as many as she could from their collective consciousness: every single Savalwoman—Sheer was the last—and all the people she knew. Her double had been instrumental in caring and protecting, in fighting and stopping Keith. A valiant Savalwoman to the very end.

Sheer leaned forward. No waves licked the foot of the cliff. Nothing but a still, glittering, pristine surface. A windy silence, an unbearable absence.

Terri's strong fingers grasped her arm. He pulled her back. She stumbled, fighting to block her grief. He held her, steadied her, until she could breathe again.

"Bibiana and Carmen showed us the way." His voice was grave, his keen eyes filled with understanding and urgency. "It's your turn now. You must unseat Keith and act in place of the kwirimok until a new one is found. And I will support you."

CHAPTER 215

Waiting

27 May 3077, Standard Time (ST), Sixth Federal Era
Redland—House in the canyon

Bent over his father's oud, which his mother had recently given him, Farren concentrated on the tune he had invented while day-dreaming about life with Jack in Earth Metropolis—rainy mornings when he cooked muffins for breakfast; gardening and sunning in the hammock on their terrace; drinking Venuvers with Jered and Roger in the pub-hub down the street.

He hummed while Jack's chest rose and fell peacefully beneath the sheet.

Since the first day he regained consciousness, Jack was adamant about working out. He exercised for hours, and slept as many. His body was responding so positively to the mhuol treatment that had stopped the poison's nefarious effect that Kilu had already diminished his daily dose. Jack found in training the will to pull out from the Reddish drug's addiction.

Friends and family speculated about the route Theo had taken. Proof of her presence was found in a qanat running below the canyons—she had camped there, eaten food and marked her presence in the qanat's log, yet she remained invisible.

Had she opted for the high plateau route or was she winding her way through the canyons?

Fern, supported by her Suni Sister friends, convinced Malcolm—and Livia, whom she was the first to intimidate—that her daughter was heading for their old home. She declined going there herself, because she wasn't ready to confront old memories. She preferred to stay in Esk Strath until her daughter came back.

So Kilu had arranged for Farren and Jack to move into the MacDougals' family house, and they had been there for six days now.

Sunbeams played shadow and light through the curtains. His fingers rested on the oud's strings. The harsh songs of the cacti wrens that abounded near the house wove sound into the stuffy air.

That morning, Jack had exercised for five hours and eaten two full meals. Farren relayed the good news to Kilu in his midday report. In her reply, she raved about Fern's course in first aid, and shared Cowan and Nujise's concern about Erlend. Would he agree to talk to him? Farren wasn't certain that his own perspective on this sad story would heal the young man's heartbreak, but his mother had insisted, and he had agreed.

He stroked the shiny instrument and returned it to its box. The large bedroom, which had once been Fern and Ian's, opened onto a landscape of boulders and cliffs which he observed often.

Where was Theo?

Hopefully close by now. Malcolm's trekkers were inside Canyon Maze, but hadn't found her yet. From the moment he regained consciousness, Jack had argued with their friends and family about their reluctance to find Theo. They defended the Long Walk, this rite of passage Farren had never done because he had left before he reached his twenties. And, as Livia pointed out, since he had not done it, where was his legitimacy in talking about it?

At dinner the day before they left Esk Strath, his mother and the others alleged that if Theo was in trouble, she would have stayed in the qanat and waited there for help. Jack's expression darkened—a sure sign that he was better—and Farren had braced himself. In a soft yet scathing voice, his brawan had told Fern and Malcolm, who knew Theo best, to think straight. Did they really believe that she was the kind of woman capable of sitting still, of being reasonable, of not putting herself at risk? Did they? Farren remembered Malcolm's face, how stunned he had been by Jack's anger.

Jack had continued, his voice rising a little, and everybody around the table stopped talking or eating. He said that he hadn't known Theo as long as they had, but he knew her to be determined and stubborn. She wasn't a quitter, and if she was hurt, she would continue walking; she would crawl if she had to. Because that was her way. She never gave up. That's how she had found Farren; that was why she hadn't stayed in the qanat. And she needed assistance because she didn't know how to ask for it, or even expect it, and probably by now thought that they had given up on her. This, Jack couldn't accept. Red irritation spread over Malcolm's face and puffed his cheeks. He told Jack he loved Theo and knew her well, and he remembered how often they had discussed the Long Walk when they were kids.

Memories had a way of sparking up, of bringing back forgotten words. A flicker in Malcom's eyes: shame replaced irritation. He thanked Jack for his words; he said he would think them over.

The next day, as they rode to Fern's canyon house, Malcolm told him that Jack's outburst had made him realize his mistake. So he had asked the trekkers to find her fast. He even admitted that Theo had never intended to do the Long Walk.

So, by not sending help, he had forced her to do it—this was Jack's indignant conclusion.

The same day they moved to Fern's house, the Eridanis left on Kirby's ship. A strained departure. Organizing one-on-ones with Ashta proved more complicated than anticipated, so they resorted to writing to each other every day through hypernet.

The vivid tension among Eridanis increased after Kirby relayed news about Eridan, whose ocean was freezing, and about Meranka, a garden planet, Eridan's closest neighbor, where hundreds had mysteriously died overnight.

Neither Farren nor Ashta wrote the word, not through their insecure means of communication, but they both feared that Keith had launched Mindrule.

The Federal Security Headquarters sent out military ships to secure the area and prevent any ship from landing on Eridan or Meranka until all risk of alien invasion or contamination was ruled out. Since Clobb never responded to his queries, Farren relied on Lonetom back in E-Met, and SpaceSS agent friends, to obtain information. While SpaceSS was still reeling from Simpson's defection and contending with a tricky leadership vacuum, a vicious power game was at play between the Guild and the Federal government in Nuong.

Smanul had joined an independent committee that was investigating the crimes and torture perpetrated in the Gold Mines by Colonel Ty and the Skodraks. Ehr, who wanted his friend to stay in Redland, was encouraging him to think about raising ponies with him.

The Guild's decision to destroy the Dome's spaceport continued to create heated debates among Redlanders and Federal representatives, as much as the forthcoming trials or Mogud's status did.

Ashta worried about Nand. So did he. He felt intensely protective towards the young woman, who had experienced so many tragedies yet had restored to him forgotten moments of his past with her visions. Ashta and he both counted on his mother, who adored Nand, to pull her out of her dismal mood.

Sunrays blurred his sight. He wiped his water-filled eyes.

He checked on Jack, now snoring, and headed down to the kitchen.

Time to cook, to invent a new dish.

Time to feel alive again.

CHAPTER 216

Frozen Eridan

29 May 3077, Standard Time (ST), Sixth Federal Era
Guild Observation ship—orbiting Eridan

The Guild Observation ship was yet another prison with its tiny screens that permitted a partial view of Eridan, which they now orbited. A prison worse than the others because this ship, which they had boarded in Nuong, tantalized them with views of their home planet.

They were forbidden to land.

Sitting on a narrow parapet close to a small window below the piloting room, her computer beside her, Nand kept a vigil as Mocean's blues morphed into white.

The Guild's scientists elaborated theories about this radical change in Eridan's weather. With no knowledge of their planet's unusual ecosystem, how could they understand anything? Ashta hounded Clobb to authorize them to go home. He rejected all her requests. An investigation was underway in Meranka, where hundreds of gardeners had died a few hours before the ocean in Eridan had begun to freeze. Until it was proven that these facts were unrelated, they would remain on the Guild Observation ship.

Ashta asked for Farren's help to sway Clobb into letting them contact Sheer and Keith. He hadn't answered yet.

Ice spread like a disease. Nand perused the distant landscape for invisible black spots, traces of kidadakh pods.

How would they survive if they couldn't break ice to breathe?

A cabin was allotted to her. Sleeping there, cooped up in a windowless bunk, added to her anxiety. So she stayed near the small window, comforted by the ship's purring quietness.

When nobody was around, she surrendered to sorrow; she grieved Erlend, she worried about Terri and Davin, about Sofini and Bibiana and her friends.

How had they fared?

Even though her visions of Farren reflected true memories, she had hoped that those related to Eridan were wrong, that the images of death and sinking that crowded her sleep simply symbolized her own unrest.

As days went by, she feared that they represented reality. And if they did, it meant that Kaipekak had not survived.

She had endured their separation; she had hoped he had done the same.

All these weeks, she had convinced herself that he had survived her absence.

But when she viewed Eridan for the first time, her heart froze.

How could Kaipekak breathe with so many ice floes?

Had he already sunk?

She could not bear another loss.

She pressed her forehead against the window pane.

She whispered Erlend's name.

She had tried so hard to be strong, to do the right thing, to protect and to heal.

And she had failed.

Eridan's chalkiness shone in the dark.

Mocean's ice drowned life, and she couldn't stop it.

She sat down, her computer on her lap. She clicked on Erlend's picture which Nujise had sent her and cried harder as she caressed his face with her thumb.

Nujise told her to move on, like mothers do, but she could not.

She missed Erlend even more than she missed Kaipekak.

What was her lover up to? Roaming across sand dunes and taming wild ponies? Trying to catch a star at dawn when the swazzi stopped blowing?

Had he met a real man?

Of course.

———◆———

Getting Derek Clobb to understand what was at stake in Eridan remained a frustrating challenge. Ashta typed her daily encrypted message to Farren to update him with the latest horrific development.

Perhaps he already knew.

Would he understand its implications for Eridan? She feared not.

In his deal with the Federal authorities, Tarbel Mogud had revealed the true nature of Keith of Rain Forest's involvement within the alliance to overthrow the government in Nuong. He had divulged the M word—*Mindrule*—which had prompted a new angle on the current investigation in Meranka.

You need to intervene before this becomes out of hand, she wrote. *Eridan is a living being, and it's dying.* Would he know how to circumvent the rules and administrative procedures? *In short,* she typed, *Eridan is in quarantine, something to do with this garden-planet, and we aren't allowed to go home. These are two separate matters: our return and the investigation. Clobb said this evening that our future is not encouraging. From the evidence gathered so far, it seems that Eridan "attacked" Meranka. If this is true, our planet will be banned. He mentioned retaliation, probation, with an appointed Federal government that would substitute itself for the kwirimok's spiritual power. We can't let this happen! Farren, we need your help!*

Almost Home

26–31 May 3077, Standard Time (ST), Sixth Federal Era
Redland—Canyon Maze

From one bend to another, the landscape changed from unfamiliar to familiar. Theo marveled at this discovery.

"Remember the cluster of mhuol trees I showed you yesterday afternoon?" Kieran, the handsome thirty-something man who organized hiking trips in Canyon Maze, pointed towards a green-crowned dented red peak. "It's opposite Painted-Caves, and we walked up that trail together yesterday afternoon. The stratified rock next to the arch, that's where we slept last night."

Theo took the binoculars he handed her and perused the red labyrinth etched against the horizon, with dusty mhuol bushes standing out like toothpicks. She recognized stern pillars and jagged boulders which overwhelmed delicate arches and admired the tenacity of the raindrops that carved and sculpted those crimson rocks.

Had she really crossed this vast and tortuous, this daunting landscape?

"Sorry for panicking yesterday … and this morning. I …" Theo shuddered as she gave him back the binoculars.

Akilah, Kieran's cheerful, athletic wife and awesome cliff-climber herself, gripped Theo's arm reassuringly. "You did fine." She winked. "Particularly for someone who's afraid of heights."

"Your mother's home is this way. A two-hour walk. We'll take you down the path and sleep at ground level tonight." He removed Theo's backpack from his shoulders.

"Can't we get there before sunset?"

Kieran grinned as he uncorked his water bottle. "Sure." He glanced at Akilah. "You win."

"What?" Theo asked.

He removed his cap, raked his tousled blondish hair then shoved his cap back on. "A silly bet. I thought you were too tired to hike all day, and Akilah was convinced of the opposite."

"We'll eat now, and get you to your home before dusk." Akilah removed her own backpack, which contained Kieran's stuff. "You've been favoring your left leg again. Does your right ankle hurt?"

"I'm fine."

"I'll check it now. Sit down over here and stretch out your leg."

The two trekkers sent by Malcolm and Farren treated her like a princess.

They had found her as she reached Painted-Caves, and carried her inside as she stumbled once again on the trail, knocking herself over. They spent three days caring for her, tending to her bruises and hurts, preparing meals and hot drinks, talking to her.

Cell coverage in Canyon Maze was tricky. They had told Malcolm that the moment they found her they would give a mirror signal when the aircraft did its daily routine over the canyons. But Theo had begged them to keep her presence secret until she felt able to face the world again, and, after much discussion, they had agreed.

They gave her a note from Farren, which brought tears to her eyes each time she read it as she basked in his loving words. While they enjoyed the hot springs' bubbling waters, Akilah and Kieran told her what they knew of the events since the crash, details mostly about her mother and Malcolm and Mogud. The debate between Farren and the Redlanders about whether or not to assist her bemused her.

Even if finding out that she had been defended and supported during her journey soothed some anxiety that she hadn't been abandoned to her fate, it also threw anger into her mixed emotions. Or, more exactly, resentment: how could her Reddish family and friends liken this survival trek across Canyon Maze to a Long Walk?

How could they decide for her?

And not think about what she had endured, her despair and loneliness?

It was walk or die. No leisurely hike.

Akilah and Kieran accompanied her on the last stretch of her journey on the plateau. Kieran lent her a walking stick and carried her backpack. Akilah led the way; she gripped her hand when Theo reeled from the height.

They left her in view of her home. They watched as she walked down the goat trail, ready to assist her if she panicked. Theo waved at them as she neared the ground. They climbed back up the cliff because Kieran wanted to sleep on the high plateau to photograph the suns' double rise the following morning. Afterwards, they would head towards Esk Strath.

The first sun had set, and Theo hurried down the trail to get home before the swazzi rose. She preferred not to imagine what would have happened if Kieran and Akilah had not waited for her in Painted-Caves. The eight days it had taken her to reach the hot spring cavern had stretched her stamina to its limit, even if finding the qanats, and thus not having to worry about water anymore, had changed the nature of her hike.

Weariness became a cumbersome companion, though. She forced herself each day to get up and walk, whether inside the qanats or outside when the solitude of the tunnels weighed too heavily.

Before leaving Painted-Caves, she spent a few hours alone, looking at the Smenns' exquisite and precise drawings on the sandstone walls: an enchantment of flowers, trees and ponies, with a few human figures outlined on the sides. Her father had introduced her to these moving murals. She remembered his lively explanations, mischievous smile, and kindness. She thanked him for his loving presence throughout her journey, a presence that had steered her away from dangerous ledges and prompted her to go on when discouragement threatened or when her weak ankle twisted.

Her backpack weighed nothing; it contained the minimum needed to get down to her home. Akilah and Kieran carried the rest of her things to Esk Strath. She teared up when she recognized the roof of her father's studio, and beyond it the windows of the house. She sat down, not minding the rising breeze or the dusty path. She wrapped her arms around her knees and gazed at her home embedded in the mountain side, amazed by its tranquil beauty.

CHAPTER 218

Despair

31 May 3077, Standard Time (ST), Sixth Federal Era
Redland—Canyon Maze

After jogging for an hour, Farren scaled the wall of a nearby cliff. He forced his quivering muscles to carry him up, while heat beat against his neck and back.

Even now that Jack was recovering, and, given his fortitude, doing so remarkably fast, he still worried. Would he ever stop being afraid that death would grab Jack while he wasn't around?

"If" had chased him day in and day out: if Jack survives the mhuol treatment, if Jack lives.

And now this.

He leaned his forehead against the hot mountain rock, one hand massaging the stitch in his right side.

He dared not climb too high as he tired easily, with headaches that laid him low. The isolation cell had left scars: during his migraines, he suffered terrifying moments of blindness.

Jack had questioned him about the Gold Mines.

Farren glanced over his shoulder. The bench where they had sat on the patio in front of the house was empty.

His sight dimmed. He blinked. He gripped the mountainside; he fought his dizziness.

Too dangerous to keep scaling the cliff. He slipped downwards and sideways to reach the trail that led to the plateau.

He trudged up to the summit. He found a flat, brownish boulder where he reclined in the light of the setting suns to watch the glowing mineral-red landscape and pinkish sky.

"We talked a lot, about me, about Talmand, and I thank you for that. For caring for me when I was delirious," Jack had said earlier as they drank coffee in the shade. "But we still need to share lots of things. What happened to each other when we were apart; what drove us to become strangers." His smile was so sad, it still hurt Farren hours later. "We have too many secrets. I tried to tell you what happened when I thought you were dead." He drew circles in the sand with the tip of his cane. "It's not easy. I'm ashamed of myself. I gave up."

"But Theo dragged you back into life, didn't she?"

"Yes. She saved my neck, and I can't wait for her to get here so I can thank her properly. But you and I, where are we?"

Fear seared Farren. What question was Jack really asking? "What do you mean?"

"Our secrets are killing us. We need to speak, however hard it is. What happened in the Gold Mines? What did Colonel Ty do to you? Why can't you say 'I love you' to me anymore?"

He had stood up, away from Jack's probing eyes, his questions. Jack did the same, and lost his balance, swearing as he steadied himself on his cane.

"Farren … why don't you trust me anymore?"

"It's not a question of trust!" How could he explain the fear that Jack would reject him? "It's …"

Words failed him.

"Is it over between us?"

He shook his head—no.

Jack found his balance. He opened his arms, uncertain, hopeful.

"I can't. I'm sorry." He no longer deserved Jack's love.

He had left.

Farren pressed his palms over his smarting eyes. Memories assailed him now: Smanul's scream when he learned about Jimmy's death. Blood running down the boy's temple.

The fight. His defeat.

Pleading with Colonel Ty to let him out when the stiffness radiating in his back grew unbearable, imploring him for light.

The only thing he had ever obtained was the acid knowledge of his capitulation.

How could he reveal this to Jack?

CHAPTER 219

Home

1 June 3077, Standard Time (ST), Sixth Federal Era
Redland—House in canyon

Jack jerked awake. The room was plunged into wind-noisy darkness. His nightmare's images faded, leaving in their wake a sense of doom. He switched on the bedside solar lamp. The room—Theo's bedroom when she was a teenager—appeared mundane in the dim orange light. He wiped his sweaty face and got up. He grabbed the cane that had once belonged to Farren's grandfather and checked Farren's room—Theo's parents' former bedroom—right next to his. It was empty. The big bed was still made.

Where was he? Was he all right?

There was light in the kitchen and his heart soared with relief. He hastened down the steps and pushed the door open. Farren was leaning over the sink, looking out of the window at the pre-dawn sky, a barely outlined figure in the room's shadows.

"Farren? Where the hell were you? I was worried sick about you."

"Jack?"

He would have recognized her husky, hesitant voice anywhere, and his heart hammered in his chest. She moved into view. She wore one of Farren's checkered shirts—it had hung the day before on the clothesline outside—and a pair of dark blue tight-fitting pants. A cap was jammed hard on her head.

Tall, thin, her resemblance to Farren was uncanny.

"Theo?" he whispered, then cleared his throat. He hobbled across the kitchen, letting his cane crash to the floor in his haste to reach her. "You made it!"

"You made it too!" She rushed to meet him halfway. Jack embraced her and she wrapped her arms around him, hugging him tightly. "I was so worried about you," she said, her voice muffled against his shoulder.

"I had nightmares that you'd tripped into a gully and broken your skull. That you were hurt and alone," he murmured, aware his voice might crack again.

She raised her head. Her cheekbones jutted out. "I can't tell you how many times I fell or twisted my ankle. My knees and hands are a mess."

He gripped her upper arms. "You can be proud of yourself. I'm so proud of you. How brave you've been." He winked. "A true Savalwoman ..."

She framed his face between her hands, scrutinizing him.

"But you? How are you? Kieran and Akilah said you were all right. But are you? Really?"

"Kieran and Akilah?"

"The trekkers you and Farren convinced Malcolm to send to meet up with me. Thank you for that." Her lips quivered. A deep-seated anxiety filled her dark eyes. "I wouldn't have made it here without them. I was too tired in the end."

"Farren is the one who convinced your cousin. He went after him every single day from the moment the sandstorm abated."

She swallowed. "Tell me about you. The Xplo-bullet poison."

"I'm still on the mend. Improving each day. Why don't you sit down? I'll brew some coffee. Are you hungry?"

She clung to him. "Can you hold me a while longer? I …"

He enfolded her in his arms. She shook. He stroked her back.

"I was terrified," she mumbled. "I thought I'd never get here."

"But you did, sweetheart. You did."

"I went a little mad. I frightened myself."

"You're not alone anymore. I'm here."

She kept shuddering. He thought he heard a sniffle, a sob.

"Rory's dead." She looked up at him, her face streaked with tears. "I was with him when he died …" Her mouth wobbled. "He was in such pain and I couldn't help him. I had to leave him under the ship. I wanted to bury him. I stayed with him, and the Fudrons returned and … I hid under the wing. They kept shooting at the ship …"

He made her sit down on the bench against the wall and sat beside her, embracing her. She laid her head on his shoulder and closed her eyes as he rubbed her arm.

"Rory is buried in the Esk Strath cemetery," he said. "We'll go there together."

"I'm sorry, I …"

"Shhhh …"

While he stroked her, he gave her more news: her mother was staying with the Suni Sisters in Esk Strath and was working at the clinic. She and Kirby had become close friends. Lonetom had left three weeks before; so had Clobb. The Eridanis had travelled to Nuong in Kirby's ship as originally planned and were now in a Guild ship orbiting Eridan. One of them hadn't made it, though—a Face Changer named Axonna. And it turned out that the young man called Aslone was in fact a young woman, Nand.

"She holds an important position in Eridani society. Declan must be so relieved that she's alive. What about Ashta?"

"She's fine. She and Farren are close. They write to each other a lot."

She wiped her face.

"And Farren? Where is he?"

"I don't know."

"You had a fight?"

"No, not a fight …" He limped across the kitchen to stoke the stove. "It's tough."

She followed him and leaned against the counter beside him. "What is?"

He put hot water on to boil in a pan. "Speaking about what happened. He's close-mouthed, and I know he went through hell." He took two tall mugs from the shelf above the stove.

"Maybe it's too soon for him. Maybe he can't."

He poured coffee into the filter.

"Jack?" Her eyes shone. "Maybe he's afraid to tell you." She bit her lip. "Or ashamed."

Could this be the problem?

Shame he could relate to.

"You're right. Maybe it's too soon. But I want us to be together again … Like before."

She covered his clenched fist with her hand.

"Give him time. Do you have any idea where he went?"

He shook his head as he poured boiling water into the filter.

"So you're worried sick." She repeated his own words.

"He's not sleeping well. I hear him walking around at night." He rolled his shoulders to remove the stitch between his clavicles. "He climbs cliff walls. Maybe he fell."

"Let's go get him."

"Now? It's still night outside!" He poured coffee into the two mugs and handed her one.

"Dawn is close and it's the best time to walk."

"But you just got back! You're exhausted. I'll go."

"You don't know the way to the cliff." Impatience filtered into her tone. "I'll take you." She took a sip and cringed.

"Too strong? My coffee's never good."

"It's perfect. What?"

She had bounced back into his life, safe and sound, and joy filled his heart.

"I'm happy you're back."

Her face softened. "So am I. Now, shall we get ready?"

He bobbed his head, curbing the urge to salute.

CHAPTER 220

Heart to Heart

1 June 3077, Standard Time (ST), Sixth Federal Era
Redland—House in canyon

Two trails led to the vertical cliff. Because of her fear of heights, Theo opted for the slow-rising large trail that wound through vegetation and rocks before reaching up to the top between two wall-like boulders.

They walked side by side, Jack leaning on his cane and Theo clutching her trekking stick.

"So, your treatment, what was it exactly?" she asked.

"Mhuol, like you suggested. It stopped the Xplo-bullet's action, but didn't dissolve all the poison floating around my body. There's still lots of it. Kilu is convinced that if I keep up with mhuol I can fight its effect."

"How long?"

"Probably my whole life." He scowled. "But she already reduced the dosage."

"Does it hurt?"

He shrugged. "Not too much. And there aren't too many

side effects."

"You're such a brave man." She squeezed his arm affectionately.

"Apparently mhuol has no effect on Eridanis."

"I'm not surprised. Even if they look like you and I, their physiology is different." She stopped. "Let's rest."

He drank from the water bottle Theo handed him. "Speaking of mhuol, Lonetom convinced the Suni Sisters to take out a patent for this cure, since it's the first time a treatment has successfully eradicated Xplo-bullet poison. Nujise is working out the legal aspects with Jered."

She chuckled. "Mhuol?"

"Since Redland is the only producer, its export is likely to generate a profitable income." He handed her back the water bottle.

"Ready?" She screwed the lid back on.

"Ready." He didn't move, though, and said, "You're the brave one. Walking through Canyon Maze." He picked up his cane. "After we find Farren, I want you to tell me everything—the crash, what you did, where you went, where you fell. Everything."

"I will. I promise."

They resumed their slow ascent.

"What about Mogud?"

"He's being questioned in Nuong."

"Why over there?"

"Federal matter. He, Simpson and Keith of Rain Forest allied in a coup to overthrow the Federal government. It was supposed to be launched the day we escaped. Clobb waited until the last minute to trigger the explosives in the Dome's spaceport because he thought the Spylady was headed for Gambling Nova, and he wanted to arrest her and Mogud at the same time. When the Guild ship crashed with you and Rory on board, he refused to send a ship to rescue you, because he didn't want to alert Mogud to the Guild's widespread presence in the air. Lonetom tried to fly out with Smanul to the crash site, but his ship was shot down by Skodrak helicopters outside of Esk Strath."

"Were they hurt?"

"Smanul broke a leg and Lonetom sustained a few burns and scratches. The spaceport exploded in the afternoon, about the same time as a huge sandstorm began. It nailed ships to the ground for nearly ten days."

"Mogud's ships shot us twice the first day, and they returned two days later through the storm."

"Are you sure?"

"Yeah. Rory was dead, and they set the shipwreck on fire."

"It must have been Mogud himself! He tried to escape in a ship hidden in a shed near the Gold Mines that day." He squeezed her hand. "I'm so sorry that Clobb was such an ass."

"It wasn't your fault!"

"No. Still!" He waved his stick. "I don't think Rory could've been saved, but you would have been spared your ordeal if the Guild fleet had intervened immediately."

Streaks of purple and orange colored the dawn sky as the last flutters of swazzi dwindled to nothing. The first sun had risen, warming them.

"You say the sandstorm lasted ten days? In the canyon, it came and went."

"It was so thick that even in orbit nobody saw a thing. Everybody was frustrated because even though Redland was swarming with Guild ships, none of them was equipped to fly through swazzi gales. They flew around the crash site nine days after the accident only. And by that time, you were long gone."

"Not far. I got lost in the beginning and had to start all over again. What about Simpson?"

"She's on the run. Farren keeps tabs on the Private Pirates Forum on hypernet."

"Who's in charge of the Dome?"

"The Guild took over with dozens of Fed agents. The Skodraks were disarmed and sent to Nuong. Civil servants replaced them to help transfer the prisoners elsewhere."

"Malcolm must be happy …"

"He is."

They grinned at each other. Theo helped him clamber up some unstable, piled-up rocks at a bend. They halted on the other side to drink water and eat strips of smoked vegetables.

"I have Rory's stockey," she said as they resumed their ascent. "He asked me to give it to you."

"Then we can bust Mogud!" he exclaimed, and slapped his cane on the ground. "He claims that Rory was unable to pilot the Guild ship. He testified that after you tried to murder him, you took over the ship's command to escape and that it's your fault it crashed. He stated under oath that his pilots' orders were to force the ship to the ground to aid Rory. We surmised that they set fire to the ship to eliminate any incriminating elements and ensure neither of you survived."

"It was so frightening …" She shivered despite the heat. "His last words were for you, and Farren, and Jethro …" Her voice wound down to a sob.

"I loved him too. Come here."

He enfolded her in his arms, thankful that she was alive.

What an effort she had accomplished to cross Canyon Maze!

They slowly climbed another stretch of the stiff path, lined on both sides by tall, smooth boulders. Half-way through, they sat on a flat stone to rest.

"Can I ask you a question?" He wiped his face with his shirt.

"Sure."

"It's about that mental battle in Pit 3."

"What about it?"

"What happened exactly?"

"You were there. You saw everything."

"Not really. How did you kill Xë? Farren explained that he participated in a … mental battle."

"Yes. I was relieved when he pitched in." She flexed her ankle. "I don't like talking about this. I'm not good at telepathy and things like that. It spooks me."

"I'm fine with the mental battle." He stretched his legs. "Even though for me it's totally surreal."

When they resumed their hike, Jack felt a strain in his calves and thighs, but his breathing was less labored than it had been two hours before. Theo hummed beside him.

The trail turned into steep steps dug into the mountainside, which they climbed slowly. Once they emerged onto the plateau, Theo took Jack to the viewpoint, surrounded by boulders, where she used to sit with her father. The second sun had risen.

"I can't go any higher. Already …" She cringed, closing her eyes.

Jack slipped his fingers through hers. "You're not alone anymore. I won't let anything happen to you. Where shall we sit? If you want, we can go back down right away. You tell me."

"No. But if you don't mind, can we wait for Farren over there?" She pointed towards a line-streaked mountain wall. "The vertical cliff is to the right."

"I recognize it from the picture in your parents' bedroom. Will he go back this way?"

"Yes. It's the shortest way."

"Is it possible to view Canyon Maze from here?"

She tucked her arm beneath his, and walked with him to a delicate ochre arch surrounded by spiky yellowish shrubs burdened with dozens of white flowers. Pointing at huge candelabra cacti and odd-shaped boulders, she detailed her trek through a series of red canyons that to his neophyte eye cloned one another: a harsh and barren landscape, with various reds and oranges mingling with patches of green weeds.

She had guts, and he felt humbled by her courage in crossing such an intricate labyrinth.

"Can I ask you a question?" Theo unscrewed the lid of the water bottle. They sat side by side in the shade near the boulder entrance.

"Sure. Shoot."

"What worries you about this mental battle?"

"I'm not worried."

She raised an eyebrow.

He tapped his cane on the ground. "Farren cares a lot about you since our escape from the Dome and that mental fusion."

"We only united energies to defeat Xë. But I see it's a problem for you. Why? You don't want us to have feelings for each other? I mean, Farren and I?"

She still knew how to get smartly to the point. He traced lines around stones. She had him wrong, though. He felt no threat to what he shared with Farren. His problem was much more difficult to admit. He dreaded losing Theo's affection; he feared that their friendship would vanish if she and Farren got seriously involved.

"You care for him?"

"Yes. I do." Her voice was husky. "Do you mind?"

"He'll be happy," Jack temporized. "He cares for you too."

"You haven't answered my question." She squinted at him under the suns' glare. "Do you mind?"

He raised a hand in a helpless gesture. "I don't know. Yes … No … Of course, I'm happy if you two get along together. That's what Farren always wanted. To be in a double relationship. With me, and with a woman at the same time. And you're the best choice he could make."

"Jack? Will you look at me?"

Reluctantly, he obeyed. She took his left hand between her own. Tenderly, she brought it to her mouth and kissed his fingers gently. "I love you, Jack," she said softly. "Whatever I feel for Farren won't change what I feel for you. You are much more than a friend to me." She wrinkled her nose. "It's difficult to define."

"It is." He squeezed her fingers. "But no less important." He considered her. "About Farren. He's my best friend, my lover, my partner. I won't ever leave him. Is this something you can accept?"

"Jack, I …" She lifted her shoulders. "We're going too fast here … I only said I cared for Farren."

"I'll fight for him if necessary."

Still holding his hand near her lips, she smiled. "And you should. We'll see what happens between the three of us. But there's one thing I promise. If things sour between us, for whatever reason, I'll be the one to leave. I won't ever come between you two."

"I know you won't." He studied the luminous landscape over Theo's shoulder and glanced back her way. "You're a complicated person, but I love you too."

CHAPTER 221

Exhausted

1 June 3077, Standard Time (ST), Sixth Federal Era
Redland—On the plateau

Farren had slept in between two boulders. They protected him from the swazzi gusts that blew strongly on the plateau, but not from the night-time chill. He sneezed himself awake and rubbed his body to warm up as dawn's light flushed the sky pink and purple.

The night before, he had decided to talk to Jack. No more procrastination. Their happiness depended upon a few words.

He started his journey before the first sunrise. Two hours later, as he skittered down a slope, he saw them, Jack and Theo, sitting side by side, holding hands.

His eyes watered. He savored a quiet moment of relief as he simply watched them, the man and the woman he loved.

Jack raised his head and they stared at each other before Theo did the same, and Farren grinned as he hurried down.

They stood up, Jack still holding Theo's hand.

Farren hesitated as he reached them. Who should he hug first? Each opened an arm and clasped him.

"You're crazy, both of you, to have climbed up here!"

"We wanted to be sure you were safe." Jack slipped a hand beneath Farren's shirt.

Theo stepped back to examine him. "Jack was worried about you. And so was I. That's why we're here."

"When did you arrive?"

"Last night. But I showed myself only this morning. I slept in my father's studio." She opened her small backpack. "Here, put on your sunglasses. Jack said there's a problem with your eyes."

"He said that?" What did his brawan know?

Jack's warm hand crept higher. Farren's skin tingled.

Theo nodded. "Why are you so surprised? He's been fretting so much about you that he can't sleep."

"Really?"

Jack pulled him closer to him and kissed him.

"Yes." He grinned as he let him go. "But now that we've found you, and Theo is back, I'm fine."

A lilting fondness warmed Jack's clear eyes. His brawan hadn't looked at him with such banked desire in days. Some tension loosened inside of Farren. Jack's hand shot out to steady him. "Are you all right?"

"Yes."

"Did you eat this morning?" Theo asked.

"No. But I'm fine."

She handed him her water bottle and mixed vegetable strips. "We only have this with us."

"Thank you." The water refreshed his parched mouth.

Jack scrutinized him. "We should head back to the house and rest, all of us. Theo is exhausted, and you look kind of peaky."

"And what about you? You are the one who's recovering." Theo handed Jack his cane and took her hiking stick. "I admit that I'll feel better once we're back at ground level."

"Theo's afraid of heights."

"Then you'll walk between us and we'll tell you stories." Farren put Theo's small backpack on his shoulders. "I've been up and down this trail every day since we moved into your home, so I'll go first."

Ten minutes later, they reached the abrupt and narrow steps dug into the mountainside.

"This is the tricky part." Farren stopped and waited for Theo and Jack. "I'm amazed that you got up here."

"Why don't you go down first, Farren, and I'll hold on to Jack?" Theo suggested. "We'll take the steps one at a time the way we did going up."

"I'm steady. My cane helps," Jack said.

"I know it does, but I don't want you breaking your neck," she said.

Jack squeezed Theo's hand. "We'll do it the way you want."

The suns beat their sharp glare upon their necks as they began their slow descent. Farren lost his balance as he reached the second step down. He gripped the stone wall to steady himself.

"I'm fine, I'm fine!" he called, looking up at Jack and Theo. His heartbeat accelerated.

"Throw the backpack onto the trail!" Theo yelled from above. "There's nothing breakable in it!"

His body pressed against the rock, he removed the backpack and let it drop. It bounced on each step before rolling a bit and shuddering to a stop. Its pounding noise hurt his head. Jack's legs dangled in front of him: his brawan had chosen to go down in a sitting position.

"Are you okay?" Jack asked as he stood on the second step next to Farren and held him. "You're very pale."

"I didn't sleep much last night." He raised his head. "Theo, your turn."

The first shudder struck Farren as he stabilized himself on the fifth step. He held his breath as three other shudders shook him. Dots of light danced in front of his eyes.

Theo's anxious voice asked him how he fared.

"I'm fine." He wiped his dripping forehead, feeling hot and cold at once. "One more step to go and we'll be on safe ground."

He glanced behind him: the trail looped down the mountainside. How would he get to the house? He shook his head to clear it: bad idea. Bile filled his mouth. Tremors jolted him. His fingers slipped; his body fell backwards. He tried to grab a mhuol shrub's protruding branch, the momentum carrying him sideways. His knees smacked against rock.

"Farren!"

Jack and Theo shouted his name in unison.

He wanted to reassure them, tell them that it was a mere cold, as he crashed against the steps. His sunglasses bumped off his nose. Light blinded him. He closed his eyes as bright green and orange streaks zigzagged inside his brain. His joints burned after each bump and shudder.

He tried to move. His head hurt and a shower of luminous dots whirled before his eyes.

Hands held him, steadied him. Words were spoken above and around him. Nausea was a relentless bitch, though. Cool fingers held his head as he retched. His mouth tasted foul; his throat was strewn with cactus needles. He lay on his side, his knees trembling against each other, sharp rocks piercing his skin. A hand wiped his forehead, stroked his hair; another tucked a light blanket around him.

Yet Jack and Theo's efforts proved ineffective at stopping the cold from winding around his aching limbs with the fierceness of stifling snake coils. When heat took over, he lost the senses of sound and sight.

CHAPTER 222

Cowan

1 June 3077, Standard Time (ST), Sixth Federal Era
Redland—Near Fern's home

Cowan searched Fern's house from top to bottom. Nobody was at home. Coffee had been brewed and barely drunk. On the patio, he listened for voices. Only the cacti wren chirped. Movement on the large trail to his left caught his eye: someone was running down the path. He reached it as the runner dashed down the last stretch.

She was leaner than in the pictures that had been handed out, and her skin had darkened, but he recognized her at once: Theo Maddiogga!

She leaned forward, her hands gripping her bent knees as she labored to catch her breath.

"You're Theo, aren't you? Fern's daughter? I'm Cowan MacRae, a friend of Farren and Jack."

She raised her head, nodding.

"Here." He gave her his water bottle. "Have a drink."

"Thanks." She poured water directly into her mouth.

"You got back now?"

"At this speed?" Her chuckle gurgled into a cough. "No. I got here last night. Listen: Farren fell. Jack thinks he has a concussion. They're up on the trail, near the top. I'm here to find a stretcher."

"What happened exactly?"

"We were on our way down, by the high steps up near the plateau. He slipped and knocked his head on a step. Afterwards, he vomited and lost consciousness."

"How did Jack get up there?"

"We climbed the trail together earlier. He's fine. It's Farren we're worried about."

"I'll take my horse up and bring them down."

"Can you really ride up there?"

"Shewn is a sturdy mount."

"Let's go."

"Why don't you rest? I'll go."

She shook her head. "We need to hurry. It's sizzling up there. I'll get some food and we should be on our way."

Cowan understood now why her mother and Malcolm had been so certain that she would make it back on her own: this was a tough and dedicated young woman.

He insisted on calling Kilu before setting out, and blurted out the news of Theo's arrival, even though he had promised to keep silent. She had to show herself on the webcam and be greeted by her mother before they left the house.

She scowled while she packed water and food. She got silently onto the horse behind him. He told her how everybody had been so worried about her since the crash.

He asked her why she was so rattled. Didn't Fern deserve to know that her daughter was safe and sound?

"You can't understand."

"Then tell me."

"Why?"

"Because I never intended to upset you like this."

"This can wait, not Farren."

They got off the horse at the last bend in the trail, where it was large enough for the horse to turn around. Cowan secured the reins between two rocks and they headed up. Jack waved his cane at them.

Theo's brisk attitude mellowed the moment she reached Jack. She pulled a pair of sunglasses from her pocket. "Here. Put these on."

"Thanks, sweetheart!" He smiled at Cowan. "Hello, my friend. How did Theo find you?"

"Kilu sent me when she didn't receive Farren's report last night and this morning."

"How's Farren?" Theo asked.

Farren lay in the shade, protected from the suns by Jack's shirt strung between a boulder and a mhuol shrub. He wriggled out of the makeshift tent. "Much better." He ran his hands through his messed-up hair. "He regained consciousness soon after you left," Jack explained. "He wanted us to walk down."

Theo hunkered down by Farren's side and laid a hand on his forehead. "You've still got a fever."

"I feel much better." He caught her wrist. "Not dizzy anymore. I can walk."

"No. You'll ride down the trail with Cowan, and Jack and I will walk down."

By the time Jack and Theo arrived in the late afternoon, Cowan had Farren resting on his bed, his scratches and bumps, nausea and aching joints cared for thanks to Kilu's advice. Bleak with exhaustion, Jack favored his right leg as he limped into the house. Theo entrusted him to Cowan, who told her that her mother was expecting her call the moment she arrived. She visited Farren instead and stayed with him for over an hour.

When she came down the steps, he insisted about Fern, mentioning respect. She glared at him and stomped out of the house.

Cowan thought she would join them when the swazzi rose. By dinnertime, she had not yet shown up.

"Should I get Theo?" he asked as he set a reheated vegetable bake on the kitchen table. Farren was already sitting on the bench.

Jack, who had taken a nap, showered and changed into a snug t-shirt and cargo pants, shook his head. "No. She needs her rest. I'll check in later."

"Fern doesn't understand why her daughter won't talk to her." Cowan sat on a stool.

Farren cut the bake into thick slices, setting three aside on a plate. "Tonight, she'll sleep without worry. That's the most important."

"They'll talk when they see each other." Jack served hot coffee. "When is the cavalry arriving?"

"Tomorrow afternoon. Sorry about that, but ..."

"Fussing mothers and family." Farren clucked. "We'll get over it, won't we, Jack?"

"You're the injured one this time. You'll see what it feels like ... Is your mother coming?"

"After the report Kilu and Fern gave her?" Farren stuffed a big piece of bake into his mouth. "I called, but she wasn't at home, so I imagine she's already packed her saddlebags and will get here tomorrow morning. Speaking of which, she told me last week that Erlend was moving in with her. Did you know?"

Cowan shook his head. "No. I suppose that's what he wanted to tell me about. I've been out of reach, rounding up the last trekkers. I arrived in Esk Strath last night. Erlend wasn't there, so when Kilu asked me if I could check on you, I was free to come."

"Lucky us. Thanks, Cowan."

"So you didn't talk to Erlend recently?" Jack cut more slices and gave each of them second helpings.

"No. He probably forgot that I was coming." Cowan snorted. "It won't be the first time. He's not good with hours and meetings. But I'm happy if he stays with your mother. I want him out of Esk Strath."

"Farren told me how worried you are about him," Jack said.

"It's never easy to get over a love affair. And in this case, his friends are as rigid as his enemies."

"You mean his gay friends?"

Cowan nodded. "Yes. They don't understand why he defends Nand."

"He broke up with Nand because he felt betrayed," Farren said. "But he still loves her—him—that's obvious. It can't be easy."

"Nujise will help him." Jack reached out for the platter of dates and placed it in the middle of the table. "And the company will be good for her, too." He glanced at Cowan. "Is Livia coming?"

"I don't see how she could avoid it."

"Does your sister know Theo?" Cowan asked.

"I don't think they ever met. Or maybe when Livia was a young girl. After all, Fern and my mother are Suni Sisters, so their daughters were bound to meet during festivities."

"It could be interesting." Cowan grinned as he grabbed a handful of dates.

Jack stood up. "I'll check on Theo."

"She must be famished. Here's a plate for her, and I'll get her something hot to drink." Farren stood up.

"Sit down! I'll do it." Cowan said. "Tell me what you want."

———◆———

Swazzi gusts slammed into Jack as he crossed the patio. Gripping his cane in one hand and the food platter in the other, he staggered twice before reaching Catdougal's studio. He pushed the door open and lurched inside with a flurry of dust.

Theo sat on an old-fashioned leather couch in the warmly lit room.

"Can I come in?" he asked.

The door banged shut behind him. She jumped to her feet to close it. She was crying. "You're already in." She took the platter, which she set on a low table. He removed the water bottle's carry loop from his wrist and handed it to her. She sat down, and patted the couch for him to join her. "How's Farren?"

"Much better. We had dinner. I brought you some vegetable casserole he baked yesterday, and some mhuol tea and honey."

"Thanks."

She put the plate on her lap.

"I wanted to give you the heads-up about tomorrow. Your mother, Kilu, Nujise, Smanul, Ehr, Malcolm and Livia, and some others I don't know are coming to celebrate your return. They should be arriving in the afternoon."

"Fine." She cut the slices into pieces with her fork.

"Cowan was out of line when he talked to you about your mother. He's sorry. He won't say what happened when you met. Will you tell me?"

She set the plate on the low table and brought her knees close to her chest. She wiped tears off her cheeks.

"What's up, sweetheart?"

"I … I know it's silly, but I wanted us to be together tonight."

"We are—together, I mean. You're not on the trail anymore."

"No!" Her shoulders tensed. "Cowan … I made him promise not to say anything to Kilu about me. I wasn't ready. And he told her I was back … And then … I had to say hello to my mother in front of him! I don't know him! I didn't want it to happen like that. I … I was so embarrassed. He doesn't know anything about me. How things are. He doesn't know about you and me and Farren … and …"

She covered her face with her hands. He put his arm around her shoulders and held her. "You're exhausted, and you need to sleep. Do you realize the effort you put in today after everything you went through?"

Regret coated her voice. "I wanted quiet time before seeing people."

"It would've been nice, but Farren fell."

"You're right …" She smiled tremulously. "I'm sorry …"

"There's nothing to be sorry about. Now, why don't you eat some more, and we'll get you to bed. Your room is ready."

"But it's your room."

"Not anymore. I'm sleeping with Farren tonight. I want to keep an eye on him."

"I'd rather stay here tonight." She leaned over and cut food with her fork. "This is where my father worked."

He surveyed the cluttered room. "You're not going to merge with that orgacomp over there, are you?"

"The thought crossed my mind, but like you said, I'm too tired. This is good!"

"Farren is a great cook."

"I remember. You told me about his cooking that day we went shopping in Nuong." She sighed. "It seems like such a long time ago."

He got up. "Didn't your dad dig a tunnel between this studio and your home to avoid the swazzi late at night?"

"He did!" She grinned. "I'll show you. There's a hidden staircase that opens in the wardrobe on the landing next to my parents' bedroom."

CHAPTER 223

Restless

1 June 3077, Standard Time (ST), Sixth Federal Era
Redland—Nujise's home

Half an hour from her house, not far from the qanat that brought water to the valley where she lived, Nujise grew vegetables and succulents in a garden where she worked daily.

Dusk rolled in, that sweet time of day when the sun-heated scents of roses and tomatoes kissed the air. She went down to the garden to choose succulents for Fern and her daughter.

Berry sniffed butterflies while Juniper dozed. Barking suddenly erupted. Both dogs jumped up, growling. Nujise winced as she stood up: despite daily stretching exercises her lower back stiffened whenever she bent over.

The uneasy feeling she'd had for two days, ever since Erlend had gone to Esk Strath to meet his brother, increased. She scanned the surrounding boulders.

Fern's call had barely alleviated her edginess. Not that she didn't rejoice at the news of Theo's safe return. She even teared up like a schoolgirl, happy for her friend; happy for her boys, as she called Farren and Jack. She promised to attend the party; she would cook a dessert and be on her way at dawn. She told Fern not to expect her before late afternoon.

Unnerved by her dogs' restlessness, Nujise grabbed the half-empty pot and headed straight for her house. She shooed the dogs inside, closed the shutters, checked the rooms and locked the door. She took Kane's rifle off its hooks and placed it on the kitchen table. She cleaned it every other day, the way Kane had taught her. She enjoyed loneliness, but tonight she wished Erlend had already moved in.

Kilu called around dinner time. She informed Nujise about Farren's fall on the trail. They agreed that it was linked to exhaustion; too much stress. Kilu said that Erlend was invited to the party, of course, and to bring him along. Nujise told her friend that he'd gone to Esk Strath to meet Cowan. He wanted his brother to help him move some of his bigger canvases.

While Nujise checked her three loads of berry fudge, Kilu called again to say that Erlend had indeed spent a night in Esk Strath two days before. She had talked to a friend of his who explained that he had received an urgent message from Cowan asking him to meet him down by Glendhu, so he'd ridden there with a group of friends heading that way.

Nujise left several messages on Erlend's cell. Around midnight, her phone rang, waking her up. A man's voice, a voice she couldn't place, told her to stop calling, Erlend was fine. And that if she didn't want any trouble she'd better stay in her house with the yellow shutters and the red flower-pot hanging from the porch and the whirligigs lined up along the rail.

As the man hung up, the lights went out.

She tried Kilu: her landline was dead. She fingered her cell. Its battery was low. She pressed Farren's number. He answered on the first ring, his voice thick with sleep, yet quick to clear. She whispered that Erlend was in trouble and she had been ordered not to interfere.

Her son told her to stay put, to keep away … from the windows, she figured, but her cell phone went dead. The dogs whimpered and scratched to get out. She hesitated. She kept Berry inside with her and let Juniper out. The tall dog dashed into the night. Berry barked and barked, and finally she relented and let the bitch loose.

She took her rifle, sat in her armchair and waited. She thought she kept her eyes open, but she had a strange dream with Nand in it. She woke up to a sense of urgency. She remembered her dream's fleeting images. In it, Nand poked her to wake her up. She shook her and shouted, but Nujise slept on, her covers smelling nice and soft, her feet seeking coolness in her bed's edges.

She thought about Nand/Aslone as she waited for the swazzi to abate. Erlend and his lover made such a nice couple. If only Nand had told him right away that she was a Face Changer … Nujise had talked at length with Erlend. He had broken up with Nand, but as days went by, as he came to grips with their unusual relationship, his love for the Face Changer increased.

At dawn, Nujise's sense of wrongness reached the limit of what she could stand. She opened the door cautiously. She gripped her rifle and stood still on the porch.

Berry burst from the trail that led to Boulder Forest. She yapped, her gray coat smeared with dried blood. Nujise checked her dog: she wasn't hurt. The bitch barked, ran away and returned, and she told Berry, yes, yes, she was coming.

Her unease grew in the pit of her stomach. She heard shouts and screams. As she hurried down the path, she charged her rifle.

After the boulders, she saw them. Juniper snarled, with Erlend crouched behind her. She ordered Berry to go, to run, to protect, too. She shot her rifle and stopped the chase. They pivoted in their saddles as she aimed her weapon at them. Anger obscured her fear. She shouted at them to leave. One of them kicked his horse towards her dogs and she shot him in the hand, the way Kane had taught her years ago, when they were young and he had encouraged her to be independent.

The man—she recognized him as the one who had threatened her the night before; he belonged to Cowan's clan—yelped. His horse reared and the whole group backed away. Cowards!

She shot her rifle again. This time, they scattered away.

"Go, go!" She said, her voice ridiculously feeble, and she hastened on as fast as her aching knees would let her.

CHAPTER 224

Confession

5 June 3077, Standard Time (ST), Sixth Federal Era
Redland—House in canyon

In the end, the Esk Strath party to celebrate Theo's arrival was postponed to a later date and replaced by a family lunch at Fern's home, with Malcolm and Livia, Fern, Nujise and the three of them.

Jack, Farren and Theo promised that they would visit Redland again once the situation with the Eridanis was solved and their presence was no longer needed.

Their next trip to Redland would be like a honeymoon, Farren said toward the end of the meal, laughing at his mother's and Fern's baffled expressions. Livia chided her brother about his fickleness, his callousness, mumbling that she wasn't surprised. Theo, rendered emotional by her ordeal, pounced on Livia, stunning her into silence. She said that the young woman's snide remarks exhausted her more than hiking through Canyon Maze. "Theo!" Malcolm pleaded, and Theo squeezed his hand and smiled at him with kindness.

"No, she's had it coming. I've been patient, but …" She stood up and addressed Farren's sister. "I finished my journey three days ago, and I've already heard all sorts of snide remarks about Jack, Farren and myself. It's not new. When I was young, people gossiped about my father behind his back. They said he was crazy." She glanced at Malcolm, who mouthed an apology. "At the time, I had no idea how to address slander. Now I do. So this is what I have to say." She folded her arms. "Jack, Farren and I are friends. We like each other, we want to live together, and that's what we'll do. We have no idea if these relationships will last, but we intend to give it a try. So when Farren speaks of a honeymoon, it could be one. Now, Livia, you and Malcolm and other Redlanders took great care of my Eridanis friends, and for this I am deeply grateful. But Livia," she paused, "you've got to stop insulting people. I heard you accused Farren of being a coward because I stayed in the Dome!" Livia blushed. "It was my decision. My mother was forced by Mogud to stay inside for years, and I wanted her out. I bet you would have done the same. At any cost. So, blame me. Call me mad, because it was truly a mad thing to do. But stop blabbing nasty things about your brother. He's a wonderful man and you're lucky that he's part of your family."

In the ensuing silence, she sat down, suddenly embarrassed. Her mother's expression showed unexpected disapproval, while Nujise's features combined neutrality and some support in the way her eyes twinkled. Jack enjoyed Farren's reaction. It was the first time his brawan had witnessed Theo's temper. He stared at her, visibly moved by her passionate defense, and when she had finished, he croaked his thanks.

Throughout Theo's speech, Livia had crumbled her muffin. Afterwards, she addressed her mother and husband. "Will you defend me, or do you agree with her?"

Always a man of compromise, Malcolm had embraced Livia and they had left the table—and dinner—together.

When Jack, Farren and Theo departed from Gambling Nova two days later, Livia didn't show up to say goodbye. Malcolm told them that Livia had gone hiking to think things over. He felt confident that she would mend her ways, particularly because, besides Theo's outburst, Cowan had told her she shared responsibility for his brother's assault.

In the uproar that followed Erlend's bashing, Cowan and Nujise convinced Jack and Farren to take the young man along. They claimed that he wanted to be with Nand. Although this was highly unorthodox, going on an assignment with a civilian—an artist—they agreed because, after all, Theo was also a civilian. Except that with her Savalwoman training and her Nexus street fighter experience, she didn't really fall into any category.

They had been dining with Erlend aboard the SpaceSS ship when she had casually dropped her bomb about belonging to the Julepa gang in Nexus, which, of course, enhanced the mesmerizing net she had cast over Farren, overexciting him about her cybernetics knowledge.

At first, Jack was worried about this three-way relationship. Could he tolerate being left out? How would he cope with Farren flirting with and kissing Theo?

To his surprise, he enjoyed himself. He basked in their affection. He felt more cherished than he ever had before.

Before their departure, he had time alone with Farren. They went for a walk up the trail, while Theo chatted with her mother. Farren wanted to show him the cliff he had climbed. Afterwards, they lay down together in the shade of an orange arch, while hawks glided in circles above them.

He clasped Farren against him.

"Not now."

"Why? We're alone. Nobody will see us."

Farren had thrown an arm over his eyes, his body tense and rigid.

"Whatever happened to you, whatever you did, I love you." Jack stroked his brawan's arm and waited.

Finally, Farren sat up and Jack did the same.

"I need to talk to you about the Gold Mines," Farren said. He gazed at his clasped hands and raised his head.

Jack had never seen such distress etched on his handsome, pale face.

He touched Farren's knees with his own as he sat up and moved closer.

"Are you sure?"

"I want you to know," Farren said. "Over there, I took care of Jimmy, Smanul's kid brother. But not well enough. There were threats, insinuations. I understood too late. Jimmy was murdered one morning. I failed Smanul. He thinks I'm brave, but …" He shook his head. "Afterwards, they stuck me in a cell where I couldn't stand up. In total darkness. I thought of you, then. The little boy afraid of the dark." He stared into nothing-ness. "If there's one thing this taught me, it's to understand you, what you went through when you were a kid. I am an adult and yet … They chained me. I thought I was going mad. One day I couldn't take it anymore. I begged for light. I broke down." His chest rose and fell quickly. "They beat the shit out of me. They said I was a wimp."

"But you're not!" He scrambled closer to Farren and embraced him from behind, his face pressing against Farren's neck. "Listen to what I'm saying. I love you. You're the hottest, the most fantastic man in the world, and you're mine."

Farren slouched forward, his voice barely audible. "Don't mock me!"

"Smanul told me how you protected his brother and defended him the day Jimmy died."

"He won't see the truth!"

"He knows you did everything you possibly could. That's when you showed your mettle. Taking Jimmy's defense, saving Smanul from himself, one against a crowd, taking the blame—that was such a brave thing to do." Jack held on to Farren, hearing his heart beating fast. He forced him to turn sideways so that they could face each other. "Look at me! That cell's only purpose was to break you. It didn't happen. I know it because you are here with me. You're such a great man. Don't ever think otherwise. And I'm honored to be your brawan."

He sustained Farren's probing eyes for long minutes.

In the end, Farren told him the words that he had waited to hear since they had reunited.

Their lovemaking on the plateau until the first swazzi blew dust into their eyes remained Jack's best memory of Gambling Nova.

After a six-day trip, they approached the Guild ship orbiting around Eridan, and Jack envisioned his upcoming confrontation with Clobb. The fact that they were traveling on a SpaceSS ship—and not just any ship, but the admiral ship—underlined SpaceSS's interest in Eridan.

Sycal Veld, who had been appointed Spylady in the interim until new elections were organized, suspected that Donatella Simpson had found refuge in Eridan. Their assignment was to find her, obtain her release and put her in the hands of SpaceSS authorities aboard the admiral ship. Simpson would stand trial with Mogud.

He talked at length with his godmother in Catdougal's studio the day after Theo's arrival. He listened to her argument, letting her trudge through the mud—their relations remained strained—before she surprised him by asking him whether they would work for SpaceSS again. Technically, Farren still belonged to SpaceSS. She didn't want to lose them to the Guild; she would raise their salaries, offer bonuses and advantages.

She needed them, and she explained why.

He had never held such a good hand. He used it without a qualm to obtain carte blanche and the swiftest ship. During this conversation, he realized he could no longer work for SpaceSS. He didn't want to be reinstated: he wanted to take SpaceSS to court. He feigned listening to her and promised to talk matters over with Farren and Theo.

Satisfaction filled him each time he remembered the sound of her breath catching. "Yes—Theo. She's back, and she's with us now, so everything that concerns orgacomps, space doors and her father's work is part of no deal. She hired us. Farren and I work for her in this particular instance."

He relished his godmother's silence, as he imagined the neurons in her brain connecting and searching for a means to bypass them and reach the gem now in their custody.

CHAPTER 225

Reunion

10 June 3077, Standard Time (ST), Sixth Federal Era
Guild Observation ship

Erlend found Nand where Ashta had told him she would be: in front of a small window, watching Eridan sparkle under the afternoon sun. He walked silently through the empty corridor until he stood behind her. He put his hands on her shoulders and whispered her name.

She reeled. She grabbed his hands with icy fingers. "What are you doing here?"

"I came to be with you. I arrived with Theo, Farren and Jack. They're already talking to Clobb. You'll soon go home."

She gazed at their reflection. "I thought I'd never see you again."

He held her fingers tightly to warm them. "Ashta said you're not eating."

"I don't like the food."

"I brought you some mhuol tea, and biscuits and stuff. Nujise gave me a parcel. She's worried about you."

Still holding him, she faced him. "What are doing here, Erlend?" She stepped closer. "What happened to your face?"

She had lost weight. Her reddened eyes were hollow in her gaunt face, her hair in disarray.

"You cry a lot, from what I heard. Does it help?"

"Who hurt you?"

"I'm fine."

She caressed his face, framed it between her palms, and searched his eyes. He had forgotten their intensity. Some tension loosened inside him.

"I'm still a girl."

"You're Nand."

She caressed his lips with her thumbs, kindling his desire.

"That I am. But …"

"Do you think you could face-change from time to time?"

"Into Aslone? I need to practise, but yes. I can do that."

She stepped closer, their bodies now touching. "Do I need to face-change to kiss you?"

"Can you?"

"That's why I'm asking. I mended my broken arm with Axonna's help, but it needs to regain its total elasticity." She frowned. "Another week, maybe …"

"That long?"

She chuckled, and he knew he had done the right thing.

"Close your eyes!" she ordered.

"No."

"You must. Otherwise I'll disappoint you. I don't want to do that today."

"You won't." He embraced her frail body. "Don't die!"

"I'm not dying!"

He stepped back. "I know about hlyks."

"Who told you?"

"Does it matter?"

She wriggled out of his embrace. He held her.

"I mean it, Nand. You're not alone anymore."

"I've no idea what you're talking about!"

"Don't you? You shared with me the vision of a frozen Eridan. Do you remember?"

She nodded.

"You can't give up."

Her blue eyes brightened. "You don't know what you're asking!"

"I'm asking you to choose between living and sinking. You want to know why I came? Because I love you; because I want to live with you in Eridan. But for that to happen, you need to live, even if your kidadakh sunk."

She closed her eyes. Tears spilled out.

He embraced her until her wrenching sobs quietened.

CHAPTER 226

Red Arches

10 June 3077, Standard Time (ST), Sixth Federal Era
Guild Observation ship

Sitting against the wall in the conference room, Clobb watched Farren Megan and Theo Maddiogga as they worked with Ashta Coral to install a connection with the Savalwomen Fortress in Eridan. So far, all their efforts had been in vain.

Jack Finch leaned against the door, arms crossed over his chest, listening to their banter. His relaxed stance contrasted sharply with the first time Clobb had met him, a destitute SpaceSS agent, in Lonetom's loft. Finch had survived, even though he would hobble for the rest of his life, his cane already a part of him.

Not far from Jack, the Master Face Changer sat at one end of the rectangular table. The lone, stiff Eridani hadn't uttered a word during the meeting, smiling only when the bone-tired Theo Maddiogga pumped some optimism into the discussion.

The more he learned about face-changing, the stronger grew Clobb's misgivings. What if, instead of pursuing spiritual growth, someone used this capacity to do evil? He shuddered at the array of possibilities: face-changing needed to be confined to Eridan.

Theo Maddiogga burst out laughing, and Megan and the Savalwoman joined in her mirth. Finch glanced their way. She winked at him. Her body language, the way she beamed at him … Clobb experienced a jolt of envy. There was more to it than what they told him, that they were living together as roommates.

Finch had flatly refused the Guild's proposition, a decision linked to the way Clobb had handled the crash of Rory's ship. Finch had interviewed everybody, from Megan to Malcolm MacDougal, from Lonetom to the Eridanis, to get an accurate assessment of the aftermath.

It all amounted to a question of trust, Finch repeated during their conversation. Lonetom and Rory had told Jack repeatedly that Clobb watched out for his agents like a mother hen, but that day, he hadn't. He had chosen Simpson's possible arrest over protecting Rory and Theo. Rory had died. Finch agreed that his friend's death could not have been prevented; his wounds were too serious. He pointed out, however, that if medics had been dispatched, Rory would have died painlessly. As for Theo, she would have been spared her harrowing hike across the canyons, the fear of being lost, of dying of thirst or hunger, not to mention the fear of falling that still jarred her awake each night.

Clobb hadn't disputed Finch. As leader, he made choices. His call was the good one. And he didn't regret aiding Finch when he asked for help.

Nevertheless, the knowledge that Sycal Veld had effortlessly won peeved him. SpaceSS didn't deserve them.

Before he and Finch joined Megan to speak about Eridan, he expressed the Guild's interest in Catdougal's research about orgacomps and space travel. Finch issued a warning: Theo Maddiogga entrusted her inheritance into his and his brawan's care.

A reassuring piece of news. The first in many days.

Finch and Megan fascinated him with the way they spoke, not always agreeing as they followed a parallel path aimed at an identical target. He wanted them to join the Guild; Finch declined. He pressed Megan to reply, too.

"Do you really think we haven't discussed this together?" Megan sounded disgruntled. "Jack told you we weren't interested. Why do you ask again?"

"Because I like the way you think, and I believe you're wasting your time in SpaceSS. They don't deserve you. Not after what both of you went through."

They shared a glance.

"So, here's the deal," Megan said, and he spoke with such authority that Clobb reshuffled his ideas about who was in charge in their couple. "We're acting on behalf of the Eridanis aboard this ship, and in Eridan. Ashta Coral, who is a Savalwoman, thus in charge of the wellbeing of her fellow Eridanis, appointed us to defend her interests and those of the people traveling with her. That's how we work. You told them that they couldn't return home. But your decision has no grounds."

"Except the ongoing investigation of Eridan and Meranka."

"The Eridanis aboard this ship have nothing to do with what happened."

"Evidence shows that Eridan committed an act of aggression against Meranka," he said. "Since Eridan doesn't belong to the Federacy, it falls under the Guild's jurisdiction, and as such the planet is considered a rogue nation. So there's a ban on all its inhabitants' movements, on the planet or outside the planet."

"This is where you're missing some data," Megan said. "Washone, the former kwirimok, applied to SpaceSS so that Eridan could belong to the Federacy. I worked with him on this file before I was sent to Gambling Nova, and registered his petition before I left. I checked the status, and the application went through two months ago. Eridan belongs to the Federacy as much as Meranka, and therefore falls under SpaceSS jurisdiction."

At this point, Clobb hated them and their smug smiles as he berated himself for forgetting about Megan and Washone's correspondence. "I need to see this."

Farren handed him his tablet.

"I don't like this. It could be dangerous."

"For a handful of Eridanis to land on their frozen planet?" Farren raised his eyebrows. "I don't think so. We're moving them to the admiral ship this afternoon, and will take them to Eridan tomorrow."

"I'll go with you. As I told you, my investigation shows that Eridanis committed multiple crimes in Meranka."

Finch asked, "Eridanis were seen on Meranka?"

"No, of course not! And you know it. It's this … Mindrule! Mogud mentioned it during his interrogation."

"It will be complicated to prove," Megan said. "But we're

willing, and so are the Eridanis aboard this ship, to find out exactly what happened. Eridanis are not people who flee responsibility. They are convinced something dreadful took place and they want to find the truth as much as we do."

"Leave me to be the judge of this. We've tried to contact them. Nobody answers. This isn't good news."

"Maybe they can't." Finch tapped the table with his knuckles. "Their planet is frozen. Their energy derives from the waves. No waves, and nothing works. Now, about Donatella Simpson."

"Yes." He realized he preferred talking to Finch.

"SpaceSS has proof that she travelled to Eridan after she confronted me in the ship bound for the Ring of Whalience. If she survived the two big waves, we'll find her there. We were asked to arrest her and Keith of Rain Forest and hand them over to SpaceSS authorities. Thus, the presence of the admiral ship."

"You want me to trust SpaceSS with their safety? Nobody in your organization wants Simpson alive. Too much bad press. There won't be any trial!"

Finch exchanged another of those charged looks with Megan.

"We're ready to take over the investigation in Eridan and in Meranka. It will take time. We could let you bring Simpson and Keith of Rain Forest back to SpaceSS aboard the Guild ship. The SpaceSS admiral ship will accompany you to Nuong, where you will hand them over to Federal authorities, thus showing how powerful the Guild is in tracking rogue spyladies and dangerous mind-rulers …"

"Why would you do that? What will Sycal Veld do?"

"She'll be unhappy, but, as you say, it's the only way to ascertain that Simpson at least stands trial."

"Which we want as much as you do," Finch said. "As far as Simpson's fate is concerned, we agree with you. Neither of us wants her to escape her responsibility, and we fear that SpaceSS might, in the end, want to eliminate her."

"So, do we have a deal?" Megan asked.

"You really don't want to work for the Guild?"

They considered him.

"No, we don't," Megan said.

"But the Guild can hire the services of Red Arches, our company," Finch suggested, and Clobb chided himself for not having envisioned this logical outcome. "Its headquarters are currently in E-Met. For now, you can contact our lawyer, Jered Bakamo. Smanul and Ehr supervise the hiring with two ex-SpaceSS agents, and Sue Miller, our former assistant, already manages the paperwork and is looking at offices to rent in the Barrios."

"And Theo Maddiogga?"

"What will she do?" Finch pushed himself to his feet. "Ask her. Farren, are you coming?"

CHAPTER 227

Space Doors

10 June 3077, Standard Time (ST), Sixth Federal Era
Guild Observation ship

"Jack said you wanted to talk to me?" Theo Maddiogga asked, interrupting Clobb's late lunch. He had found a quiet table in the cafeteria. She sat down opposite him. "Actually, I have questions myself."

"Do you want something to eat, to drink?"

"Thanks." She picked a small raisin bread from the basket.

"About what?" He wiped his mouth. "Eridan?"

"Yes."

"You're afraid I'll find out what awful things happened over here?"

"I'm afraid you'll ask questions and get answers that you won't understand. I don't want you to reach the wrong conclusions."

He sprinkled pepper over his fried seitan and noodles. "Why do you care so much?"

"Eridan is beautiful. And I like the people. They welcomed me when things were hard for me."

"I'm as concerned as you are about this planet." He chewed a mouthful. "Washone contacted the Guild when Keith of Rain Forest first became out of control. He wanted our help. He mentioned you." He pressed his lips together. "I was relieved to learn you were still in Eridan."

She leaned forward. "Still in Eridan? What do you mean?"

"Catdougal, your father, approached the Guild nearly thirty years ago about his discovery. He and this kwirimok were friends. He told him about our organization, and that's how the kwirimok contacted us in July 3074 and we learned your father had passed away. He was concerned about Keith. He informed us about your arrival in Eridan in May 3075."

She frowned. "But it was Jack who came to get me."

"Yes." He sipped some wine. "We advised Washone to ask Megan for help, since they were already in touch about the federal application. Megan and Finch were busy investigating Eridan and Gambling Nova. It seemed the wisest thing to do."

"You used them to reach me? Because of my father's discoveries?" She dug the raisins out of the bread. "Do they know?"

"I told Finch before he landed in Gambling Nova. He was worried about the Spylady going after you."

She sat back. "So you've been tracking me since Gambling Nova? And you set Rory on my tail?"

"Finch told you that?" Of course he had. Would Theo Maddiogga turn out to be as paranoid as her father? Clobb hoped not. "With Megan dead and Finch in Iglölü, you needed protection. The Guild provided it. Like I said, we have an interest in your wellbeing. We lost track of you shortly after you left Gambling Nova. Where did you go?"

"You manipulated all of us so our paths would collide." She banged her fist on the table. "Why?

"You're entitled to be angry. Yet, in the end, isn't being alive the most important thing?" He raised his glass to toast her and drained its contents.

"Are you saying that I should thank you?"

"No. I'm saying that perhaps you should reconsider your decision about your inheritance."

"What do you mean?"

"You want Megan and Finch to handle it for you. However, they don't know anything. We do. Your father discovered a way of crossing the universe through doors that open thanks to an orgacomp network. This discovery can't fall into the wrong hands."

"So that's why you've been so insistent about having them join the Guild." She made a steeple of her fingers and pressed her chin onto them. Her stare sent shivers up his back.

"It would make things easier. The main reason is that we value them."

"And yet you don't think they can handle my father's work for me. Are you one of the sharks my father warned me about?"

He choked on his food. "No!"

"What about Sycal Veld? Rory told me SpaceSS and the Guild don't trust each other."

"We didn't when Donatella Simpson was Spylady. Things will probably change now." He waited a beat, then asked the question that had been nettling him. "So, what will you do at Red Arches?"

She grinned.

CHAPTER 228

Face Changer

10 June 3077, Standard Time (ST), Sixth Federal Era
Guild Observation ship

Declan examined his appearance in the bathroom mirror. He darkened his features, and toyed for a moment with the leather string. In the end, he left his black locks of hair brushing his shoulders. The peach-colored shirt bought in Nuong didn't seem like such a good idea, but he owned no other. He forced a grin, hating everything about this face, this man, who had stolen the love of his life, the foreigner who had enthralled Nand and Ashta.

What better way to get Evetha to realize how much he cared for her than to take his enemy's appearance and show her?

Her visit to his cabin half an hour before had decided him.

Instead of napping after lunch in Ashta's cabin as she had told everyone, she knocked at his door.

"We must talk, you and I," she said.

She flirted with Megan, and had the gall to question him about the day she left Eridan. The only thing he remembered with clarity was her attempt to burn Keith's mind to ashes.

He told her instead that he loved her, that she must give him a second chance, because things couldn't possibly work out with Megan, not with Finch in the picture.

She brushed off his words. She ignored him.

Like Ashta and Nand.

She spoke of his future, about Mocean and Eridan.

How could she possibly think he still had a future?

Fury forced its way down his throat as mightily as ice stifled Eridan into stillness. It awakened memories engraved into his soul, memories that slashed through his nights, that bathed him in gloom: his slain disciples and Half-Masters, their glassy eyes, their cut throats, their stink.

In his nightmares, blood seeped up, mixing with sand, covering the beach, drenching him.

Why couldn't Evetha realize how horrified he was by Xë's death?

How could he have any future in Eridan after bringing down a Major Ring?

She stood close enough for her lemony perfume to tease his nostrils. Her tight-fitting clothes molded to her lean body. He wanted her.

She said in her sexy voice that Eridan and Eridanis needed him.

Her lips shone, inviting a kiss.

They retained their suppleness, whereas her harrowing journey had left lines on her forehead and dusted gray through her frizzy hair.

Now that he was healed, he could restore harmony, she said.

Harmony!

He didn't care about harmony; he cared about her.

She thanked him for allowing Finch and Megan to work for them in Eridan, a shy softness wrapping these men's names when she pronounced them.

Declan smashed the mirror with his fists.

Evetha was infatuated.

He would change her mind.

———

Jack found Ashta in the sports facility. She was practising moves on a plastic rug with a stick.

"Hey, Jack! I could use a partner."

He joined her in the middle of the room.

"What kind of martial art is this?" he asked while he put on his glove wraps.

"Thumo. That's what Savalwomen do. I learned other stuff and wanted to try out some steps."

"I did mostly karate and boxing when I was younger. I can show you some moves later. Right now, it's speed bag time." He lingered.

She wiped her sweaty face with a towel. "What's bothering you?"

"I won't ask you how you figured that out."

"I didn't read your mind. But something's off."

"It's your Master Face Changer."

"Declan? Why?"

"I don't like the way he watches Theo."

She nodded. "You noticed … It's a problem. He's obsessed with her."

"She's just mentioned general things about him so far. Were they ever in a relationship?"

"Not exactly. They were friends. Declan had feelings for her, but before anything happened between them, Theo was kidnapped by Keith, and Declan received a mindblinder blast. Afterwards, she left Eridan with you, and that was it." She smiled. "Can you teach me how to hit the speed bag?"

"Sure. Let's find you some wraps so you don't hurt yourself."

"I'll talk to Declan."

"Or I will …" He raised a fist in the air.

She playfully punched his arm. "Face Changers are pacifists. Words are enough, I assure you!"

***

Declan opened his cabin door: nobody. Ashta's cabin stood between the sports facility and the cafeteria. He strode down the corridor, boosted by Megan's self-confidence. In the cafeteria, Erlend sat at a square table, drawing. He stopped.

"How did the meeting go?" Erlend raised his head. "Is Nand all right?"

"The Master Face Changer is furious … There is concern about you."

"Why?"

"Eridan is cold now. Inhospitable. Not fit for a Redlander. The Eridanis don't want you around tomorrow."

"Even Nand?"

"She told me she doesn't understand why you came."

Erlend stilled. "What?"

"She's upset. Couldn't you have been kind to her when you two patched things up?"

"I was. It went fine. I—"

"Don't bother. They convinced me. We should have left you in Gambling Nova."

The man's wounded eyes buoyed his spirits.

———

Declan had soured, and Theo regretted her initiative. She hurried back to Ashta's cabin. Her first feeling was disappointment. But once she reached the safety of her friend's cabin, a pervasive uneasiness filled her.

She had learned to listen to herself, to her body's perceptions, to its hints. She leaned against the door for support. What made her so wary and faint?

Something in the way Declan had ogled her mouth while they talked. He hadn't listened to her. He had watched her with purpose.

In a way that reminded her of Logan.

She swallowed.

She pressed her trembling, clammy hands against each other.

She was safe. Nothing could happen to her. Farren and Jack would never let anybody hurt her.

She stepped away from the door. Her legs shook.

Maybe she was imagining things. Maybe it was her.

She settled herself on Ashta's sofa and pulled a blanket over her body.

There was nothing to worry about. She would stay away from him from now on.

Could she confide this to Ashta?

Or broach the subject with Farren or Jack?

She pressed her hands against her eyes.

She didn't dare.

She opened her new Tatimori and triggered her advanced hypernet connection. At mid-afternoon standard time, she would reach Annie for an instant—if crazily expensive—and chat.

Theo to Annie: Knock, knock.

The answer arrived less than a minute later.

Annie to Theo: Theo! I've been waiting to hear from you for ages.

Theo to Annie: We've been busy. We're on the Guild platform and tomorrow we land in Eridan. It's my time off.

Annie to Theo: How are you?

Theo to Annie: Still exhausted.

Annie to Theo: I found out why Lonetom doesn't answer your messages. He quit SpaceSS and lives with his brother now.

Theo to Annie: Do you know why he did that?

Annie to Theo: He told Jered and Roger that SpaceSS cost him his best friends.

Theo to Annie: I think Jack forgave him. But not Farren. It will take time. He doesn't want to talk about him at all. Have you tried to reach Lonetom?

Annie to Theo: I'm still looking for an address.

Theo to Annie: Tell me when you find one.

She would ask Clobb eventually, if Annie's research came up blank.

"Theo! It's Farren. Can you let me in?"

Theo to Annie: Listen, Farren's knocking at the door. Send me Lonetom's coordinates when you can, and give me news about everybody I know in E-Met. Don't wait after me. The next days will be busy. Dance well and take care. Love to your mom.

Annie to Theo: Love you, Theo.

Theo closed her Tatimori. Farren knocked with insistence.

"Coming!" she shouted.

———◆———

Finally, Evetha opened the door.

"Farren? I'm trying to rest here." She raised her eyebrows. "What happened to your shirt? Where did you find this one? It's gross!"

Declan entered the cabin and shut the door.

She yawned. "What are you looking at?"

"You!"

"Is that why you're here?" She shrugged. "Silly man!" She chuckled and stroked his cheek.

He held her wrist.

"You're beautiful."

She blushed. "A compliment from Prince Charming! Lucky me."

He pulled her towards him. He smiled and enfolded her, pressing his body against hers.

"What are you doing?"

"Loving you!" He slipped his fingers inside her shirt.

"Farren! No! Not here! It's Ashta's cabin."

He spread his hand on her warm skin and fondled her breast, loving her lemony scent.

She stepped back. "Farren, you promised!"

Farren found Jack and Ashta shrieking with laughter beside the speed bags in the sports facility.

Jack grabbed his speed bag. "Is everything all right?" he asked.

"No. Ashta, where's your cabin?"

Ashta's smile disappeared. "What's going on?"

"Declan took my appearance."

"No!" She shook her head, but she had already removed her glove wraps. "I don't believe you."

"Ask Erlend to repeat the words I supposedly told him about Nand and Eridan! Declan's made a mess of things. I'm worried about Theo. I want to check that she's all right."

They strode across the sports facility. Ashta stopped to pick up Jack's cane and hand it to him. A grim expression replaced her merry one.

"This way."

"You love me, don't you?" Farren nuzzled her neck.

"I do, but …" Theo pressed her hands against his chest. "I'm not ready. I …"

He crowded her; he crushed his body against hers; his hands groped her.

"Farren!"

"You're mine!" He held her tighter.

"Stop!" She struggled harder. "We agreed to wait."

He wasn't listening.

He crushed his mouth against hers. "I love you!"

The wrongness from earlier returned twofold. It petrified her.

She turned her face away, hating his touch, his smell. "Let me go!"

"I love you, Evetha!"

His hands moved lower. They fumbled with her pants.

"What did you call me?"

"My love. You're mine!"

"Never!"

Pressing her index into his clavicle, she shoved him away from her and jammed her knee into his groin. He groaned and folded over. She hit him in the thigh and he fell back. Instantly, she straddled him. She tore his shirt open and sat back, panting, still unbelieving. "Declan?"

He closed his eyes.

"How could you do this to me?" She slapped him. "I hate you!"

She stood up and kicked him.

He moaned and rolled to the side. "Evetha, I—"

"Shut up!" she yelled, unable to curb her rage.

The cabin door slammed open behind her.

CHAPTER 229

An Eridani Matter

10 June 3077, Standard Time (ST), Sixth Federal Era
Guild Observation ship

Theo whirled. Her dark eyes stood out in her blanched face. She stepped back, raising her hands as if to ward them off. "It's Declan. He—"

"Why, you lowlife, barbarian clod!" Jack lunged towards the Master Face Changer.

Ashta stepped in front of him. "Jack, no! I'll handle it. It's an Eridani matter."

"Are you kidding?" Jack tried to move past her. She spread her arms wide, her feet anchored in the ground for balance. She heard more than saw Declan struggling to stand up.

"I know how serious this is." She faced the Master Face Changer, trying unsuccessfully to contain her anger. "Are you out of your mind? This is Theo! Do you realize what you've done here? The consequences for all of us? How do you think Clobb will react?"

Farren put his hand on Theo's shoulder. She flinched and

retreated, bowing her head as she struggled to button her shirt. "I'm sorry." Her voice quavered, and Ashta glared at Declan.

"He's the one who should be sorry, not you," Farren said quietly.

"You need to understand." Theo bit her lip. "I thought it was you." She gazed at him. "But then he didn't … He wanted …" Her voice broke. "He touched me, and, you know, we said we …"

"Why, you …!" Jack's face tightened. "Let me!"

Ashta stood her ground. "Stop!" She ordered. "I'll handle this!" She grabbed Declan's arm and pulled him to his feet. The Master Face Changer cowered when she forced him to walk by Jack, who snarled at him, and sit on her bunkbed.

"It's all right." Farren stood next to Theo, his arms by his sides. His calm voice showed none of the turmoil that he must be experiencing. "Can I hold you?"

Theo shook her head, her body shuddering.

"Why don't you sit down?" Jack placed the cabin's only chair behind Theo. He gently pushed her into it and, grabbing the bedspread, placed it around her shoulders. "I'll get you something hot to drink."

"I'll do that." Farren headed for the hot beverage box. "Stay with her."

"I'm tired," Theo said.

"Of course you are." Jack sat down on the floor beside her.

Theo hunched under the bedspread. "It's my fault, what happened."

"I don't think so, but tell us," Jack said.

Farren brought her a mug of tea with lots of honey, then knelt on the floor.

"I wanted to make peace with Declan, so I went to see him

in his cabin. We used to be friends in Eridan. Close friends. I cared for him, so when I had to leave, I asked him to come with me to Earth Metropolis, and he turned me down."

"It wasn't like that," Declan mumbled, hiding his bent face behind a trembling hand. "Let me face-change and I'll answer all your questions."

"Not now," Ashta said. "You took this appearance, you stay in it until we're done."

Declan's shoulders slumped. "Evetha nearly killed Keith that day."

Theo gaped at him. "You chose Keith over me? Why?"

"He's my cousin."

"But he hates you! He wanted to kill you! And he tried to read my mind that day. I had to protect myself." She clenched the mug with such force that she spilled some tea.

"What you probably don't know, Theo, is that Sheer and Washone forced Declan to say he attacked Keith," Ashta said.

The Master Face Changer crossed his fingers over his forehead to hide his face.

"Why did they do that?"

"To protect you."

"But they forced me to leave Eridan."

"They hoped you'd come back. Declan took responsibility. It was public, and his family banned him. Lots of people turned their backs on him. Then Keith massacred the Face Changers." Ashta fought her displaced sympathy for the man sagging beside her. "He hurt Declan so he wouldn't be able to face-change again."

Theo handed the mug to Farren and leaned forward. "Declan? Why didn't you tell me any of this in Gambling Nova?"

He let out a harsh breath. "What for? You didn't care about me anymore."

"Didn't I deserve an explanation?"

"There's nothing to explain."

Theo sat down and bounced back to her feet. In two strides she stood in front of Declan.

"Look at me!"

He put a hand over his eyes.

She pushed it forcefully away and bent forward to meet his eyes.

He had somewhat face-changed. His reddened face no longer resembled Farren's. It wasn't his own yet, except for his purple eyes.

"You face-changed into Farren to have your way with me." Theo's voice boomed in the cramped cabin. "You frightened me! You hurt me!"

"Evetha, I … I'm sorry!"

"I don't want to hear that you're sorry! I want to know why you did this to me. You betrayed me! I trusted you. You were my friend."

"I wasn't thinking straight." He sighed. "I was angry."

She eyed him grimly. "How far were you ready to go? What would have happened if I hadn't realized it wasn't Farren kissing me but someone else?"

"I—"

She cut him off. "If you had succeeded, I would have betrayed Farren. That was your intention, wasn't it? To break us apart."

He shifted his eyes. "No …"

"Don't lie to me! And stop lying to yourself. You don't love me."

"I do …"

She shook her head several times. "It's not because you take the appearance of a living man that you can replace him. Farren is …" She glanced over her shoulder at Farren, now standing beside Jack, and her smile was small, but it was a smile. She faced Declan again. "He's nothing like the man you tried to be. He smells different. He kisses different. He holds me different. Farren loves me. He would never assault me. And for the record, your face-changing was wrong. Farren has tattoos on his body."

Ashta joined her and, a hand on her arm, studied her from head to foot.

"What?" Theo asked, with some trepidation.

"You did well."

Tears appeared in her friend's dark eyes. And with them, shock.

Her quivering lips and flushed cheeks signaled a deep need to rest. Fast.

"What do you want to do?"

"About pressing charges?" Theo rubbed her eyes. "I need time. I'll tell you tomorrow."

"Theo …" Jack said. Farren held him back.

"I know. But I agree with Ashta. It's an Eridani matter."

CHAPTER 230

Sharing a Memory

10 June 3077, Standard Time (ST), Sixth Federal Era
SpaceSS ship

"I'll be right out!" Theo answered when Farren knocked at the bathroom door, asking after her.

Even though she had spent the last half hour under hot water scrubbing her skin to wash the feeling of Declan off her body, the memory of his hand cupping her breast and fondling her body remained. His touch had rekindled the memories linked to Logan, and brought with them traces of the nauseating scent of crushed roses.

She caressed her cheeks and her neck as she examined herself in the mirror.

She had not faltered. She had put into practice the Julepa gang lessons, Thumo lessons, everything she had learned. And even if she recoiled at the blows inflicted on the man she had thought was a friend, she felt no regrets. She had come to her own rescue and stopped rape from entering her life again.

Rape!

The word seared her with shame. Her nose tickled. She gulped. Grief trapped her again. Would she have the stamina to endure it? Even though she slept long hours at night and napped in the afternoons, she was still recovering from her harsh journey through Canyon Maze.

She stared at her anguished eyes, her drawn face.

Would she rue what she intended to do?

It had to be done.

She combed her hair, checked her clothes and walked out of her hideout.

Farren and Jack sat on the couch, conversing in that quiet manner that she found so comforting. They had welcomed her into their couple, strong enough in their mutual faith and love to accept her and give her space. They had become her home, and they deserved to know everything about her.

Farren stood up. "Theo, we ordered food. I can warm it up."

"I'm not hungry." She cleared her throat. "I need to talk to both of you." She sat in the armchair facing the sofa. "Now."

"You don't have to," Jack said. "You're tired, and—"

"I must."

She flattened her palms on her thighs because she didn't want them to see her shivering like a leaf in the wind. Her heart pounded in her chest. "I didn't tell you everything about myself."

"And we haven't either!" Farren handed her a tall glass of apple sissli, and caressed her fingers as she took it.

"Each of us has his secrets. It takes time to share them." Jack sat up.

The inside of her mouth went dry. "I want you to know my story so you can understand why I nearly killed a man this afternoon."

Jack slapped the arm of the sofa with his fist. "He attacked you! You were within your rights!"

His growl heartened her.

"Theo, you don't think we're judging you or anything, do you?" Farren asked, leaning forward.

She steeled herself for strength. "Mogud was always interested in me. He had that way of leering at me. As if his eyes alone could heat my skin. My mother noticed, and when he forced my parents to move under the Dome, she told my father." She swallowed. "My father is the one who organized my trip to Eridan. My mother was supposed to travel with me, but Mogud forced her to stay. My father knew I couldn't be told the truth because I wouldn't have left. So he pretended to hand me over to Mogud, and I believed him." She wiped the corner of her eyes. "And I also believed he preferred to die than to protect me. I found out the truth when I returned to Gambling Nova."

"I am sure your father loved you dearly," Farren said.

She nodded. "He did. He arranged everything—the ship, money in a bank account in Nuong, and men's clothes—because he figured it would be safer for me. But I was stupid. Old Jim landed somewhere to fuel up. I was starved and lonely. I left the ship to buy food." She drank some apple sissli and held the glass tightly between her hands. "There was a raid, and I was kidnapped with many other people. They piled us onto a ship to another place. I had nothing with me, barely a few fedgads."

"Theo, I am so sorry." Farren sat closer to her, on a square table. He brushed her fingers again. "You're freezing!" He took off his sweatshirt and handed it to her. "Here, put this on."

"Thanks."

"Who kidnapped you? Do you know?" Jack asked.

"Logan," she whispered, and pulled Farren's sweatshirt tighter around herself. It carried the faint scent of his after-shave, his warmth.

"Logan? You mean you were a Scavenger worker?" Farren asked.

She nodded. They knew about Logan, and this mere fact brought her stress level down a notch. "I found out later that Mogud and Logan were friends. When Mogud sent out bounty hunters after me, he told Logan. I didn't stand a chance." She felt her cheeks warm up. "He raped me." Her bland voice shook. She remembered the vast dining hall where she had been brought with other girls to dance; it had been a kind of banquet with men and women sitting at long rectangular tables on three sides, but it wasn't about dancing; they had laughed and clapped as she and the other girls fled around the hall. She remembered the persistent smell of roses rotting in vases, the cold floor freezing her back. She remembered his weight. "Other men raped me too. Afterwards, he told me I could go. I was so naïve I thought he was telling the truth. He wasn't." She coughed, conscious of the silence, afraid to look at them. "I was able to leave only be-cause some workers …" She paused. "The Scavengers used dogs to keep workers in line. One day, some of them set the dogs free, and lit fires all over the compound."

"The Fire Revolt," Farren said. His strong, kind voice brought her back to the present.

"Yes. I was still inside Logan's palace when it exploded. I escaped with one of the girls. It was night. There was lots of smoke; I coughed for days afterwards. We ran. There were dogs everywhere, and Scavengers fighting with workers. It took us three days to reach the closest city on foot. She asked me to wait for her near a building, and …" She closed her eyes. "I didn't. I wanted, you know, to find something to eat, I was so hungry, so I slipped inside a covered market. I heard voices not far from a stand. It was Logan. He and the girl were talking, and she told him that she had found me. I ran through the market. They chased me. After crossing a fish market, I found myself in the middle of a nomad camp." Of Zineb, she remembered laughter and warmth. The tall woman with pendants and necklaces stood at a tent's entrance. She waved at her and when Theo, famished and panting, didn't move, she sent two children to grab her by the hands and drag her into the tent. "They sheltered me. They made me part of their group, and they took me in their ship packed with goats to Nexus. They entrusted me to the Julepa gang, and I stayed with them long enough to learn how to defend myself. I couldn't imagine traveling to Eridan without knowing how to protect myself." She finished her glass of apple sissli. "I bought an Exploplan jacket and this time my disguise was a good one. I traveled from Nexus to Eridan on cargo ships. I was constantly afraid that Mogud's bounty hunters would find me. I hid. I did things I'm not proud of to survive. And I finally reached Eridan. I was so angry, so upset with life. So uncontrolled." She chuckled bitterly. "I disrupted their lives." She raised her head. The affection and understanding in Jack and Farren's eyes unraveled her senses. She fought to keep her composure. "I don't want to disrupt your lives. I am bad luck." Would she be brave enough to tell them everything? "I'm not a good person. You saw what I did to Declan. I'm not …"

"Yes, you are." Farren pulled her into his arms. "You're beautiful."

She bowed her head. "No. I'm not. I can't make you happy. I'm not right for you."

"Let me be the judge of that." He raised her chin. "You're so courageous. You humble me." He wrapped his arms around her.

She had to break up with him, with them.

"Don't!" she pleaded, her voice weak.

"Don't what?"

She pulled away and he let her go. She glanced at Jack, who was standing nearby.

"Farren is not Declan," he said.

"I know!"

"Well then, let him hold you. You need it, and so does he."

"Why?"

"Because he's hurting. What you told us. I don't know about him, but I want to tear the pain from your heart and squeeze it until it shrivels to dust."

There was no pity in Jack's eyes. No pity, but anger on her behalf, and something else. An understanding, as if …

"Theo …"

She faced Farren.

"Thank you for your trust," he said kindly. "It can't have been easy to tell us about Logan." His voice became urgent, vibrant. "What he did to you, that's not what you are. It's two different things. I heard the story of a young woman who managed to cope against terrible odds and kept on going, who traveled and basically made it all by herself. So I'll repeat myself. You are a beautiful woman, Theo. And I want to be the man who makes you understand that."

He held out his hand and she grabbed it, as well as the tingling promise in his dark velvet eyes.

CHAPTER 231

A Frozen Mocean

*11 June 3077, Standard Time (ST), Sixth Federal Era
Eridan (207th Cycle, Cuttlefish Season, Whirlpools' Blue
Year)—Savalwomen Fortress*

Sheer and the New Council members were attending a meeting in the Fortress when roaring sounds stopped Roisin-the-Bold short in his Shallow Seas assessment. They rushed to the window. Coming from the horizon, two aircraft flew at close range over Oniraveen Bay. They circled the bay, then went south.

Sheer pulled on a jacket. "We need to get ready to welcome these visitors, whoever they are."

"Who says they will land here?" Roisin asked.

"Eridooneen is stuck under an ice siege, and people live here."

"Who do you think it can be?" Mona wondered as she pulled on her mittens.

"We'll soon find out."

"Do you think they know …?"

Sheer glanced at Issavern, still unsure about the old yeold's loyalty. "We must assume they do. Be prepared."

———

The aircraft returned faster than anticipated and, after circling Oniraveen Bay, landed on the frozen harbor, beyond the line of sailboats stuck in ice.

Sheer and Terri, followed by Joos, Cass, Roisin-the-Bold, Mona, Issavern and Davin, hurried down to the pier, while Oniraveen inhabitants milled towards the shore from all directions.

Snuggled in a heavy jacket, Ashta appeared at the top of the biggest aircraft's gangway. She stood still for a moment, then raised her arms towards the sky. As she walked down, people showed up behind her.

"It's Ashta and the Face Changers!" Terri said. He scanned the crowd, heart beating because he couldn't see Nand.

"And there's Evetha too!" Sheer hastened forward. "Good."

"There are only five of them. I don't see Nand. Can you?" Davin asked.

"Maybe she's in the other ship. There's someone coming out," Mona said.

A man wearing a black cap that covered his ears walked out alone. He joined the other, taller man waiting at the foot of the first gangway.

In the meantime, Sheer sprinted down the path dug into the ice. She reached the two Savalwomen, eyeing them with pleasure as she drew the welcome sign.

"You made it."

"It's been a rough ride." Ashta coughed. "And we're not in the best of shape." She pointed at Farren and Clobb. "We have company. Much needs to be discussed."

"Who are they?"

"The handsome one on the left is Farren Megan," Evetha said. "He was Washone's contact at SpaceSS. And the scowling one, his name is Derek Clobb. He belongs to the Guild and is overseeing a Federal investigation of Eridan. He's trustworthy to an extent. He needs to be convinced that Eridan isn't dangerous."

Sheer grimaced. "I didn't know about Washone's involvement with SpaceSS. What is it about?"

"Ask the Master Face Changer." Theo's voice derailed. She blew on her fingers. "Or better still, ask Farren for details."

"From what we've learned," Ashta explained, "Washone petitioned for Eridan to be part of the Federacy."

Sheer nodded. "I'll need a detailed report about this as soon as possible." She eyed Evetha, not liking the brittleness that clipped her tone, the way she evaded her eyes. "Are there other foreigners with you?"

"Jack Finch is here too." Evetha's tone softened. "He's the man who came here to get me."

"And there's Erlend," Ashta added. "He's Nand's lover."

Sheer remembered the first time she had met Nand, the lasting impression the teenager had made on her, and she rejoiced inwardly.

Ashta searched the crowd, then spoke to her. "Sheer, we must arrange a quick meeting with Theo and Farren. Things are complicated. Since Eridan is suspected of attacking Meranka, I took it upon myself to appoint Jack and Farren as our representatives in our relations with the Federacy, and particularly the Guild."

"You did right. I'll get this underway. Do we need to organize lodgings for everybody?"

"We hope to get Clobb to leave later today," Theo said. "It depends on this discussion. The rest of us will stay awhile."

Declan and the Half-Masters were greeted by Joos and Cass, and the six of them stood slightly apart, in a circle, rubbing shoulders.

Ashta followed Sheer's glance.

"They are the only ones who survived."

"We feared that none would make it. And the Master Face Changer carries no scars. He seems fit. That's good. We need him. Thank you, Evetha!"

The two Savalwomen's smiles were as frozen as the ice they stood upon.

What had happened?

Ashta spotted Mona several arcs away waving at her.

"I'll be right back!" She headed towards Bibiana's beaming older sister.

"What's going on with the Master Face Changer?" Sheer asked.

Evetha rubbed her hands. "I wasn't expecting it to be so cold."

Sheer liked the new self-confidence she perceived in the foreign Savalwoman. "I'll need a full account from you and Ashta."

"She knows everything that happened to the Face Changers and Nand. I don't. She's the one you need to talk to."

"I'd like to hear your take on things. For instance, do you share her misgivings about the Master Face Changer?"

This time, Evetha looked at her squarely, and didn't hide her anguish and anger. "Now is not the time." She then greeted the two young men who had joined them.

"I'm Davin, Nand's brother, and this is Terri. Our cousin. Did Nand make it?"

"Yes. She's unwell. She'll join us later."

"Define unwell." Terri said.

"Sad. Weak."

"Can we see her?"

"Sure. I'll take you to her." Evetha faced Sheer. "Don't say anything to Clobb without either Jack or Farren around. Warn people. He's curious and friendly. He'll get people to talk to him easily. You don't want that. Not immediately, and not to this man."

"You know him well."

Evetha nodded. "He's cunning and brilliant. He won't stop until he gets what he wants. Ashta did the right thing when she appointed Jack and Farren. They have clout and they'll know how to protect Eridan's interests during the investigation."

"So, what we've done is known abroad?" Davin asked.

"This is what I mean," Evetha said. "Keep silent until Clobb leaves, because anything anybody says can be held against Eridan." She glanced at the three Eridanis. "There's an inquest about Eridan. My friends Jack and Farren will help you with that, but for this they need everybody's full cooperation."

"You'll have it," Terri said.

Farren and Clobb walked cautiously on the ice cap beyond the sailboats' line.

"I'll get things underway and meet you at the Fortress in an hour," Sheer said.

———◆———

Ashta hugged Mona for a long time.

"How are you coping?" she asked. "I'm so sorry about Aslone."

Mona swiftly brushed her eyes. "I'm fine now. I've been working a lot, with the Face Changers. The few who are left. Lots needed to be done. And you? We were so worried."

"I'm happy to be back home, finally."

"Joos and the others must be ecstatic. They feared the Master Face Changer wouldn't survive."

"How's Bibiana? I've sent her mental messages since we landed, and she doesn't answer. Is she all right?"

Mona grimaced. "We can't receive or send mental messages anymore."

"Why? When did this happen?"

"When Mocean began to freeze." She bit her lip and gripped Ashta's hand. "Bibiana lives with Terri and Sofini. She—"

"What?" Worry flickered through her like fire. "What happened to her?"

"That day—night … she and Carmen stopped Mindrule. Carmen was so weak with the greens, she sunk."

Sorrow and sympathy brought tears to her eyes. "Oh, no … Sheer didn't say a word. She must be devastated."

"She doesn't show anything." Mona smiled. "Sofini feeds her, and Terri keeps her busy. There's so much to do. Organizing ourselves to find food and fresh water."

"And Bibiana?"

"She lost her voice because she screamed so long and so

hard to wake us up. She collapsed, sprained an ankle, and stayed under the waterline for several days." Mona smiled. "She's better now, but she can only whisper."

"Where is she?"

"With Sofini. They're glued together."

A shout drew their attention.

"Over there!" Mona said. "I was sure they would join us."

A kite buggy skidded over ice.

"They're inside of that thing?"

"Yup. Terri, Davin and some of Davin's friends construct all sorts of wind-propelled engines to get people around."

Ashta's eyes misted over when she recognized Bibiana sitting beside her twin in the kite buggy. She waved and ran to meet them, nearly slipping on the ice.

Sofini stopped the kite buggy. She got out of it to help her sister, but Ashta was already there. She quickly hugged Sofini and jumped inside next to Bibiana, wrapping her arms around her lover, her head over her breast, happy to hold her, to listen to her heart beat its steady, lovely song.

———◆———

Nand sat with Erlend and Jack at the back of the SpaceSS aircraft. Despite the cozy, safe interior, she felt the outside air slowly sprinkling its icy flakes inside her as she tried to reach Terri, Davin and Kaipekak mentally.

Every attempt was met by a vacuum, deepening her despair. A glacial emptiness in which she could easily lose herself if she wasn't careful.

"Nand!"

She looked up: her brother and her cousin were rushing down the aisle, followed by Theo.

"Why are you crying?" Davin asked as he reached her side.

"Why didn't you answer me?" she cried. "I thought you were dead. That you had all sunk!"

"We can't communicate mentally anymore," Terri explained. "But we're alive. All your friends are."

Erlend helped Nand to her feet. Davin pulled her into his arms. He smelled of iodine, seaweed and freshness. She closed her eyes, dizzy with those long-forgotten scents.

He held her tight, burying his face in her neck. "What happened to you? You're so thin."

"My turn!" Terri said.

Davin reluctantly stepped away. Nand knelt on the ground to hug Terri.

They gazed at each other.

Can't you hear me?

Terri smiled with a melancholy that pierced her heart. "I know you're trying. But our minds are as frozen as Mocean." His eyes were haunted with unfathomable grief. "It's our punishment."

She held his shoulders and pressed her forehead against his.

Are you sure you can't hear me?

"I love you, Nand."

"I'm sorry about Aslone."

"It's getting better." He chuckled bitterly. "In a way. Why don't you sit down and introduce us to your friends?"

They all squeezed themselves into a booth, with Nand between Erlend and Terri, and Davin, Theo and Jack opposite them.

"Erlend," she said, "this is my cousin Terri and my brother Davin. Erlend and I met in Redland. And the handsome man beside Theo is Jack. It's his second time in Eridan."

"We've been expecting outer space visitors since …" Her brother's eyes clouded and he glanced at Terri.

"Since … Eridan began to freeze. We'll explain. You must be present when we do, Nand. We need you."

She blew her nose and wiped her cheeks. Tears poured from her eyes.

"I can't."

"Why? Are you hurt?"

How could she explain the fear threatening to choke her alive?

Terri picked up her left hand and stroked it.

"It's complicated."

"Everything about Eridan is complicated," Erlend said, and he tugged at her right hand. "That's what Nand always said when I asked her about her life when we met. It's complicated."

He knew how to pull her away from the brink, and she was grateful.

"I'm afraid," she admitted.

"Because Mocean is frozen?" Davin asked.

She shook her head.

Erlend laced his fingers into hers. "Nand fears her kidadakh has sunk," he said, and his words, however harsh, pulled her further back into the realm of the living. "Until this morning, she forced herself not to think about it. Since we landed, she's been trying to communicate with him. She can't hear any kidadakh. She's scared that the grief of losing Kaipekak will be too much for her to bear."

She tried a smile as she gazed at her brother, at Terri beside her. "I can't face this."

Davin touched her knees beneath the table. "You're not alone. I'm here with you, with Terri and Sofini, Bibiana and all your friends. Your family. We'll support you."

"You can't, not in the way I need …"

"Remember what Mamerwen told you a long time ago, after we helped the Master Face Changer," Terri said with some urgency. "Hlyks always survive their kidadakh's death. She did, and she's still alive."

"That's not true. It depends on the bond. With Kaipekak, our bond is called fusion, and it's stronger than other bonds. If he sunk, I've no idea how I'd react."

"If you need mental strength, I'll support you," Theo said.

"But Ashta said you couldn't use your mind anymore."

"It does hurt when we communicate, but drawing energy from me, that's different."

"Don't you hate using your mind?" Nand asked, in answer to the worry which had flared in Jack's eyes.

The daunting and magnificent woman, who had pugnaciously countered Clobb's prejudice about Eridan at every step, grinned. "For you, I'll make an exception."

"Why?"

"Because you're special."

Heat invaded her cheeks. "I wouldn't know how to reach for your mind," she murmured, as she finally grasped why so many people around her adored Theo.

"Ask Ashta. She'll give you my imprint."

"Thank you, Theo. I'll do that."

She leaned back against the wall. "Do you think we could

drink something before we go outside?"

Jack read his cell. "Farren says everybody's walking slowly. He's with Clobb; Ashta found her girlfriend; the Face Changers haven't budged. So yes, we can do that."

———◆———

While Erlend recounted Farren's feats after the Dome escape to Jack and Theo, things their lover hadn't bothered to explain, Nand led Terri and Davin to the front of the sleek aircraft, to a wider area where they could all sit together.

"I want to try something," she said. "Close your eyes, both of you."

Axonna, you heard everything. Can I heal their minds?

What do they look like?

Emeralds. Hard and green, with dark veins. This is Terri's, and here is Davin's.

They don't need healing. They need to be thawed. Like Mocean.

How?

Flood them with Mocean's waves. Warm their minds.

"Nand? What are you doing?" Terri asked.

Now wasn't the time to mention Axonna.

"Relax. I have an idea."

What will you do?

What I did with Erlend when I showed him what it was like to swim in Mocean.

She held Terri's hands and engulfed the green emerald that was her cousin's mind with memories of swimming in bluewater with Kaipekak.

I like these images!

So do I!

You're not alone to face the grief of Kaipekak's sinking. You have me.

You're right.

"Did you feel or see anything?" she asked.

Eyes closed, Terri nodded imperceptibly.

"Keep the memory," she ordered. "Your turn, Davin."

Her brother's big hands warmed her own.

No emerald with Davin, rather jade. She suffused his mind with fluttering, colorful anemones swept by underwater currents, phosphorescent jellyfish lazily twirling through coldnight. Twice he tightened his fingers, and she injected his mind with fluid memories from their childhood.

Feeling dizzy, she stopped.

Can you hear me? she asked both at the same time.

"You still can't hear me, can you?" she repeated, trying unsuccessfully to suppress her disappointment.

"Not the usual way. But I did feel something." Terri hid his face in his hands, then he appraised her. "This is different. How did you find this canal?"

"One night in Redland, I wanted to show Eridan to Erlend. His mind is like a diamond. Hard and smooth. Impenetrable. I searched and found this sideway, somewhere between memories and awareness. It worked well." Sadness filled her as she recalled how it had ended. "My memories turned into a vision. We both saw Eridan as it is now. With frozen waves."

She wiped away new tears.

"How about you, Davin? Did you feel anything?" Terri asked.

"Moving colors," her brother said.

His expression was so perplexed that she experienced a twinge of fear.

"I didn't hurt you, did I?"

"No." He shrugged. "They tickled me. Very strange."

"I'd forgotten how noisy waves are." Terri focused. "But still no mind movement."

"We'll try again. I'm sure there's something I can do." She stood up. "I'm ready."

C H A P T E R 2 3 2

———————

Prisoner

11 June 3077, Standard Time (ST), Sixth Federal Era
Eridan (207th Cycle, Cuttlefish Season, Whirlpools' Blue
Year)—Oniraveen

Donatella knocked her forehead against the glass, her fingers like useless claws. She moaned; she hit the solid window pane with her fists, grazing her knuckles.

Three days after the second wave, they had locked her inside this large, bare room, on the upper floor of a tower within the Savalwomen Fortress, and she had not been allowed out since. Sunlight poured into her elevated prison. However, even at noon its strength didn't match the need grinding at her guts.

The dull landscape stretched its dirty white up to the horizon. An immutable flat plain capped with a light blue sky. As boring as the days that passed by. An exhausting void. Donatella had nothing to do, nobody to talk to. They fed her the same seaweed soup and bread each day, with pots of bukni, a bitter tea that nauseated her.

A spasm shook her. She folded over, her arms compressing her stomach. It was too early to let the quivers shake her body until her teeth rattled her brain to mush. She must walk. She forced herself to move. Her legs shivered; her arms shivered. Her head hurt.

The need for light that Keith had planted deep in her brain had a will of its own.

She had stumbled a few steps, half of the bay window's length, when she convulsed with another spasm and collapsed on the cold floor.

She needed light.

The short bitch who visited her each night stated that no Eridani could give light anymore. That Keith had destroyed Eridan and Eridanis.

They were dying because of him.

So would she.

That pitiful leader said that they didn't have an alternate drug, that she would have to cope with her need.

How?

Lying on her back, Donatella recoiled as she recalled her humiliating confrontations first with Keith, then with The Kresdan. How could she have been so weak, so gullible? She shook. How could she root out the tantalizing memory of the warm and soothing light which fulfilled her every need? Could memories turn into a semblance of reality? If only she knew how to retrieve the substance of the light Keith had used.

She forced herself to sit, to look outside.

She was a strong, capable woman. She was the Spylady.

Not an addict. Nothing like Max.

She grabbed her thin thighs, disgusted by her jutting bones, her gray skin and angularity. The last time she had lost so much weight dated back to the year her symbiont died. The pain of that loss had evaporated. Impossible to retrieve! She grieved it; she tried to remember it. But it was gone.

She bit her bottom lip until she tasted blood. How could she still be a Symb and not remember what it was to have and lose her symbiont?

With his blissful light, Keith had succeeded in erasing her trauma. This should be enough. This was all she wanted, wasn't it? She grinded her teeth. No, she wanted this shard of torment to still exist.

Madness had overcome her that day. She craved more; she enjoyed his gift too much to know when to stop.

Keith had replaced the symbiont loss with an inescapable need.

It inhabited her bones.

She stood up and forced her feet to lift up one after the other as she leaned against the window pane.

She glanced down at a group of Eridanis playing music on Oniraveen's little square. She heard nothing, she smelled nothing, she could only see.

And remember. Her thoughts sizzled relentlessly over the sting of her disgrace at the hands of Keith's second-in-command, the pervert named The Kresdan.

She moaned. This memory woke her up when she dozed off; it suffocated her when she drank; it shamed her.

Her need had been extreme that day, her senses fiercely overcoming her reason. She had crawled at this man's feet; she had pleaded with him, ready to submit to whatever indignity for a glimpse of bliss. He had toyed with her, giving light, then taking it away. Even though she was trained to keep silent under torture, she had spilled out answers to his questions. She had told him secrets that could endanger SpaceSS. She was his puppet, an open-eyed puppet, tingling with an insatiable need.

A puppet she remained, even though she had not seen either man again.

She brought her fists to her eyes. How could she remove mortification from her brain? That moment around midnight when she had stripped off her clothes and let The Kresdan have his way with her. How could she have erased her self-esteem?

She was trained by the best, and yet …

She had accepted his proposition, promising herself that it would happen only once. And it had, but not because she didn't want it to happen again. In exchange, while he pawed and pinched her body, while he fucked her with a dismal lack of imagination, he had suffused her brain with a continuous stream of weak light. Barely what she craved, but she dared not protest for fear of losing this much-needed respite.

And suddenly, the light had increased. He gaped at her, and he didn't seem to know who she was or what he was doing. He jerked up. He grumbled and scrambled to the floor. He held his head between his hands.

The bright light did not resemble what it had been earlier with either man. It shone steadily; it soothed her.

For a moment, she thought normally.

Just as she realized what she had done, awe grabbed at her brain and jolted it. The light increased in a manner that differed completely from what Keith and The Kresdan had forced her to experience earlier. It encompassed her; it sucked her energy. She saw herself crash to the floor.

It was as if a multitude of screaming souls had swarmed around her like bees escaping from a hive while incandescent bubbles popped in the background.

The buzzing increased, creating static. She opened her eyes with effort.

Huge in the middle of the room, The Kresdan swayed like a reed fighting a strong wind, back and forth, scratching the air with his rigid fingers.

She remembered his swinging figure. The light suffocated her with its intensity and something else—something morbid; a sense of decay, of putrefaction—was sown in her brain that day and had kept growing since.

Before darkness fell with a loud roaring sound, The Kresdan's knees folded. His mouth opened and closed like that of a suffocating fish.

The roar increased as light faded, until noise overcame all her senses.

And now it penetrated the soundproof room.

She peeped outside. Two aircraft flew by.

One of them carried the SpaceSS mark.

How had they found her? What did they know?

She had been cautious when dealing with Keith and Mogud, left no trace, not even in the orgacomp.

The ships landed on the ice cap.

Farren Megan and Theo Maddiogga stepped out. Their body language, hands touching. Together! She chuckled. If only Finch was around to witness this blatant betrayal!

She waved. She called. Her gravelly voice grazed her ears.

Another spasm.

No. Megan would not see her like this. She raked her hands through her tangled hair.

She was his boss. He would not get away with siding with her enemies.

She must ready herself.

Settling Matters

*11 June 3077, Standard Time (ST), Sixth Federal Era
Eridan (207th Cycle, Cuttlefish Season, Whirlpools' Blue
Year)—Oniraveen*

Clobb liked Sheer and this unsettled him. He had expected a fight to get custody of Donatella Simpson, not for the Savalwoman leader to readily let her go.

Two hours after they landed, Ashta and Theo took him and Megan to the Fortress, which was the Savalwomen headquarters and, from what Clobb gathered, the current operational center. They introduced them to Sheer Tellu, the grim short-haired Savalwomen leader, whom they obviously respected, and at her request left the three of them together in a freezing room overlooking Oniraveen bay.

He liked this sharp-eyed woman's directness when she asked them what to expect from their presence. He presented her with facts: the scientific results found in several Meranka meteorological stations which showed intense ocean activity in Eridan during the hours preceding the rise of a big wave, and the abnormal number of deaths of Meranka inhabitants during this wave rise until it reached its peak. Once the wave collapsed, Meranka people stopped dying, and the ocean began to freeze. The ocean's activity in Eridan had been monitored since another tsunami-like wave several weeks before. No deaths were recorded at the time.

He explained afterwards about the Federal investigation. A deliberate attack against Meranka was suspected. Still and silent, Sheer watched him. Megan told her that Keith of Rain Forest was involved in an alliance with Donatella Simpson, ex-SpaceSS leader, and Tarbel Mogud, Gambling Nova's former governor, to overthrow the government in Nuong. She absorbed this news with stamina. Keith of Rain Forest was suspected of wanting to overcome populations with the power of the mind. Something called Mindrule. She pinched her lips, and a life-threatening grief briefly lit her gray eyes. For the first time, Clobb admitted to himself that Theo and the Eridanis he had already lengthily questioned could be right: Mindrule was one man's crazy ambition. Yet Keith of Rain Forest could not have done it without the population's support.

Megan also told Sheer that Ashta Coral had appointed Red Arches to act as Eridan's representatives in its relations with the federal government in Nuong, and their lawyers, headed by Jered Bakamo, would act on their behalf. Red Arches would investigate what took place in Eridan and Meranka, and report to SpaceSS and the Guild.

Sheer thanked them for their presence. Emotion coated her first words, but soon she talked with stark clarity. She informed them that she had already launched an in-depth investigation in Eridan to understand exactly what had taken place and how. Every single Eridani would be interviewed. She then dropped her own bomb: not only had Keith of Rain Forest sunk, as Eridanis defined dying, but many Eridanis as well. And several more each day, mostly infants, because of the harsh living conditions.

She knew nothing about Donatella Simpson except that she claimed to be some important leader. Sheer's disparaging tone left no doubt that she distrusted this statement, which titillated him. And Megan as well, from the man's greedy half-smile. What was going on with the SpaceSS leader?

She had landed in Eridan before the water wall, as they called the first big wave. From what Sheer gathered, she had divulged sensitive information about SpaceSS to Keith of Rain Forest's commander-in-chief, a man called The Kresdan. Something he had confirmed when he was questioned after Mindrule.

Clobb asked her what Mindrule was exactly, and Megan told her not to answer. Then he sharply rebuked him. It irked Clobb, but he conceded stepping over the line.

The Savalwomen leader looked at each of them in turn, once again assessing them with her winter-gray eyes that missed nothing. Keith of Rain Forest's commander-in-chief had done nothing with these revelations, she added, because he hadn't had time. He was under arrest. As for Donatella Simpson, her presence burdened them. She was imprisoned in a Fortress tower. She would be willing to release her into Clobb's custody. The woman was in a state of severe withdrawal due to a mental light overdose. They had tried to reduce her need by dosing her food and beverages with akol, with no tangible results.

Megan asked about this overdose of light. Sheer told them what The Kresdan had revealed: Donatella Simpson had negotiated a deal for herself and a group of people called the Families with Keith of Rain Forest by which Eridanis would give them mental light to soothe their anxiety due to symbiont loss. Since their mental communication was as frozen as their ocean, none of them could alleviate her need in any way.

Clobb asked about Simpson's means of transport, and Sheer said that it was a small aircraft piloted by a cyborg. Both the aircraft and the cyborg were caught in Eridooneen's deep freeze, and inaccessible.

Should the ocean melt, Megan said that they would handle it. His too-casual expression alerted Clobb. He made a note to question the former SpaceSS agent later, and accepted the Savalwomen leader's proposition to visit Donatella Simpson.

CHAPTER 234

The Spylady

*11 June 3077, Standard Time (ST), Sixth Federal Era
Eridan (207th Cycle, Cuttlefish Season, Whirlpools' Blue
Year)—Oniraveen*

They entered a wide room with glistening white walls, while Sheer stayed outside.

Donatella Simpson stood, feet apart, her fists clenched at her sides. She seemed taller, perhaps because she had lost so much weight: she floated in ill-fitting clothes.

They had never met, so, of course, she ignored him and pounced on Megan.

"What took you so long?" she screeched. "I've been imprisoned here for nearly a month. That damn woman won't let me go." She took deep, audible breaths, probably to control her shivering body. "You must apprehend Keith of Rain Forest for conspiracy. He tried to kill me when I arrived here to arrest him! He's a dangerous man. Well, move! Do something! I've been drugged, and I want to sue Eridan and its leaders. Look at me!" She showed her trembling hands. "I'm in withdrawal and they merely watch!"

Megan introduced him. "This is Derek Clobb. He's a Guild leader."

She barely bestowed him a glance. "So what? I don't like the Guild. A bunch of useless do-gooders. Why did you involve them? This matter concerns SpaceSS exclusively."

"I'm here to arrest you and take you to Nuong, Ms. Simpson," he said.

"No way! I'm going to E-Met with my SpaceSS agent. My ship and my pilot are out of order. Megan, you are taking me over there right away."

Megan folded his arms. "No."

Two spasms shook her body, but she stood firm.

"I order you, Agent Megan."

"You can't. I quit. I don't belong to SpaceSS anymore."

"What do you mean? You landed in a SpaceSS aircraft. I saw you."

"My company was hired by Eridan to defend their interests in the upcoming investigations. SpaceSS lent us this aircraft."

"What company? This is preposterous! What of the debts you incurred with your studies? I'll sue you too. You botched your assignment in Gambling Nova! It's because of you that I had to try to stop Keith of Rain Forest all by myself!"

Megan's eyes widened in disbelief. "Sue me?"

Her teeth chattered. "Sue you. Unless you tell Clobb the truth. That Finch forced you to betray me and SpaceSS. Your brawan's dead. You don't need to protect him anymore."

"What are you talking about?" Clobb asked.

She whirled his way, flapping her loosely-clothed arms like a monstrous bat. "It's Megan you should arrest. Not me! He and his former brawan double-crossed SpaceSS. They wanted to murder me!"

Megan and Finch had bet him that if cornered she would go against them. They had now won themselves a hefty sum of fedgads.

"Megan and Finch betrayed SpaceSS?" He had to hand it to her, Donatella Simpson possessed a honey badger's rage.

"Yes. Finch was a mole. That's why I had to separate them. It was my duty to protect Megan from Finch's bad influence. So I sent him to Gambling Nova. He was the best choice for this undercover mission, since he was born there. A little before that, I discovered that Mogud had organized an alliance to overthrow the government in Nuong. That's also why I wanted my best field agent over there. To keep an eye on Mogud. As for Finch ..." She shrieked with laughter. "He had it coming." She scratched her head. "I admit I resorted to extremes to get him arrested. But you know what it is to govern. You need to set examples from time to time. There were breaches within our network, and stopping him and putting him on trial was the best way to stop the hemorrhage. Don't you see?"

"Jack was sent to Iglölü because he was a mole?" Megan's wide-eyed disbelief matched his tone.

"Of course. If I hadn't stepped in, he would have murdered you for real. Don't you understand? I protected you. I saved your life."

Rage took hold of Megan. A muscle ticked in his cheek. Clobb could almost hear his teeth grinding. "You're insane!" he shouted as he pounced on her. Clobb stepped in front of him. He raised a hand as if to ward him off. "What?" Megan growled. "Don't tell me that you believe what she said about Jack and me. She tried to get me killed in Junk City!"

"That's a pack of lies!" Simpson's high-pitched voice had the same effect on him as a knife scraping a bottle. "Why would I do that? I like you. You're a good agent."

"Stop it!" Megan had obviously reached the limit of what he could take. "If you don't shut her up, I will." For all his aloofness, the man was still battling his own demons, and probably some of Finch's.

An emotional bomb Clobb needed to defuse.

If only he had gone over this confrontation with Megan before! He counted on him to draw Simpson out of her comfort zone. However, the former SpaceSS agent still didn't trust him completely. Too bad!

He took a pair of handcuffs from his belt.

"What are you doing?" She walked away from him.

"Taking you into custody," he said.

Beside him, Megan expelled a breath.

She stood against the window pane, her hands behind her back. "On what charges? I've done nothing but protect SpaceSS since I became its leader. That's my job. To protect. And if it means acting illegally, then you should read the terms of my contract."

"And yet you traveled here to work with Keith of Rain Forest to launch Mindrule."

"How else could I arrest him?"

"You didn't. You stayed here, even after the Dome blew up. You didn't contact SpaceSS."

"I couldn't!" Her face was mottled; exhaustion drew dark lines beneath her eyes. At close range, Donatella Simpson had lost lots of her luster.

"You wanted retribution for your participation in this alliance. That's why you stayed here."

"What are you talking about? Keith of Rain Forest is a madman. Completely immature and unpredictable. I pretended to side with him, of course. But he attacked me. That's why I'll press charges against him and Eridan."

Even cornered, even in the throes of withdrawal, her cunning impressed him. He looked forward to interrogating her.

"You mean sue the Eridanis for providing what you wanted to obtain for you and the Families—light?"

"Don't say that word!" she hissed as she squeezed her eyes closed. Her face visibly paled as she shuddered.

He approached her. When she realized how close he stood to her, she recoiled, with no place to go.

"As far as Eridan is concerned, Megan's investigations and mine will determine how involved you've been." Her eyes darted around. "But Tarbel Mogud, your brother, Max Simpson, and Theo Maddiogga have all given us information that has already been confirmed."

"They're not reliable, neither of them, and certainly not that bitch." She eyed Megan with a mixture of plain meanness and disgust. "You're in trouble. You should have stayed on my side. When I'm done with you and your Miss Maddiogga, you'll wish you hadn't betrayed me. She's a fraud!"

Clobb pulled her by one arm and she offered no resistance. "We have the transcript of your conversation with Megan when you forced him to go undercover in Gambling Nova," he said quietly, "and with Finch when you tortured him in the ship for the Ring of Whalience. We even taped your conversation with Mogud about Megan and Finch in Gambling Nova."

He smiled. "You see, the Guild has been monitoring you for a long time." He clicked the handcuffs around her wrists.

The noise woke her from her passive state. "You can't do that! I want a lawyer."

He gripped her shoulder. "We know you're a Symb. We questioned the Families. We know about their involvement, what you promised them."

"Leave them alone. They've nothing to do with all this!"

"You tried to kill Jack Finch to avenge the Families because of Kanner Talmand."

"Well, I hope he died in great pain. It's only justice. We suffer because of Talmand." She cackled with glee. "But you can't prove anything now that he's dead. You have nothing against me."

"We'll see about that. Now, let's go."

He propelled her out of the room. Megan followed.

The late afternoon sun shone orange as they crossed the frozen bay to the Guild ship. Finch was waiting for them at the foot of the gangway.

Surprise followed by fury blotched Simpson's lean face. She stumbled, forgetting her handcuffs as she raised her hands.

"You bastard! You should be dead!"

Leaning on his cane, Finch smiled.

"Your brawan is cavorting with Theo Maddiogga!" she cried. "I saw them!"

Simpson turned towards Megan. "You did right, breaking up with Finch. You should've heard him in my office or when he yelled in the ship. A cry-baby. No dignity. It's good SpaceSS is rid of him."

Megan joined Finch and placed his arm around his shoulders in a possessive manner. They made a striking couple, proud and powerful as they stood side by side. Silent and smiling, Finch watched his former boss with a prowling shark's intensity.

"We are suing you and SpaceSS," Megan said. "Our lawyer has already begun the procedure."

"I have immunity," she scoffed, raising one shoulder. "You can't do anything against me."

"You don't have it anymore." His satisfied grin equaled that of his brawan. "We're no longer part of SpaceSS and you aren't either. You've been discharged by the new Spylady in interim." He paused. "Sycal Veld."

"No!"

"The Guild supports Finch and Megan's cases," Clobb said as he pushed her forward. "We have all the proof we need that you betrayed your own agents and SpaceSS. I advise you to remain silent now."

"No!" She struggled as quivers shook her body. "You can't do that! I'm the Spylady!"

"We'll be in touch," Clobb said to Finch and Megan as he handed Simpson over to two Guild guards. "Take care, and keep me informed."

"Thank you, Clobb," Finch said.

"Yes, your trust is appreciated," Megan added.

He saluted them. "Good luck!"

CHAPTER 235

Women Talking

*11–12 June 3077, Standard Time (ST), Sixth Federal Era
Eridan (207th Cycle, Cuttlefish Season, Whirlpools' Blue
Year)—Oniraveen*

Terri found Nand on his balcony, staring at Mocean while the sun set. He joined her, stepping on the elevated plank before placing a sweater over her hunched shoulders.

"How are you?"

His cousin stared ahead. "Kaipekak sunk. I can't hear him. I tried all day." She gripped the rail. "It probably happened soon after we left for Gambling Nova. I should have believed the many visions of his death I had. But, you know, I hoped …"

He embraced her. "You're not alone."

Her fingers whitened. "When I was up there, in the ship, and I watched Eridan, I thought I was dying myself. I've had this feeling, this sinking feeling, since we left. I tried. I really tried to fight it."

"What you told us during dinner, the battles in the ship. You were so brave." He kissed her cheek.

"That was survival. For me, the hardest took place in Pit 3, with Xë. He hounded me; he baited me. Declan forbid me to face-change back into myself, and I lost it. I didn't know if I was Nand or Aslone anymore." She wiped her eyes. "Erlend …" Her voice softened. "He fell in love with Aslone, and for me … it was—it is—love too. He listened to everything I said. He took my side until he couldn't." She leaned over the rail. Below, the waves were frozen into curls.

He grabbed her hand and pulled her towards him. "What happened with the Master Face Changer?"

She hesitated. "Things … When Axonna died, he became my elder."

"You're a resh?"

"Apparently! He gave me his healing gift and taught me how to use it. So I healed Declan when we were with the Redlanders because he was still suffering so much." She sniffled. "He hurt Erlend because of what I did. He hurt me. He didn't want to be healed. I tried very hard, but I can't forgive him. I'm sorry."

"Why do you say that you're sorry?"

"Because he's your friend, and I know how much you like him."

"But you're my cousin, my favorite cousin."

They hugged, and they both leaned over the rail.

"So that's what you tried to do to Davin and me this morning? Heal us?"

"It didn't work, did it? I tried all day to reach out to people I know, the kidadakh, the fiskiorps …" She blew her nose. "Everything is frozen. Dead. I had this idea of fixing things …"

"Don't cry." He embraced her. "You've had a long day. Come inside. You need to rest."

"Declan expelled me from the Face Changers. But I must face-change again for Erlend. He needs Aslone, not Nand, and I don't know how anymore."

"I'll help you. I'm good friends with Cass. She'll teach you again."

"Won't you mind if I take Aslone's appearance?" Her eyes were bright. "I don't want to hurt you."

"We'll find a way. Don't worry. Now, let's get you to bed."

Nand told Erlend that she would get them breakfast. She snuggled in a warm sweater and headed downstairs. She found Mona mixing batter for half-cakes and Theo perched on a stool next to her, her hands around a mug of bukni. Nand drew up another stool and sat next to Theo, who told her it was the right place to be, near the cook to taste the half-cakes.

When Mona asked her about her sleep, Nand admitted being disturbed by the silence. Mona agreed that she experienced the same kind of disquiet. Not hearing waves breaking on the shore often woke her up. It even troubled her during the day. Terri, who had lived for many tenens in the Northern Abyss, had a different opinion about silence. He said that ice cracked when you listened carefully. Theo explained that during her first weeks in Eridan, the rolling of the waves had kept her awake at night and that it took her a whole season to get used to this constant uproar.

Mona was half-way through her frying when Bibiana and Ashta showed up, holding hands. Bibiana rushed to Nand and embraced her.

"Thank you!" she said in her normal voice. "I feel wonderful this morning. It's not hurting anymore. Thank you!"

Sofini, who had entered the kitchen, smiled at her twin. "You're talking! How?"

"It's Nand! Nand has the healing gift," Bibiana said. "Ashta, you tell them. I'll set the table for breakfast."

"Bibiana wasn't feeling well last night." Ashta greeted Theo. "You're alone?"

"They're still sleeping. Yesterday was tough on both. That meeting with Donatella Simpson and the horrors she spouted. They didn't show it last night, but they were extremely upset. They need time together. I came to get a pan, and Mona was alone, cooking. So I stayed. To keep her company."

"About Bibiana?" Sofini prompted as she spread a tablecloth on the table.

"I asked Nand if she could help Bibiana." Ashta took mugs from the shelf. "Perhaps heal her throat or fix her vocal cords. This type of healing is different from trying to get your mind to function again for telepathy. So she joined us, with Erlend in our room."

"With Erlend?"

"We were both awake, and so he came, yes." Nand blushed.

"Don't listen to Sofini … she's teasing you." Bibiana winked at her sister as she set plates and forks on the table. "I confirm that he's a gorgeous young man. Nice, and funny, and he's an artist, like me. We'll show each other our work today."

"Nand cured Bibiana," Ashta said. "It didn't take long."

"You never told us you had the healing gift," Sofini said as she poured bukni into everyone's mugs. "It's ready."

The women sat around the small, round table. Mona placed

the dish full of half-cakes in the center and served each of them.

"There's wapui sauce for the half-cakes. Theo, they're better with it."

Nand picked up her fork. "I didn't have this gift before. It's new. Axonna gave it to me when he died."

"You're a resh?" Mona sat down between Sofini and Nand.

"He made me one." Nand smiled shyly at Theo on her right. "Axonna was a Face Changer. When he died, he … became part of me."

"You mean like an elder?"

"You know about elders?" Bibiana poured wapui sauce and handed the small pitcher over to Theo.

"Washone told me." Theo trickled wapui sauce in circles over her half-cakes. "I never liked that notion. How do you stand it?"

"Axonna is quiet most of the time."

"So you could be a kwirimok." Theo took a big piece of half-cake. "Mona, your half-cakes are delicious!"

Nand blushed and chuckled. "No … I couldn't."

Ashta addressed herself to the young woman. "I've been thinking, Nand. You're the hlyk. What if you reached out to Whitecur? Don't you think you could try to heal Mocean? Stop the freezing? Sheer told me yesterday that the process began when Mindrule stopped. It has to be linked."

"We're sure it is." Sofini handed the dish of half-cakes around. "The freezing is Mocean's reaction to Mindrule."

"We've talked a lot since that awful night." Mona took a sip of bukni. "And most of us have come to the same conclusion. At least, everybody in the New Council. Yet Mocean is an entity that can't be reached at will. Only kwirimoks can. And there's none left."

"Terri said you met Whitecur during your travels with Kaipekak." Bibiana licked wapui sauce off her finger, grinning at her older sister's frown.

"It was a long time ago, and I don't remember where." Nand warmed her hands around her mug. "Whitecur is what its name says. A cold current at the ocean bottom. It's like a snake; it moves constantly. It's never in the same place."

"I always thought kwirimoks could exchange thoughts with Whitecur …" Mona piled two more half-cakes on her plate.

"Did you? I don't think it's possible," Sofini said.

"I do, because I saw Washone raise a wave with his hand once. And I know where Whitecur can always be found." Theo finished the last bit of half-cake on her plate. "I met Whitecur there, and I fought it, and Washone got upset with me." She grimaced. "He yelled in my mind!"

"You did?" Sofini opened wide eyes.

"Where?" Bibiana asked.

"In Niumi. Beneath his studio."

"That seems rather logical," Mona said. "Someone wants to finish the half-cakes? I'll cook another batch for the boys."

Theo held out her plate. "The studio is where Washone's orgacomp is."

"Tell us your story!" Sofini smiled. "Please …"

"Washone wanted me to trace mentacomp configurations to Earth Metropolis with the orgacomp's help. We reached Farren's computer that day."

Mona turned around from mixing the batter. "Farren? The same Farren who's sleeping downstairs?"

"The same."

Ashta winked at her friend. "You never told me this story."

"Didn't have time. In any case, while I created the path, the orgacomp choked. So I went down in the water beneath the studio. It's not deep. There was green moss all over the orgacomp pipes. And while I pulled it off, a cold current tugged at my legs." She looked at Ashta. "Do you remember the Wansha ritual? That's when I encountered Whitecur the first time, and I didn't like it at all. I felt as if that … entity wanted to overpower me. So that day in Niumi, when Whitecur tried again …" She drank some bukni.

"What?" Bibiana asked.

"I struck back, and Washone yelled at me."

"You struck Whitecur?" Nand opened her eyes wide.

"With my feet, and mentally too … Washone had told me about Keith tampering with Whitecur, and I thought I was fighting Keith, not Whitecur."

"What a story!" Ashta said. "When did this happen?"

Theo smiled wryly at her friend. "When you were unwell. I stayed with Washone for several weeks."

"Well, in retrospect, I'd say you got it right—you were fighting Keith." Mona flapped several half-cakes onto a large dish. "Obviously, even the kwirimok hadn't realized it. Which explains why he was so angry."

"Oh, he knew, but not the extent of Keith's influence." Theo brushed invisible crumbs from the table. "I made a mess of things when I was here last. I'm sorry."

"Don't blame yourself." Nand leaned over to grab the pot of bukni and smiled at her neighbor. "You didn't know. Washone should've told you how Eridan functions."

"Nand," Mona asked, "what do you think of Ashta's idea?"

Nand poured some bukni into her mug. "I've been trying to reach out to every one of you, every sea creature, since yesterday, and I can't get through. I've been doing the same since I woke up this morning. It's not working at all."

"Whitecur is different." Bibiana entwined her fingers with Ashta's. "You should give it a try."

"If it's not risky." Sofini picked up the plates. "Terri and Davin would never let you endanger yourself."

Nand shrugged. "I don't see how it could be risky. I experienced the same thing as Theo, cold coils around my feet and body, and some sort of mental distraction. I didn't pay much attention to it. I'm more worried about Mocean itself. How do I get beneath Washone's studio if it's frozen?"

"It's been freezing from the top, with free water beneath the ice almost everywhere, even in the Shallow Seas," Mona turned around to explain. "That's why we can still find crabs and gather seaweed."

"I'll warm the water for you," Theo said. "With the orgacomp."

Nand touched her throat. "You can do that?"

"Yes. Its roots go straight from the studio to the ocean bottom. Like pipes. I'll merge, and we'll warm the water for you."

"What do you think, Nand?" Ashta asked. She rubbed her thumb over Bibiana's soft skin.

"I can try … but I'm not a kwirimok. I've no idea how to communicate with this entity." Tears brightened her eyes. She swallowed as she clenched her hands before her. "And I'm not worthy of its purity. I broke the Law several times. I participated in Xë's killing. And when we fought him, all of us in Pit 3," she glanced grimly at Theo and Ashta, "we provoked the waves in Eridan."

Theo blinked. As she stared at Nand, memories of that day in Pit 3 resurfaced. She gasped. "By the Winds!"

"It wasn't your fault! You didn't know," Ashta was quick to say. "None of us knew Mocean was that powerful."

"What happened exactly?" Sofini asked.

"How could you have provoked waves in Eridan?" Bibiana asked. "You were too far away."

"Xë tortured Farren to find out where Jack was," Nand explained. "He did it in front of our cells. He used his mind and an instrument called a stondor."

"Farren's mind is strong like Theo's. He invaded mine while we were on our way to free Nand and the Face Changers," Ashta added. "So, to protect me, Theo helped Farren find the tools to fight Xë in himself. But when we reached Pit 3, things got out of control."

"Farren sustained Xë's torture. Xë tried to shatter his mind, just when Ashta, Theo, Jack and their friend Smanul arrived. Theo …" Nand turned to Theo. "What did you do exactly? The waves I perceived were so strong, my mind blanked."

"I took him with me inside Mocean, I think." Theo pressed her hand against her mouth for a moment, reflecting. "When I received the mindblinder blast, I went into a coma. But for me, it wasn't a coma. I could think, and I was like a river flowing down into an ocean. So when Xë went after Farren, I took Farren with me deep into Mocean as a river. I sought protection within this mental Mocean, in a place where I'd been before." She frowned. "I never thought I … intruded in any way."

"How could you? Declan told me Mocean reacted to your presence with these rogue waves that filled our minds, and he ordered me to stop protecting you," Ashta revealed. "That's how he followed you inside this mental Mocean, and so did Xë. It was noisy, full of static. In Pit 3 and in our minds. In the end, I don't know who killed Xë."

"I think Farren did. I'm not sure." Theo folded her arms. "Afterwards, Declan mentioned a rogue wave, but he couldn't perceive Mocean or Eridan anymore."

"We had two huge waves," Bibiana stated. "One rose like a water wall. I saw it. I was in my sailboat. I'll never forget what it looked like before it crashed over me." She squeezed Ashta's fingers. "The second wave is the one Keith provoked, mental and physical. It's the one that caused the freezing."

Theo looked at all her neighbors. "I don't know how I can apologize. I …"

"There's no need." Nand reached out to pat Theo's arm. "I was ready to go against Xë myself to protect Farren. I would have, but thankfully you were strong enough to do it when I collapsed." She smiled.

"I would never have thought Mocean to be that powerful." Mona poured more batter into the pan.

"Xë still felt its pull years after moving to Redland. And so did we. Leaving Eridan doesn't mean severing ties with Mocean as we always believed." Nand caressed her fingers.

"Which means that you can still reach out to Mocean through Whitecur," Bibiana pointed out. "None of the Eridanis who were part of Mindrule can. But you, you still possess your strong, luminous mind." Nand turned a deeper red. "So if you can try to reach out to Whitecur, please do." She coughed to clear her voice. "Waves need to roll again, and life to return. The rest … We've lost it. We know we have."

Nand looked at Bibiana across the table. "But Keith is responsible for Mindrule, not the people …"

"Yes, and no. If one day we're once again able to think thoughts to others, we'll show you what we did, what we felt."

"Bibiana's right," Sofini added. "We had beauty, and we shattered it. Broken mirrors can't ever be repaired. Too many shards to find, to gather."

"But Mocean isn't a mirror. It's water, and waterdrops aggregate into something larger." Nand nodded at Theo. "Let's try."

CHAPTER 236

Assaulting a Savalwoman

12 June 3077, Standard Time (ST), Sixth Federal Era
Eridan (207th Cycle, Cuttlefish Season, Whirlpools' Blue
Year)—Oniraveen

Sheer appraised the Master Face Changer as he entered her sparse office, determined to keep her disappointment in check. She had hoped to work with him to restore Eridan. It wouldn't happen.

"Declan! I wondered where you were."

He had avoided her since his return, staying with the Face Changers and then spending the evening with his cousin Roisin-the-Bold.

He pressed both hands over his chest and bowed his head. "I'm so sorry about Carmen." His voice shook. "She was such a loving woman. I'll miss her."

Her double would have been horrified to learn how wrong she had been about this man whose petty reactions Carmen had tended to forgive with fond benevolence.

Sheer rubbed her hands to warm them, unable to get used

to the cold. "Thank you for your words. She's missed. What do you prefer? That we stay here, or walk outside?"

"I should be saying outside, since I have longed to be in Eridan for days. But quiet is what I need right now."

She carried Carmen's armchair in front of the bay window, and he took one of the chairs he disliked. She handed him a down blanket and tucked one around her own shoulders. There was no heating in the Fortress.

"I'm leaving," he said. "I wanted you to know."

"Why so soon? Eridooneen is stuck in ice. You can't resume your university classes yet. We're working on creating access to The Towers."

"I'm heading for Vatatui. The others, they're going home to their families."

What did he think? That he could do as he wished?

What would her double's take on this situation have been? Carmen would have insisted on attending this meeting, and Sheer would have said no, this was a matter she had to deal with alone: show who was in command, who took responsibility, what forthcoming changes to expect. They would have argued about his every word and attitude, as they often did, while they cooked dinner later, and Carmen would have surprised her with a kiss, grabbing her hand, pulling her down the corridor to their unmade bed, saying it's time to love and share and be strong.

Sheer pulled herself back to the present. "What about the Master Face Changer?"

"He's dead."

"What do you mean?"

"He died the day of the massacre." His gaze was direct, his voice strong, words probably thought and said to himself many times since the tragedy. "I sunk with my disciples and Half-Masters. The man you're talking to, he's a shadow. I survived because Xë needed to be defeated. But my soul stayed in Vatatui. Caught in a spiral I can't escape."

She was the only one left to be held accountable for the decisions that had probably led to the slaughtering of so many. Like Declan, she had rehearsed her words, and she voiced them without trembling. Carmen would have been proud of her.

"Washone and I share responsibility in this massacre."

His eyes fluttered and he sat up straighter. "You're right. Thank you for saying it. But do Eridanis know?"

What did he think? That she had reflected and come to this conclusion only to hide it?

"They will. I'm telling you first. There's lots of work to do; lots of questions need to be answered, investigations to be made. We must find out where we stand, what happened during Mindrule, what happened before, even if for the massacre, we have already gathered lots of information."

He flattened the down blanket over his thighs.

"Words can't describe the horror of that day."

"Drawings can."

He snorted. "You're relying on works of imagination?"

"I was suspicious at first, like you. Carmen opened my eyes."

"How?"

"She supported the rebels led by your friend Terri. It turns out that Nand sent him snapshots of the carnage before you departed."

"Nobody could communicate mentally that day."

Ashta had conceded during their long conversation the evening before that the Master Face Changer may feel threatened by Nand's mental strength. Her free mind and independence also antagonized him.

"Nand found a way. She's the hlyk, after all. That's how Terri, Sofini and Bibiana sailed to Vatatui and rescued the surviving Face Changers. That's how Bibiana drew those drawings, which have circulated widely among Eridanis. That's how people learned about the massacre."

"Split loyalty for the Savalwomen, then?"

She silently cursed him. He knew her well.

"Thanks to the thought-twisters, we spotted the masked archers," she said. "The majority hid in The Towers. Some of them couldn't stomach what they did. They returned, mostly to the Shallow Seas, where Bibiana's drawings were first shown. One of them attended a meeting; later he spoke to Davin. He gave us many names. The archers were arrested the day after Mindrule." She stood up. Shriveled blue sky, dirty-white landscape, a pallid sun. She missed the mixing blues of Eridan's waves, their energetic movement. "Astriv and The Kresdan are in custody here as well. The Fortress has turned into a prison."

Declan nodded. He got to his feet as well.

"Ashta talked to me yesterday." She willed the tall man beside her, the one Carmen used to call her friend, to face her.

He pressed his forehead against the window pane. "So, you know." His voice sounded hollow.

"I want to hear it from you."

He glanced her way without meeting her eyes, his hands in his pockets. "I can't. I need to think, and I can only do this alone."

"Do it here. We have rooms in the Fortress."

"And see Evetha every day? That's impossible!"

"What happened with her?"

He clenched his jaw, his fists, annoyance rising with his voice. "You said you talked to Ashta. Didn't you? Didn't she tell you?"

"I want you to tell me."

"I can't."

"Then I won't allow you to leave."

He whirled. "I can't stay here!"

"Evetha is a Savalwoman."

"I know."

"Do you? I don't think so. Otherwise, you wouldn't have come here to tell me that you were leaving." She clasped her frozen hands behind her back. "You assaulted a Savalwoman by taking the appearance of her lover. You, the Master Face Changer! Did you think I would let it go?"

"I told you I'm not the Master Face Changer anymore."

She stepped closer. "But you are, Declan. You acted as the Master Face Changer throughout your trip to Gambling Nova and back. It is the Master Face Changer who committed this despicable act."

He shook his head. "I don't understand what came over me."

"Weak defense. What I think is that you wanted to scuttle your order!"

"Of course not! It has nothing to do with the Face Changers."

"It has everything to do with them. And it spells a bleak future for all of us."

"What do you mean?"

She let her turmoil enter her voice. "Don't you get it? Nothing ever happened like this when we were all connected to Mocean. We were monitored. Enslaved in a kind of wellbeing that satisfied us. We lived, we slept, we sunk, our minds returned to our collective consciousness. We led our happy lives on a beautiful planet. Mocean prevented us from committing evil acts until your cousin became kwirimok. He had been tampering with Mocean for a long time."

"How did you find out?"

"Astriv and The Kresdan talk a lot. I know what took place, and when, and for how long. Your cousin sullied Mocean. He changed it. Nand warned us. Remember? She told us about erratic tides, smelly seaweed. Those were Mocean's reactions to Keith's intrusions."

He nodded, remembering that not long before Nand became the hlyk, her mother had warned him about erratic tides as well.

"And then Mindrule. We murdered people in Meranka."

"That's what Clobb hinted at. I don't believe it for one second."

"You should. It happened. Nightmares wake us up at night." She paced her office. "They reveal agony; they make us see our deed's stark truth. We can't rely on Mocean's soothing anymore. We are on our own. The same way you have been since you left. Severed from Mocean. And it is up to us to set our own limits. To decide between right and wrong. To take responsibility and not say, 'I can't explain what came over me.' Is this also your defense for outing Nand and trying to break her relationship up with Erlend—twice?"

He turned away from her, but she stepped into his path, forcing him to face her.

"Evetha's friends will help us put a judiciary system into place, and when it's organized, Savalwomen will find you and bring you back here. You'll stand trial for assaulting a Savalwoman, the same way Astriv, The Kresdan and the archers will be judged for their crimes."

"You're doing the right thing."

Flattery wouldn't work. "Think hard about what you'll say. A fair trial means having a lawyer to defend your interests. Find a person you trust, tell this person what you did and ask this person to defend you."

"I can defend myself."

"By stating that you don't know what came over you?"

The aircraft rose from Oniraveen Bay's frozen surface with a roar and flew low towards the open ice-sea.

"Where is it going?"

"To Niumi."

"For a visit?"

"No. There's a plan underway involving Nand's friends, and Ashta and Theo. Jack is a pilot, so he's flying the ship, and Farren and Nand's boyfriend are accompanying them."

"What plan? Is it dangerous?"

A bitter chuckle escaped her. "Dangerous? Have you not examined your surroundings? Eridan is dying. What could be more dangerous?" She collected a few documents on her desk. "Interviews about Vatatui are underway. We need your testimony."

"Can it wait?"

"No. But it can be done in the next few days."

"I'm not allowed to go?"

"No. Not before I talk to Evetha."

CHAPTER 237

Whitecur

*12 June 3077, Standard Time (ST), Sixth Federal Era
Eridan (207th Cycle, Cuttlefish Season, Whirlpools' Blue
Year)—Niumi*

Neither Nand nor Theo wanted to postpone the attempt to reach Whitecur. So, after they laid out their plan to the boys—as Mona nicknamed Terri, Davin, Erlend, Farren and Jack—the latter suggested taking everybody to Niumi with the SpaceSS aircraft, instead of a two-day trip in wind buggies.

After obtaining Sheer's go-ahead, they left Oniraveen before noon. Jack landed the aircraft in between the numerous hilly ice mounds that surrounded the island. They tramped across the still landscape. Many frozen wave curls cupped the shores. The buildings didn't seem to have suffered from the extreme climate conditions. Terri agreed with Farren that Niumi would be an ideal location to gather Eridanis for the upcoming interviews.

Theo led the group through the kitchen down to Washone's studio.

Nand stopped on the threshold and briefly closed her eyes while she gripped the doorframe.

"Are you all right?" Terri asked.

"Much pain lingers here." She braced herself and stepped inside. "It's different from the last time I visited. It was long ago." She shrugged. "The kwirimok didn't believe what I said about Mocean, so I stopped coming."

They had agreed that Davin, Terri and Ashta would accompany Nand to the bottom of Mocean. The four of them already wore ippini-lined bodysuits. They got ready, clipping feet-fins and caps over their heads and ears, and each fastening a diving headband light. Erlend helped Sofini and Bibiana carry the couch closer to the large hole in the center of the studio, and sat down with them. Straddled on a stool beside the orgacomp, Mona texted a message to Sheer on Jack's cell. Farren had lent the Savalwoman his own cell.

Theo caressed Llgun's dusty pipes before sitting in front of the orgacomp on another stool.

"Whatever happens," she told Jack and Farren, who were sharing Washone's armchair at her right side, "don't interfere; don't force me out of the merge. Even if I mumble, if I frown and grit my teeth. It can happen, and it doesn't mean anything; it's just a reaction. I never suffer when I merge. All right?"

"I'll try," Jack said. "But I don't like it."

"You never did." She grinned. "Farren, you promise?"

Farren nodded.

"Say it."

"I promise not to interfere in your merge."

"Good." She gazed at her lover and at her friend. "Stop worrying, both of you. I'll melt water with Llgun's help. It's nothing."

"If you say so." Jack folded his arms over his chest.

Responding to his concern, she embraced them both. "Trust me."

They hugged her back, each in his fierce manner.

She waved at the Eridanis. "I'll merge now." She plugged the corbilical, clipped on her headband and drew initial power from her Tatimori. She placed her hands over the spongy board and closed her eyes.

The energy drive surged stronger than anticipated and she reeled as she merged with Llgun again, sharing with *shehe* her many faceted experiences since their last fusion. She struggled not to enter an immediate, total merge. So much depended on Washone's young orgacomp.

When she had brushed her fingers over the keyboard before starting the merge she had feared that Llgun might have frozen up like the rest of the planet. Now that she wore her headband and was connected through the corbilical, she experienced some tremors.

She used Ian/Catdougal's imprint, and Llgun rejoiced, welcoming her with a shadowed energy that revealed the fear of eternal loss.

Her father's key to the network was composed of a series of pictures intermingled with numbers that she transmitted, opening her mind wider than she had ever done before, delving deep to retrace her past merges' imprints.

She first called forth Mmram, her father's orgacomp. Worry seeped into her at the lack of immediate connection: so much was at stake. Shyly, Llgun ventured forward, casting its feelers through space to reach out to the orgacomps whose imprints she carried inside her brain. Like its his counterparts,

Llgun probably knew about the network, since her father had experienced it with all the orgacomps he had met.

Galvanized, she let Llgun lead the search, and soon the connection with Mmram was established. She could now rely upon her father's orgacomp to gather momentum through the network.

She let *shehe* into her quest: to combine the orgacomps' energy and light to melt ice and return Mocean to motion.

Llgun's merge with Theo generated warmth. Ice melted around its roots.

Mmram agreed in her (*shehe* was in a female period of her existence) serious manner, and connected with OOtk and Vugeen. Leaning on the strength of her intimate bond with her father's three home orgacomps, Theo directed them towards the memory of her merge with Sham, Keith's orgacomp. The four orgacomps linked through her.

Theo expressed reservations about Ggov, Simpson's orgacomp. An enthusiastic Mmram overcame them. She reminded Theo that she disliked the way she had treated Ggov. Bathing their lonely companion in light was the orgacomps' aim.

Ggov, like Sham and Llgun, hadn't merged in a long time. The older members of the species, those who expanded with Catdougal's incentive, enveloped the younger orgacomps in ethereal colorful nets, tearing them away from intrusive dark thoughts provoked by bad merges and thrusting them into sharing's bouncy light.

Remembering Mmram's fascination with the rainrocks, Theo shared her experience with Iglölü's soul-painters. Data sparks flashed back and forth among the orgacomps. Theo gave up following, much less understanding.

When the cloud dissolved, Mmram shared a thought about Sprinkked Kwartz: he and his fellow dreamers had joined the network.

Theo became aware of her physical surroundings as if she had her eyes open. She saw Farren; she experienced his watchful stance, which, unlike Jack, he kept hidden, letting his brawan express their common concern.

She had no idea how long she had merged, but needed to find out the status. She removed her hands from the board. With an effort, she turned around. "Davin, can you check what's going on below?"

"Sure!" Davin, who sat near the edge of the hole with Nand, Terri and Ashta, slipped into the water.

The thin ice layer they had found when they entered Washone's studio had melted and water now reached the rim.

"Is it cold?" Farren asked.

Ashta tested it with her hand. "Tepid," she said.

Davin reappeared five minutes later, and Terri helped him out.

"There's plenty of water," Davin said. "It's freezing going down, but once I reached the bottom, it was warmer. Our headlamps will be useful. It's as dark as Abuion down there."

"It because of the ice covering the surface," Terri said.

"Exactly. There's an impressive white mass blocking the sun. The phosphorescent anemones are shriveled up. Ashta, do you really want to go down with us? It's like coldnight."

The Savalwoman grinned as she checked her fins. "I'm in for the experience."

"I saw the orgacomp pipes, Theo," Davin continued, "and most of them are ice-free. The water is warm next to them. So if you can keep doing what you're doing, we should be fine."

"Sure. Nand, Ashta?" Theo called. *I will be there for you if you need me. You can draw from our energy as much as you want.*

Nand and Ashta raised their heads and stared at Theo.

How did you do that? Ashta asked.

Do what?

Have a warm mind, Nand thought.

Theo smiled. "I've no idea! Must be the orgacomps. Good luck!" She turned towards Llgun and placed her fingers on the board once again.

"Let's go." Nand crouched in front of Erlend. She held on to his knees. "Erlend," she said. "It's true that I miss Kaipekak more than I thought would be possible. But I have you now. I'm not alone. Don't worry. I won't do anything stupid. I promise. And tomorrow, I'll face-change into Aslone." She smiled at Sofini and Bibiana. "Take care. Take care of Erlend." Erlend lunged forward and hugged her.

"Save your world," he whispered in her ear, "and come back to me quickly."

One after the other, they dove into the water.

You must let me stay as long as I need to, Nand thought to Ashta. *Terri and Davin will want to bring me back after a while, but I'm the one who decides. Can I trust you?*

This time, I'm your bodyguard. I'm here to protect you. If I feel that you're gone too long or too deep—I mean, if you don't answer me—I'll bring you back.

Nand nodded. She signed at Terri and Davin that she was fine.

Do you hear me? she repeated. There was not a flicker. She persisted. *I love you.*

They reached the ocean bottom. Davin was right. They bathed more in coldnight than bluewater.

Nand swam away from the pipes around which hot water now sizzled. Theo and the orgacomp were doing a great job. Warmth tucked at her bodysuit. She waved at her cousin and her brother and signed her departure into the ocean.

I won't intrude, but I'll watch out for you.

Nand nodded at Ashta and swam away.

The further she ventured, the colder the water. When the ice block above her dipped closer to the bottom, trapping her, she stopped. She closed her eyes and, holding herself upright against a protruding rock encased in ice, she stood still.

How would she notice a difference in the temperature with the water so cold around her already?

She uncurled her mind to encompass the mute ones surrounding her.

She thought of the kidadakh. She remembered the first time she had heard Kaipekak, Krilli, Kunnolik, Kaigalakval and Kahkval, the day of the hunt, the morning her life changed; she remembered reaching out to Kaipekak when she was forced to stay in Abuion—such a luminous day, when their minds had fused for the first time—how she had experienced the taste of krill, Kaipekak's sounding and breaching, the songs he sang. She remembered swimming beside him; she remembered clutching his fins; she remembered Firoloo and her smooth white skin; how they had fought zuglans near the coral barrier and saved a pod of fiskiorps; she remembered the slimy feel of schools of fish, and fiskiorps' whistles and clicks as they gathered together to catch mackerels and herrings. She remembered the tickling swish of green frothy waves, and the

softness of her mother's kisses; she remembered her melancholy. She remembered swimming and giggling in the lagoon
with Davin, Terri and Aslone when they were children. She remembered meeting Whitecur in the Abyss, once in the
Shallow Seas, often around Eridooneen and Oniraveen.

Cold water wrapped around her body.

Nand opened her eyes.

A frail, transparent young girl stood in front of her.

The distant rumbling of waves echoed.

Who was she?

Whitecur.

I thought Whitecur was male.

The girl's head dipped sideways.

Nand held out her hand. The girl floated away.

I'm afraid too, Nand thought. *And sad. Eridan is dying.*

The girl swam closer.

Nobody minded when I got sick.
Foul seaweed.
Stray tides.
Hot with fever.

Her slim shape shimmered before Nand.

Except you.
You cooled me with your winter-landscape dreams.
You listened to my songs, to my creatures.
You dreamed about me, you cared.
You left.
My waves no longer mine.

Nand raised both hands. *I'm back now. I want to help you again. Warm you this time.*

I am frozen.
I can't hear myself anymore
I can't feel movement.
It's too late.

It's not too late! We can help you melt your waves, save all your creatures.

I can't stop.

Listen to the sound of your waves. Nand brought sound to her memories of swimming with Kaipekak, breaching and splashing loudly. *Listen to the pops, the cracks, the bubbles. Remember seaweed's softness as it dances through your currents.*

The girl stood so close now that Nand could distinguish the outline of her eyes and hair, the same shape as hers.

I heard you when you returned.
You tickle me.
Yet why exist?

I miss the sound of your waves. I want to hear them again. Let me, let us—Nand remembered that she wasn't alone; she perceived Ashta, and Terri and Davin in the distance—*help you. Warm you.*

I won't be tamed anymore.

> *I won't be linked to those who used me,*
> *who scared me.*

Nand's tears dissolved in the water. Bibiana was right; Eridanis' loss was irremediable. *You won't. They can't reach you anymore. You're free.*

The girl lightly touched Nand's face, and her caress burned with the fire of ice.

> *But you can.*

Only if you want.
She swam away and returned. She stood in front of Nand.

> *You're not alone.*
> *Call the others.*
> *I want to meet them.*

Ashta? Can you join me with Davin and Terri? Whitecur wants to meet you too.

Whitecur? Ashta's mind was sprinkled with a mix of snowflakes and awe.

Terri, Davin and Ashta swam to where Nand stood.

Nand raised her hands. She signed for her friend, for her brother and cousin, to stay still and to wait for Whitecur to appear again.

This time, Whitecur's coils rose from between her feet. The girl uncurled like a fern's frond until she stood gracefully facing Nand.

Nand, the hlyk.
Heal me,
Heal them.

Whitecur turned towards Terri, standing on Nand's left, and morphed into a man his size. He opened his arms wide.

Terri, the poet.
You speak.
Make them listen.

Whitecur moved to Ashta and took the shape of an older woman. She smiled.

Ashta, the friend.
You protect.
Stay.

Whitecur faced Davin, with the appearance of a tall young man. He stood proud.

Davin, the hunter, the gardener.
Seek balance.
Always.

Whitecur morphed into the translucid young girl again when she turned to Nand.

River woman.
I like her lazy, lone waters.

She's warming me.

Theo, Nand thought. *Her name is Theo.*
Whitecur stayed a moment longer, then dissolved, and the cold surrounding them vanished.

A Strange World

*12 June 3077, Standard Time (ST), Sixth Federal Era
Eridan (207th Cycle, Cuttlefish Season, Whirlpools' Blue
Year)—Niumi*

Ashta emerged from the hole and Erlend helped her hoist herself up onto the margin. Nand appeared soon afterwards, followed closely by Terri and Davin. Sofini and Bibiana poured bukni in mugs; Mona served half-cakes.

Erlend embraced Nand, not minding her wet and cold skin, just thankful that he could hear her heart beating. He had kept his concern to himself, Nujise's warnings, what she feared—that Nand would sacrifice herself for her planet's wellbeing—after a literal reading of Eridan and Yelun's founding myths.

She had not. She held him, alive, exhausted, with a light in her eyes he had never seen before. Something loosened inside of him—the fear that had choked him since he had first seen her in the Guild ship, a forlorn figure grieving her frozen planet.

He hugged her, and she hugged him back. And he wondered about this strange world where he had followed her. She said that she needed to change, the bodysuit was too tight, and she walked out of the studio, promising to return at once, to recount what had taken place below.

The Eridanis beside him were subdued, those who had gone down lost in thoughts they seemed unable to share. At least not immediately. Erlend perched on a stool and took his sketchbook out. Terri and Sofini shared the couch with Bibiana and Ashta; Davin still sat on the margin of the hole, his legs dangling in the water, a handsome and grave athletic figure. He raised his head as Erlend outlined his position and he smiled, and this smile soothed some of Erlend's longing. He did not miss Redland, though. Only Cowan and Nujise, and some friends and landscapes.

He resumed his drawing. His hand shook: the memories of his bashing were still too raw to be put to rest.

"Everything all right?"

Erlend nodded at Jack, who had this spooky way of knowing when to pull him away from the edge.

"Did Theo finish her merge?" he asked as he closed his sketchbook.

"Not yet. How's Nand?"

"She seemed fine. She went to change."

"Did she tell you anything?"

"No. But something happened down there. They all have strange expressions."

Jack thumped him on the shoulder and walked away.

Two hours later, they sat together around a large table in the kitchen. At first, caught up in an excitement-linked general exhaustion, they postponed any discussion about Nand meeting

Whitecur, and Theo and the orgacomps melting ice, while they helped themselves to the heaps of food Mona had cooked.

Erlend sat opposite Nand. He kept his sketchbook at hand while words slowly began to be exchanged around him. Theo's merge had ended nearly an hour after the four Eridanis had returned to the surface. They admitted having encountered Whitecur—a sea-water Face Changer. Jack asked many questions about this mental and physical encounter, and Farren teased him relentlessly. Their banter eased the tired, uncertain mood. Theo and Llgun had indeed warmed water beneath the studio, and Nand had exchanged thoughts with Whitecur, but the challenge remained huge, given the planet's scale.

Theo tried to stay awake and eat her fish soup. Erlend portrayed her sluggishly holding her spoon, holding her head up against her raised hand, her eyelids fluttering as she slowly slipped into sleep. Farren and Jack didn't hide their worry when they carried her to bed, and she didn't wake up. Generally, she was a light sleeper, Farren explained when he came by later to wish the rest of them a good night.

Before Theo and her men went to bed, Terri recited Sorja'u's prophecy. He explained the importance of Whitecur's words, giving the four of them an attribute.

Life in Eridan would never be the same again, Nand's cousin said, a catch in his voice. Mindrule had severed their link to Mocean, and it could not be revived. He hoped that, thanks to Nand and Theo, the freezing process had stopped. Maybe one day they could restore some form of mental communication among themselves. Their former joyful life, always connected to the collective consciousness, was over. Memories to be grieved while new ones were created. When the ice melted and Mocean became a moving ocean again, they would find a different meaning to their lives.

CHAPTER 239

The Call

*13 June 3077, Standard Time (ST), Sixth Federal Era
Eridan (207th Cycle, Cuttlefish Season, Whirlpools' Blue
Year)—Near Niumi*

The call originated from the deep.

It tore Theo away from her sleep, away from Farren's warm and secure embrace. She rose from the bed and tiptoed out of the room. Jack opened an eye as she crossed his room. She winked and pressed a finger over her lips.

On the landing, she opened the common wardrobe and found a bodysuit in her size. She put it on, picked out feet-fins and a swim cap, and walked out. She hastened along the side of the building in the crisp early-morning air, then down the steps leading to Washone's studio.

The call spurred her on.

Inside the lit studio, she caressed the orgacomp and walked to the hole.

The call sang in her head as she sat down on the margin. She clipped the fins onto her feet and tied the light headband over her swim cap.

She entered the warm water. She took her time, her hands gripping the edge as she took deep breaths to prepare herself.

"What are you doing?" Jack rushed to the side as she let go of the ledge. "Where's your oxygen tank?"

"I don't need any."

She somersaulted and dove into the dark waters.

The call's intensity diminished as she swam deeper.

She reached the bottom and examined her surroundings. At dinner, the Eridanis had described a dreary underwater landscape. Her heart tightened as she discovered its drabness. Too soon for umbelliferous anemones to sway, for enchanting colors to brighten rocks.

The water temperature was mild, and a slim beam of light poured from above. Maybe someone had dug a hole in the ice cap. She checked the orgacomp's wet roots: smooth and clean. Holding herself upright on a protruding rock, she waited.

As the call faded, a cold current wrapped itself around her legs and arms.

Something nudged at her consciousness.

Different from her experience during the Wansha ritual.

This time, it stayed at the door of her mind.

She let go and plunged her hands into the cold current, feeling its power through her pores, her limbs.

River woman.

The echo of a sound, a thought, an emotion; too remote, too flimsy, too alien for her to grasp.

We'll never mix.

And yet … the something poking at her mind reminded her of daydreaming with the rainrocks. Except that they celebrated motionlessness, and Mocean was all about movement.

Evetha, the Lonely One.

Theo remembered getting lost in the ocean during the Wansha ritual, fighting Whitecur.

This time was different.

She caressed the current.

No numbness; no need to surrender.

Teach them to be unique, alone.
Teach them about living and sinking,
about being one.

Far away, a wail crossed the ocean.

A kidadakh!

Theo opened her eyes.

The cold current's coils vanished.

Had she dreamed?

Where was she?

Nothing seemed familiar. Above her, ice covered the surface.

Theo?

She looked around. To her right, Nand waved at her.

She joined the young woman and followed her as she swam towards the left. The ice sheet gave way to ice floes, and they emerged from the ocean to hoist themselves onto a floating ice block.

Theo breathed deeply to quieten her thumping heart. "How did you find me?"

"Jack woke me up. He worried because you didn't come back. You swam far."

"It was Whitecur. I thought I hadn't moved at all. Where are we?"

"See the trees over there to the right? That's Niumi. We're about one hundred arcs from the shore, opposite the small cove by the pine trees. Look at them! They found canoes. They'll soon be here."

"I heard a kidadakh, I think."

"So did I, when I searched for you. It's good news; it means that some ice melted."

Theo rubbed her arms and jumped up and down to keep warm. The ocean had been milder than the nipping breeze.

"Was it Kaipekak?"

"No. I'm almost sure now that he sunk. I can't reach him. I don't know if it's related to Mindrule or if he just forgot how to communicate with me in my absence." She blew on her fingers. "He's a young kidadakh, and he's like me. Nobody taught us to be hlyks."

"Will you be all right?"

"I think so. I understood this other kidadakh's image-thoughts. Mocean's creatures need me."

Around them, the floes drifted on the slowly melting blue-green waters.

"So you're feeling better than yesterday when we arrived?"

Nand nodded. "Much, thanks to you. There's so much to do.

I want Erlend to see Eridan as it was before." She shrugged in the dainty manner Farren was so fond of. "I restored some of Davin's and Terri's ability to exchange thoughts last night. We found another canal after meeting Whitecur, so I'm hopeful."

"They must be relieved, and so must you."

Wavelets lapped the sides of their unstable ice block.

Nand smiled.

"It's a beginning."

THE END

REVIEWS OF *TROUBLE*:

Trouble is a book about fascinating worlds, difficult choices and destiny.

—Fany Van Hemelen, *Goodreads*

I found the storyline interesting and the character development was great. The style of writing was spot on. I really enjoyed it.

—*Lisa's Books, Gems and Tarot*

Hybrids takes place in a unique sci-fi world filled with ideas and norms common to humans. Jennie Dorny writes a delightful story shimmering with the beauty of possibility.

—Amanda Murello, *Indies Today*

This book gave me definite water-world feels! I loved the story and plot, I loved the writing and I felt like the author has a real talent for this! The characters were also very well developed.

—Paige Green, *Goodreads* and *Reedsy*

REVIEWS OF *VENGEANCE*:

Jennie Dorny has a vast imagination and a precious gift in the ability to paint an exquisite picture with words. (…) *Hybrids Volume 2: Vengeance* is a whimsical and deeply philosophical fiction novel that proves that a sequel can be even better than the first!

—Amanda Murello, *Indies Today*

REVIEWS OF *FEAR*:

This riveting novel relies more on interplanetary action and rectifying a crime than on world building or character development. The plot moves quickly and the stakes are high. Although the book takes readers to a wide variety of stunning scenery, my favorite location in these vibrant Hybrids novels is always Eridan. From the salty air to the intimidating Saval-women, the small planet is a delight to visit by means of Jennie Dorny and her winsome words. Jennie Dorny has hit her stride with Hybrids, Volume Three: Fear, which is a real treat for fantasy lovers.

—Amanda Murello, *Indies Today*

This book is filled with more action than the other ones and is a fast-paced story. Nevertheless, the author does write, like usual, with a touch for detail and it is again a beautiful fantasy story. Jennie Dorny has written again an original book and by reading more editions of this series I am more and more confident this could be a wonderful series on screen too. (…) So just dive into the first stories to follow the background and be completely blown away.

Just a warning, when you start reading this captivating fantasy series you will enter a world that you will never forget anymore and just like me you get hooked to the books.

—Fany Van Hemelen, *Goodreads*

GLOSSARY

Abuion: Underwater city in the Southern Abyss (Eridan).

Abyssans: Eridanis who live at the bottom of the ocean.

Adonine tea: Herbal tea (Redland).

Airmob: Aerial motorcycle (E-Met).

Airvan: Swift flying car used by Skodraks (Gambling Nova).

Akadongo: Series of breathing exercises practised daily by Eridanis living in coldnight.

Akol: Bubbly green alcoholic beverage (Eridan).

Apple sissli: Exquisite non-alcoholic fermented beverage combining apple juice and yellow sissli pollen (found everywhere).

Aqualing: Word to designate Eridanis.

Aquaport: Platform where off-planet spaceships land and take off in Eridooneen (Eridan).

Aquastreet: Water-filled streets in Eridooneen (Eridan).

Aquatrain: Underwater train that runs along the Kerven Archipelago (Eridan).

Arc: Unit of measurement between a meter and a yard (Eridan).

Archipelagian: Eridani living in the Kerven archipelago (Eridan).

Asparadish: Crunchy vegetable (Earth Metropolis).

Astrocloggs: Action figures.

Bananor: Banana-shaped red fruit (Eridan).

Barrios: District surrounding Rezghan's City where non-SpaceSS members reside (Earth Metropolis).

Battersea: Ground-level spaceport where ships for hire are easily found (Earth Metropolis).

Bissub: Underwater vessel for two people (Eridan).

Blue Alagafa: Sea lettuce that grows in Oniraveen Bay. Main ingredient in Blue Alagafa soup.

Blue Exan: Tall building where SpaceSS agents work (Earth Metropolis).

Bluewater: Middle level in the ocean's depths where most marine creatures swim (Eridan).

Bodysuit: Piece of clothing worn by Eridanis. It covers their whole body, regulates their temperature and protects them.

Brawan: Term used between married homosexual men. The lesbian equivalent is Koban. Used mainly in Earth Metropolis.

Bubflat: Underwater apartment in Eridan (name comes from bubble, because of their round and aggregated shape).

Bukni: Bitter tea (Eridan).

Charlattee: A card game that resembles poker (Eridan).

Choctea: Hot beverage mixing dark cocoa and black tea.

Clearwater: First level in the ocean's depths where all colors are visible.

Cluexxan roast: High-protein vegetarian dish served mainly in spacecraft.

Coldnight: Deepest level in the ocean's depths, where people from the Abysses live.

Corbilical: Wire used to connect a person to a computer.

Cycle: In Eridan, each cycle is composed of twelve years. The cycle of years is an association of colors and worlds. There are four colors—orange, brown, blue and white—and three worlds—vegetal, marine and aerial. An element of each of the three worlds corresponds to a color.

Dadoo: Name for father, daddy (Eridan).

Darrapi: A network of wagons that brought prisoners from one part of the Dome to the other (Gambling Nova).

Dip3: Interstellar payphone.

Dome: Name of the prison erected in Gambling Nova. Off-planet visitors access it from the spaceport situated at its summit.

Double: Among Savalwomen, the name given to each partner in a couple (Eridan).

Druska: Derogatory word to define homosexuals (Redland).

Dwetwal: Eridani name for orca.

Earth Metropolis (E-Met): Name of the city-planet where SpaceSS is located.

Elders: Dead Eridanis who are the kwirimok's counselors. They talk in his head.

Eridan: Small planet covered by a living ocean. Inhabitants: Eridanis. Adjective: Eridani.

Eridooneen: Eridan's underwater capital backed against the main island in the Kerven archipelago.

Executive Exan: Square building where the Spylady works (Earth Metropolis).

Exploplan: Nuong-based company that sends out volunteers to explore uncharted planets.

Face Changer: Eridani who can change gender and appearance at will. Face-changing is a spiritual search.

Fadjiggle: Flat crêpe eaten in Redland.

Fedeconocs: Company that uses Federal convict labor.

Federacy: Organization that regroups planets under Nuong's executive and political rule.

Fedgad: Currency used around the Federacy.

Fegÿ: Pinkish, stinky perennial flower that cures rotflu. Found in Tlelgäü.

Fiskiorp: Eridani name for dolphin.

Flar: Flame-thrower weapon (Gambling Nova).

Frenink: A stupid person (Eridan).

Frybrain whistle: Device used in Nexus to eradicate infrared connections and computer circuits in cyborgs' brains.

Fudron: Small jets (Gambling Nova).

FuzFuz: Small compact home computer.

Gambling Nova: Federal prison-planet where political prisoners are sent. The prison itself is a hermetically enclosed Dome erected in a desert. By extension, Gambling Nova is Redland's common name for those who live off-planet.

Garden-island: Islands scattered all over the ocean in Eridan where Eridanis grow plants and vegetables.

Genuine: Hand-held computer used by Metropolice officers (Earth Metropolis).

Gikodalh: Eridani name for sperm whale.

Gobrinee: Shellfish found in the sand (Eridan).

Gold Mines: High-security district outside the Dome where the most dangerous prisoners are sent (Gambling Nova).

Greens (the): Incurable disease (Eridan).

Guild: Independent political organization which fights corruption and settles disputes.

Half-cakes: Eaten at breakfast in Eridan, half-cakes resemble pancakes.

Half-Master: Among Face Changers, rank allowing former disciples to teach.

Herhis: Possessive adjective used in relation to orgacomps.

High-City: In the Dome, the upper level that houses the greenhouse (Gambling Nova).

Hlyk: Mental bond between an Eridani woman and a sea mammal. By extension, the name of the woman who shares the bond.

Iglölü: Continent on Tlelgäü where fegÿ is cultivated. By extension, the name of the federal penitentiary housed on it.

Ippini: Eridani name for seal.

Jilong: Green tea (Earth Metropolis).

Julepa: Name of a gang of street fighters in Nexus, specialized in cyborg tracking.

Junk City: Thriving salvage-yard hub (pioneer settlement in a mining planet).

Juno Rap: Name of one of the Julepas' mottos.

Jutuq: Famous revered warriors in Reddish nomad lore (Redland).

Kerdakulik: Eridani name for rorqual.

Kerven: Eridan's main archipelago.

Kidadakh: Eridani name for humpback whale.

Korok: In the Abyss, collective reproof of an individual after an action that discredits the community (Eridan).

Kqad: Strong coffee (Gambling Nova).

Krandemon: Equivalent of "My God"; originates from Ochrock.

Kwirimok: Spiritual leader (Eridan).

Kwisimok: Spiritual leader (Yelun).

Law (the): In Eridan, law that prohibits an Eridani from reading another Eridani's mind without permission.

Low-City: In the Dome, the ground level that houses the districts where prisoners are held (Gambling Nova).

Mamin: Name for mother, mommy in Eridan.

Master-Buffer: An Eridani whose mind protects and heals others.

Mentacomp: Mental link established with an orgacomp.

Metalaz: Gang in Sub-City (Gambling Nova).

Metropolice: Police in Earth Metropolis.

Mhuol: Desert plant used as a drug or a medicine (Redland).

Mindblinder: Weapon used by Savalwomen, which combines laser and brain waves to harm someone's mind (Eridan).

Mind Men: Name for Keith of Rain Forest's followers (Eridan).

Mindread (to): To read the mind of another without permission (Eridan).

Mindrule: The use of Eridanis' collective consciousness to control other worlds.

Mocean: Sentient living entity whose appearance is the ocean in perpetual movement. Eridanis are linked to Mocean through their dreams.

Monosub: Underwater vessel for one person (Eridan).

Nexpee: Cyborg police officer (Nexus).

Nexus: Planet known for its gangs and cybernetics activity.

Norinori: Expensive, card-sized miniature computer, carried on one's wrist.

Niumi: Island where the current kwirimok resides (Eridan).

No-Ringer: Kwirimok's status (Eridan).

Nuong: Federal capital and planet.

Observers: Name given to Guild agents.

Octonitron: Small bomb.

O'dahb: Necklace worn by Nomad men (Redland).

Omniliner: Cargo spaceship.

Oniraveen: Aqua-troglodyte city in Kerven, where the Saval-women's Fortress is situated (Eridan).

Orgacomp: Hermaphroditic organic computer.

Ourlane: Town set in an icefield in the Northern Abyss (Eridan).

Outersuit: Garment worn over the bodysuit (Eridan).

Ovolgane: A stringed instrument (Eridan).

Paradox doors: Invisible doors that open on secret corridors inside the Dome (Gambling Nova).

Pepper sweetzers: Spicy crackers.

Pistolaz: Laser gun (Gambling Nova).

Pixodrum: Drum made with coconut shells (Eridan).

Plasteck: Material used to build sailboats (Eridan).

Pubhub: Pub (E-Met).

Rainrocks: Sentient beings living in Tlelgäü.

Redland: Name of the planet where the Gambling Nova prison is located, so named for the color of its deserts. Inhabitants: Redlanders. Adjective: Reddish.

Resh: An Eridani belonging to the Major Rings who can welcome another's thoughts and memories before that person dies and returns the memories to Mocean.

Rezghan's City: Earth Metropolis district only occupied by SpaceSS staff and their families.

Ring of Mindread: Circle that spins around an Eridani's iris when she/he mindreads. Each ring has a different color. They are revealed during the Tanhassee ritual and determine an Eridani's mental strength. There are four Minor Rings (Kelp, Night, Wind, Fire), four Major Rings (Earth, Sky, Sea, and the No-Ring, the kwirimok's invisible ring). Declan is a Ring of Sea; Washone is a No-Ringer.

Rockrowdies: Group of prisoners living in Sub-City (Gambling Nova).

Rotflu: Deadly flu that causes a swift deterioration of the internal organs.

Rotweed: Eridani curse word.

Rovigon: A shawn-like instrument (Eridan).

Savalwoman, Savalwomen: Female warriors in Eridan who handle the defense of the planet and its inhabitants.

Sbogbone: Zneecat food.

Season: There are four seasons in Eridan: Oyster Season (spring), Cuttlefish Season (summer), Jellyfish Season (fall) and Green Spray Season (winter). A season is made of eight tenens (eighty days), with the seasons each separated by a holiday: krill day (between Oyster and Cuttlefish), sand day (between Cuttlefish and Jellyfish), star day (between Jellyfish and Green Spray) and fog day (between Green Spray and Oyster).

Sharm: God's name (Redland).

Shean: Material used for clothes (Earth Metropolis).

Shehe: Pronoun used to refer to an orgacomp.

Shield-Master: Major Rings who protect Minor Rings during mental blasts (Eridan). Both Declan and Washone are Shield-Masters.

Shoshosh bar: Bar where Eridanis can work and drink.

Sink (to): Verb generally meaning "to die" in Eridan.

Skodrak: Guards in charge of security and defense in Gambling Nova.

Slunks: Carnivorous beasts, half-lynx, half-wolf (Yelun).

Smenn: Name of Redland's first inhabitants.

Smooze: Cracker.

Soyouna: Cigarette brand (found everywhere).

Spacebooze: Alcoholic beverage available everywhere.

Spaceport 21: Spaceport in Earth Metropolis.

SpaceSS: Space Secret Services. Founded by Shadaran Alvez. Its headquarters are in Earth Metropolis. Its Academy is in Ochrock.

Spylady: Name of the SpaceSS leader. Masculine: Spylord.

Stockey: Device used for data storage.

Stondor: Pen-like object used to pry into prisoners' minds (Gambling Nova).

Sub-City: In the Dome, the underground level where prisoners who have finished their term live (Gambling Nova).

Suni Sisters: Women's sorority in Redland.

Suprasub: Underwater vessel for several people (Eridan).

Swazzi: Strong wind which blows in Redland at night.

Sweetzers: Tasty appetizers (Sub-City/Redland).

Symb: Person who lives with a symbiont.

Symbiont: A sentient pet-like being that lives in symbiotic relationship with some human beings.

Tanhassee: Ritual by which Eridanis find their Ring of Mindread.

Tatimori: The best laptop available.

Tenen: A ten-day sequence (Eridan). Each tenen in a season has a different name: seaweed, night, wind, sun, earth, sky, sea, salt.

Th'an(s): Name of the people living in Yelun.

The Towers: Keith of Rain Forest's current underwater residence in Eridooneen (Eridan).

Thought-twister: Young person in Eridooneen who hides instinctive reactions under unrelated thoughts and fights Keith of Rain Forest, usually in groups or gangs (Eridan). Mainly Rings of Night, Wind and Fire.

Thumo: Savalwomen movements and exercises (Eridan).

Tlelgäü: Planet where the rainrocks live and where the Iglölü penitentiary is. Tlelgäüin: name of the inhabitants.

Tlelgow: Old language spoken in Eridan.

Venuver: Beer available everywhere.

Volcano kiss: A chocolate cupcake with melted chocolate sauce inside.

Wadda: Huge hairy quadruped (Yelun).

Wansha: Ritual by which a novice becomes a Savalwoman (Eridan).

Wapui: Sweet and juicy orange fruit (Eridan).

Whaldan: Abyssmen who stay at the bottom of the ocean during a kidadakh hunt (Eridan).

Whauld: The Abyssman who organizes kidadakh hunts (Eridan).

Whitecur: A cold current which is Mocean's physical expression, its essence (Eridan).

White Ring: Abyss people's genetic deficiency (Eridan).

Xnig: Strong Eridani alcohol.

Xplo-bullet: Bullet containing a lethal poison which slowly dissolves into the blood and cannot be extracted.

Yelun: Cold planet. Yelun's inhabitants are called the Th'ans.

Yeold: Name of community leaders in the Abysses (Eridan).

Yimdo: A word in Tlelgow used by a kwirimok to sustain Mocean's mental presence.

Znamuz: Grandmother zneecat, responsible for its descendants' wellbeing.

Zneecat: Alien cat originating from Nexus, used to detect cyborgs.

Zuglan: Eridani name for shark.

(first name alphabetical order)

Aïlin Borgen – Mona, Bibiana and Sofini's younger sister. (Eridan)

Alk – Tamia Stewart's granddaughter. (Redland)

Ameli – Terri and Aslone's mother; Nand's aunt. (Eridan)

Anabel – Face Changer, Half-Master. (Eridan)

Annie Miller – Sue's daughter; Jack and Farren's goddaughter. (SpaceSS)

Arika – Sign language teacher. (Eridan)

Arthus – Sharra's husband; Nand's and Davin's father. (Eridan)

Ashta Coral – Savalwoman. (Eridan)

Aslone Misruni – Terri's older brother; Face Changer. (Eridan)

Astriv – Face Changer, Half-Master. (Eridan)

Axonna – Face Changer, Half-Master. (Eridan)

Beruk Xë – Eridani renegade. (Eridan and Gambling Nova)

Bibiana Borgen – Sofini's twin. Artist. (Eridan)

Bill (William) Morning – Head of the Department of Foreign Diplomacy. (SpaceSS)

Captain Kirby – Smuggler.

Carmen – Savalwoman. Sheer's double. (Eridan)

Cass – Face Changer, Half-Master. (Eridan)

Clive – Face Changer, Half-Master. (Eridan)

Colonel Ty – In charge of the Gold Mines. (Gambling Nova)

Cowan MacRae – Clan leader; Farren's friend. (Redland)

Crazy Moon – Silver Blue's sister. (Yelun)

Cyand Emmett – Cyborg. Real name Jeff Taylor. (SpaceSS)

Darran – Lonetom's brother. Husband of Elimar. (Turtle Planet)

Dave Remesh – Sycal's lover and advisor. (Ochrock)

Davin Kahini – Nand's brother; Sharra's son. (Eridan)

Declan Reel – Keith's cousin. Master Face Changer. (Eridan)

Deirdre – Declan's mother. (Eridan)

Derek Clobb – Guild leader. (SpaceSS)

Didi – Face Changer, Half-Master. (Eridan)

Donatella Simpson – The Spylady; Max's older sister. (SpaceSS)

Dylan – Declan's uncle. (Eridan)

Ehr – Archer and musician; Smanul's friend. (Redland)

Elimar – Darran's wife. (Turtle Planet)

Erlend MacRae – Cowan's brother. Artist. (Redland)

Ethelwin Gorani – Poet and artist, member of the Wind Followers clan. (Redland)

Farren Megan – Jack's partner/brawan. Livia's brother; Nujise's son. SpaceSS Agent. Also calls himself Dag Smith. (Redland and SpaceSS)

Fern Maddiogga – Theo's mother; Ian MacDougal's wife. Nurse and weaver. (Redland)

Feyn – Face Changer, Half-Master; Declan's assistant. (Eridan)

Finn – Declan's father; Deirdre's husband; Master Face Changer. (Eridan)

Firoloo – Dolphin. (Eridan)

Ggov – Donatella's orgacomp. (SpaceSS)

Heris – mythical character. (Yelun)

Ian MacDougal – Theo's father. Also known as Catdougal. (Redland)

Issavern – Northern Abyss yeold.

Jack Finch – Farren's partner/brawan. SpaceSS Agent. Also known as Kane Budrock. (SpaceSS)

Jered Bakamo – Lawyer. (SpaceSS)

Joos – Face Changer, Half-Master; Declan's oldest friend. (Eridan)

Kaipekak – Nand's whale. (Eridan)

Kane Megan – Nujise's husband; Farren and Livia's father.

Kanner Talmand – Jack's grandfather. Owner of the Talmand Factories. (Ochrock)

Keith of Rain Forest – Declan's cousin. (Eridan)

Kij – Face Changer, Half-Master. (Eridan)

Kilu – Suni Sister. Friend of Theo's mother. (Redland)

King Ystffan – Keith of Rain Forest's brother. (Eridan)

Korund – Face Changer, Half-Master. (Eridan)

Lady T'ang – Homeless. (SpaceSS)

Laura – Jack's aunt. (Ochrock)

Lilrain – Keith's grandmother. (Eridan)

Linda Blake – One of Jack's colleagues. (SpaceSS)

Livia Megan-MacDougal – Farren's sister. Malcolm MacDougal's wife. (Redland)

Llgun – Washone's orgacomp.

Logan – Scavenger leader.

Lonetom Winter Creek – Jack's oldest friend. Librarian. (SpaceSS)

Lottie – Jack's mother. (Ochrock)

Malcolm MacDougal – Theo's cousin; Livia's husband. (Redland)

Max Simpson – Donatella Simpson's younger brother. (SpaceSS)

Mmram – Ian MacDougal's orgacomp.

Mona Borgen – Oldest sister of Bibiana, Sofini and Aïlin. (Eridan)

Nand Ath Sharra – Davin's sister, Sharra's daughter. Hlyk. (Eridan)

Nora – Adoptive child of Captain Kirby.

Norwen – Ashta's ex-double; Declan's ex-lover.

Nujise – Farren and Livia's mother; Theo's godmother. Belongs to the Wind Followers clan. Husband was called Kane.

OOtk – Theo's orgacomp. (Redland)

Priest (the) – Sons of God Leader.

Rianne Dove – Freelance spy. (SpaceSS)

Roger – Jered's partner. Dancer. (SpaceSS)

Rogerod – Southern Abyss yeold. (Eridan)

Roisin the Bold – Declan's oldest cousin. (Eridan)

Rory Boyle – Farren and Jack's friend. Former SpaceSS Agent; Guild Observer. (SpaceSS)

Samosa (Fagan) – Prison governor. (Iglölü)

Shadaran Alvez –Radical lesbian who founded SpaceSS. Sil Anchoressa is her other name. (SpaceSS); Astrallan is her brother.

Sham – Keith's orgacomp. (Eridan)

Sharra Ath Erwen – Nand and Davin's mother; hlyk. (Eridan)

Sheer (Sheeroia) Tellu – Savalwomen leader. Paired with Carmen. (Eridan)

Silver Blue – Crazy Moon's brother. (Yelun)

Smanul – Jimmy's older brother. Ehr's friend. (Gambling Nova)

Sofini Borgen – Bibiana's twin. (Eridan)

Sprinkked Kwartz – A rainrock. (Iglölü)

Sue Miller – Annie's mother; Jack and Farren's assistant. (SpaceSS)

Sycal Veld– Dean of the SpaceSS Academy; Jack's godmother; Dave Remesh's lover. (SpaceSS Academy)

Tarbel Mogud – Governor of Gambling Nova. (Gambling Nova)

Terri Misruni – Nand's cousin. Aslone's brother. Good friend of Carmen. (Eridan)

Thedda Thorn – Works in the Department of Foreign Diplomacy. (SpaceSS)

The Kresdan – Keith of Rain Forest's second-in-command. (Eridan)

Theo Maddiogga – also known as Althea MacDougal, Evetha the Solitary One, Theodan Alvez. (Redland, Eridan, SpaceSS)

Timaï – Empath teacher. (Eridan)

Valenta Thibb – Farren's best friend. Saskia's girlfriend. (SpaceSS)

Vilmar – Face Changer, Half-Master. (Eridan)

Vugeen – Ian MacDougal's orgacomp. (Gambling Nova)

Washone – Kwirimok. (Eridan)

Wendella – Keith of Rain Forest, Roisin the Bold and King Ystffan's mother; Dylan's wife; Declan's aunt. (Eridan)

Willi – Captain Kirby's oldest adoptive son.

Yunu – Beruk Xë's father. (Eridan)

Yussu Johnston – Leader of the Wind Followers, the storytellers' clan. (Redland)

Zineb – Nomad leader. (Nexus)

ACKNOWLEDGEMENTS

Thank you, first and foremost, to my dearest friend Hélène de Coustin, who read and read again, over many years, the numerous drafts of *Hybrids*, first in French and then in English. Thank you for your advice, enthusiasm and readiness to talk about the characters and plot. Thank you also for boosting my spirits when discouragement threatened.

Thank you to my wonderful English editor deRaismes Combes, who edited this mammoth book (now published in four volumes) and thank you to Catherine Dunn for proofreading this book and giving it its much-needed professional touch. Thank you to Maureen Cutajar for the layout and typesetting, and to Robin Vuchnich for the covers.

Thank you to my family supporters: Alice and Jildaz, my mother Anne; and thanks to Jean-René.

A special thanks to John Thompson, John Donatich, Ines ter Horst, Asbjørn Overas, Tina Hegeman, my "work" friends, who have known about this project for years and who question me each time we meet in Frankfurt and London: I finished it, and it's published now!

And thank you to my friends, always there to support me and help me, thank you for being there in good times and hard times: Stéphanie Beaupré, Barbara Le Goff, Antonella Di Trani, Marie-Claude Bianchini, Laurent Samy and Dominique Renoux.

Jennie Dorny was born in 1960 in Newton, Massachusetts. She lives and works in Paris with her three cats. She is both French and American. She studied American literature and civilization, Italian and history of art at three Parisian universities. She wrote her Master's thesis about contemporary Irish poetry after spending a year in Dublin. She loves words and languages, and can spend hours exploring a thesaurus. Over the years, she has studied Spanish, Japanese, Hindi and sign language, and recently took up Italian again. She has published in French *Gambling Nova* (1999), *Eridan* (2002) and *Les Cupidons sont tombés sur la tête* (*Mischievous Cupids gone Crazy*, 2007). *Gambling Nova* and *Eridan* are partial, earlier versions of *Hybrids*; science-fiction novels that in many ways deal with the question of gender.

TITLES IN ENGLISH
BY JENNIE DORNY

Hybrids, Part 1: *Trouble*

Hybrids, Part 2: *Vengeance*

Hybrids, Part 3: *Fear*

Hybrids, Part 4: *Hope*

I hope you enjoyed the four volumes of Hybrids as much as I enjoyed writing this whole book. I invite you to connect with me at any of the coordinates below. I look forward to hearing from you!

Visit my website:
www.jenniedorny.com
Email address:
contact@jenniedorny.com
Facebook Author Page:
www.facebook.com/Jennie-Dorny-Author-Auteur-778974449200881
Amazon Author Page:
https://www.amazon.com/Jennie-Dorny/e/B004MOC2TW?ref_=dbs_p_ebk_r00_abau_000000
Smashwords Author Page:
https://www.smashwords.com/profile/view/Jennie1203

www.ingramcontent.com/pod-product-compliance
Lightning Source LLC
LaVergne TN
LVHW042346190726
843493LV00005B/935